NORA'S KRAKEN

Leigh Miller

* * *

This is a work of fiction. Names, character, places are either products of the author's imagination, or used fictitiously. Any resemblance to actual persons, living or dead, events, or locales, is entirely coincidental

Copyright © 2023 Leigh Miller

All rights reserved. No part of this book may be reproduced in any manner without written permission of the copyright owner

ISBN: 9798387705472

Cover design by Leigh Miller

authorleighmiller.com

To A — You told me I didn't need to dedicate another book to you. I didn't listen. Did you really expect me to? This one's for you.

1

Nora

My world comes crashing down around me on a Friday afternoon.

Sitting in a nondescript beige and gray office at the Paranormal Citizens Relations Bureau, I stare open-mouthed at the Bureau agent across the desk from me.

"I've been *what*?" I ask, sure I must have misheard him.

"Recognized, Ms. Perry. As a kraken's mate."

"I didn't… I wasn't… how did this happen?"

Mr. Blair, the agent who called my workplace three days ago out of the blue and asked for this meeting, looks at me with patience and understanding, a soothingly calm tone to his voice.

Like that would do anything to take the edge off the bomb he's dropped in my lap.

"I realize this all must be very unexpected," he says, "but I promise you everything will be alright."

This has to be a joke. I glance at the shut office door behind me, half-expecting Kenna or Holly or one of my other friends to burst through and tell me I'm being pranked.

It certainly wouldn't be any more of a surprise than getting the call to come here.

This place didn't even exist a few years ago, not until the government's passage of the Paranormal Acts, allowing all sorts of different beings to come forward and join the mortal, human world.

It was a shock for everyone, to put it mildly.

One day all those creatures were the stuff of myths and legends, and the next they were all too real. The Paranormal Citizens Relations Bureau oversaw it all, smoothing the way for paranormal folk to find their place in this brand new world.

Some paranormals definitely look it. Orcs, winged fae, and naga, among others. Some, though, move through the world indistinguishable from humans. Shifters, vampires, nymphs, and demons, they have the choice whether they ever want to come forward and reveal who they are.

Mr. Blair is one of the latter types of creatures. Sitting in front of me, he looks almost entirely human, except for his eyes. Sharp, amber, and with thin, oblong pupils, I don't know what they make him, and I don't know what to make of the fact those eyes seem able to see right through me.

"Unexpected is one word for it," I mutter. "How was I... what did you call it? Identified?"

"Recognized," he corrects gently. "Your mate saw you three days ago at a coffee shop, and immediately knew who you were to him."

My stomach lurches. It must have been the Second Cup Cafe, just down the street from the bookstore where I work. That was Tuesday, which I only remember because it's the one day each week I splurge on something coffee-related that doesn't come from my pot at home. I hate Tuesdays, and Second Cup's chai lattes always make them a little better.

"How did you find out who I am, and how to get in touch with me?"

The question gives him a moment of pause, and his golden eyes flicker as he comes up with an answer.

It triggers a warning deep in the back of my brain.

How *did* they find me? I've spent these last few years trying to make myself as unnoticeable as possible, and they were not only able to discover who I am, but where I work, in a matter of hours. I got my latte at half-past seven, and the phone in the shop was ringing before noon.

The realization puts a sheen of sweat on the back of my neck.

"We have investigators," he says finally with a small, apologetic smile. "They get assigned to cases like these."

The silence between my question and his answer makes me think that's a lie.

And just like that, I don't know if I can trust anything he's saying. The old instincts kick up hard. Who is he, really? What does he want from me? Do I even have a mate out there somewhere, or am I being set up for another reason entirely?

"Your mate's name is Elias Morgan, and he's very eager to meet you," Mr. Blair goes on when I don't respond. "He's a kraken shifter, to be more specific, and all krakens are very steadfast and loyal. They can live for up to a thousand years, but only ever take one mate. That makes them just the slightest bit territorial, but…"

Whatever else he says is lost to the rushing sound in my ears.

Territorial.

It's just one word, but the implications behind it make my lungs constrict and my heart race. Other adjectives spring up around it, bringing a wave of panic with them.

Territorial. Possessive. Jealous. Controlling.

My thoughts spiral, sucked into a deep well of memories and fears and long, black nights. Unable to take a second more of this conversation, I push my chair back. The movement is so abrupt it startles the agent out of his monologue.

"Ms. Perry? Is everything alright?"

"I'm not interested. Please tell Mr. Morgan I don't have any interest in meeting or being mated to him."

Mr. Blair's brow creases in concern. "Have I said something that's upset you? I didn't mean to, and having a kraken for a fated mate really is—"

I wave my hands in front of my face. "Enough. Please. I'm leaving now."

Before he can get another word in, I grab my coat and head for the door. I have to get out of here. I need fresh air, space, and to get the hell away from this place.

Following the exit signs through a maze of hallways and forcing myself not to break out into a run, it takes everything in me to keep my breathing even and my panic down. I've just reached the lobby and the relief of seeing daylight so close, when my distraction causes me to run right into a tall, broad stranger.

His breath leaves him in a slight *oof*, he braces a hand on my shoulder for balance, and my cheeks heat immediately. He's got at least six inches on me and I have to crane my neck a little to look up at him, opening my mouth to offer a hasty apology. My words, however, die in my throat when I meet his eyes.

They're the bluest eyes I've ever seen.

Dark, intense, and the color of waves in a tempest, fathomless seas, and the deepest maritime twilight, they look down at me with dawning recognition.

"Lenora," he whispers in a soft, warmly accented voice.

I don't know how he knows my name, don't know how I know exactly who he is, but I back away immediately. Those blue eyes widen in surprise, then narrow slightly with focus as he tracks my retreat.

"I'm not..." I start, trailing off as I take a few more steps toward the door. "You've got the wrong person."

He shakes his head slowly, and I can't help but take inventory of the rest of him. His ink-black hair has a bit of roguish messiness to it. There's a couple days' worth of dark stubble growing over the hard line of his jaw, and his nose is a little crooked, like it's been broken a time or five. His build is tall and broad, not bulky but streamlined and elegant—a swimmer's body. He also has a long, jagged scar running down the left side of his face, all the way from his temple to the middle of his cheek.

He looks like a damn pirate.

Maybe that makes sense. Aren't krakens known for bringing down ships?

No. *No.* I'm absolutely not thinking about pirates or krakens or any of it. I have to get out of here.

"Lenora. I'm—"

"No," I say firmly, raising a hand. "You've got the wrong person, Mr. Morgan."

His eyes flash. "Elias. Please call me Elias."

Elias Morgan, the kraken who thinks I'm his mate. A shiver runs through me.

"Mr. Morgan, I'm sorry, but I'm not the woman you think you're looking for."

He looks like he's about to speak again, try to stop me, keep me from leaving and feed me the same bullshit about fate and mates and all the rest. I'm fully prepared to just turn and run, when something in that deep blue gaze of his makes my blood chill.

It's there, right there in his eyes.

Territorial. Possessive. Greedy.

It sends a shot of fear all the way down to the bottom of my soul. I can't do this. Not again. Not when I've just gotten my life built back to something I'm proud of.

Whatever he sees in my face gives him pause, and though some of the possessive edge leeches out of his expression, it does nothing to calm me.

"*I'm* sorry, Ms. Perry," he says softly. "Forgive me."

I've got nothing else to say, and nothing to do but give him a single shaky nod before fleeing out the Bureau's front door.

2

Elias

My mate has just fled from me.

Lenora Perry. The treasure my heart has been searching for these past three hundred years. My fate.

As the front doors of the Paranormal Citizens Relations Bureau—the *Monster* Relations Bureau in most peoples' vernacular—swing shut behind her, the hunter's urge in me flares to life.

I need to go after her, track her, keep my eyes on her so I know she's safe. It's not just a polite suggestion, either. It's an imperative, a command riding me with every breath I take.

My mate is fleeing, and I need to follow.

Still, I hold myself back.

She looked terrified. Gods, what did she think of me?

I know I look like hell. I've barely slept in the three days since I first saw her. I've barely had the motivation to do the bare minimum to keep my life together, much less indulge in extravagances like shaving.

Standing alone in the Bureau's lobby, all I can do is stare at the shut door she's left behind, aching to go after her. It's not until a soft voice says my name from somewhere behind me that I finally shake myself out of it.

"Elias? Can I see you to Mr. Blair's office?"

I turn to find Ruthie—one of the Bureau's receptionists, a forest sprite with a waterfall of mossy hair and deep black eyes—looking at me with her brow creased in concern.

Clearing my throat, I work up enough composure to answer her. "Yes, Ruthie, thank you."

All the way to Blair's office, I barely see my surroundings. No, all I can see or think of is Lenora.

Where is she? Is she alright? She looked so panicked, so afraid. Is it safe for her to be out in the world like that?

I'd imagined this day going very differently. Humans don't have the same concept of mates as many paranormal creatures do, but these last few years have certainly proven humans and monsters can pair successfully and happily. And even before that, there have always been times and places in history where paths have crossed and soul-deep bonds have been forged for monster-human pairings.

How I'd hoped that would be the case for Lenora and I.

Entering an office, I find my oldest friend leaned back in his chair, running a hand through his hair. He stands to greet us both, and Ruthie, definitely not oblivious to the tension in the room, leaves with a final concerned glance.

"What the fuck did you say to her?" I ask as the door closes, forgoing a civilized greeting. "Why did my mate just run terrified from this building?"

After two and a half centuries of friendship, I hardly feel the need for pleasantries.

"Did you run into her in the lobby?" Blair asks, settling

back into his chair.

He shifts a stack of papers to the side of the desk. From a brief glance, I catch my name and Lenora's, along with a bunch of other Bureau red tape.

Blair seems to have noticed the conflict in my expression, because his own hardens into suspicion.

"Elias," he says warily. "Whatever you're thinking... don't."

"I don't know what you're talking about."

The lie earns me a small, sardonic smile. "I've known you long enough to read that intent in your eyes, friend. You're already calculating the time and distance it would take you to get to her."

He's not wrong.

When we were both young—well, when *I* was young, he had a couple hundred years on me, even then—we'd spent enough time chasing riches and treasure and other boons for him to know full well what I look like on the hunt. And there's never been anything in my hundreds of years that called to me the way she does.

The instinct that drew me to her—the one that had me going out of my way on Tuesday morning, drawn a couple of blocks down from my normal route to the office—flares in me once more. It pulls and insists, commands me to go, do, seek.

"And if it was your mate, what would you do?" I ask before I can think better of it. I know the words are a mistake the moment they've left my mouth.

The dragon in him goes utterly still. A lethal, waiting sort of calm.

"You think I don't understand what it means to lose a mate?"

Blair doesn't sound angry, nor threatening, but something much, much more sinister and ancient. Krakens have nothing on dragons in the need to possess and protect our treasures, to keep them safe and sheltered from all harm. Knowing what I do about his own history, that was exactly the wrong thing to say.

I bow my head in a show of respect and contrition. "I'm sorry."

The silent seconds stretch long between us. This is familiar, too, the reminder that in the grand scheme of our shared history, we've never fully been equals.

"I took this case as a favor to you," Blair says, still with that ageless calm in his voice. "I did so out of respect for our centuries of friendship and because I know just how much she already means to you."

"And I thank you for that. But—"

"No buts," he cuts in. "You will abide by our laws in your pursuit of her. She comes to you of her own free will, or you leave her alone."

My very soul flinches at the idea. Leave her alone? Never. She'll never be alone again.

Blair, some of that frozen fire in him receding, gives me another tight smile. "You never were good with rules."

"At one time, as I recall, neither were you."

"Then it's a good thing we've both grown up over the centuries."

Another beat of silence. Some of the tension leeches from the air and Blair lets out a long breath.

"Tread carefully, Elias. I can't tell you why, but all of this could turn into a huge problem for the Bureau if it's not handled properly. After everything we've achieved for advancing monsters' interests over the last few years, I'm not about to see our reputation damaged because one kraken thought he could go off half-cocked in pursuit of a mate."

An oily, sinking suspicion seeps into me. "You make this sound like it could cause some sort of geopolitical incident. Who is she?"

I barely know anything about Lenora. She works at Tandbroz bookstore. She gets coffee at the Second Cup Cafe. Her light brown hair and hazel eyes might be lost in a crowd for anyone who wasn't looking closely enough.

It doesn't even scratch the surface of what I want to know.

I want to know her coffee order and what makes her tilt her face up at the rainy sky and smile like she did on the day I first saw her. I want to know all the books she recommends to the customers she speaks with. I want to run my hands through her impossibly soft-looking hair and see her stunning eyes looking back at me with trust.

Blair's eyes harden. "You'll have to find that out for yourself."

My instinct perks up at the challenge in the statement. "Will I? I can at least guess she's important if she's warranted this level of scrutiny."

Blair grimaces, but doesn't contradict me. It's not every day the Director of the Bureau gets himself involved in casework.

"You and your mate are a special case, Elias, and I'm more than happy to supervise and make sure you don't fuck it up."

Special case. So she is important. Why, or to who, I can't even begin to guess, and the mystery of it just adds to the building need to seek, to know, to find.

"Anyways," Blair continues. "We'll try to reach out to her again in a few days, once things have gotten the chance to cool down. She might just be overwhelmed and need some time to process everything."

Yes, or she might be letting all that fear and doubt harden into a resolve never to see me again, never to speak to me again, never give me the opportunity to show her who I am and why I would make a suitable mate to her.

I hold the words in, even though I know Blair reads them on my face. Damned dragon. He can't read minds, but the deep well of instinct he possesses and the way he can see through peoples' artifice are pretty close.

"In the meantime," Blair says, apparently unbothered I still haven't said anything, "stay away from her. And take care of yourself. You're not going to convince her of anything looking like that."

Apparently done insulting me for the day, he stands and gestures toward the door. An unmistakable 'get the hell out of here'.

I stand as well. "You'll let me know as soon as you've spoken to her?"

At that, the rest of the authority and hard resolve on his face melts into understanding and a deep sense of loyalty, of friendship.

"I will. And because I haven't told you yet, congratulations. I know this isn't the way you would have preferred things to happen, but I speak for myself and the rest of the monsters who count you as family when I wish you nothing but good fortune with this blessing."

Family. Gods above, the creatures I've kept company with these last three hundred years will have a field day with this. One in particular who I know will be frothing at the fangs to learn I've finally been captured in a female's net.

I grit my teeth. "Have you told Casimir?"

Blair lets out a low chuckle, the sound of it tinged with smoke and char, and gestures again toward the door. "No. Though I imagine he'll be just as thrilled for you as I am. Now, if you don't mind."

Dismissed, I give him a curt parting nod. Leaving the Bureau a couple minutes later, I breathe the mid-afternoon air deep.

There. Just there. The faintest hint of her on the breeze. It's barely discernible, maybe not even enough to track, but I close my eyes and cling to every tiny piece of her I can.

Lenora smells unexpectedly like the sea.

Crisp and clean, the slight saltiness is mixed with something else, something floral and earthy that makes me think of remote isles and densely packed forests. It's underpinned with a note of sour fear, and I frown, wishing like anything that it wasn't.

Lingering on her scent was a mistake.

All of that essence makes me want to break into a run, to follow the strands until I find her, speak to her, make her understand.

How would she react to that? Poorly, I imagine, but there was a moment between us in the lobby... It was over before it really began, but when our eyes met, I could see it for a bare second. Warmth, curiosity, the widening of her eyes and the parting of her lips as she studied my face. So small, so fleeting, but... there.

It's enough. It has to be enough.

For now.

With colossal effort, I turn away, push down the instinct that's still howling in me, and silently vow to let my treasure come to me in her own time.

3

Nora

After the disaster at the Bureau, I do a pretty admirable job of keeping it together during my Saturday, Sunday, and Monday shifts at Tandbroz.

It's hard not to be jumpy, hard not to expect that every time I round a corner downtown or every time the shop door opens when I'm working *he'll* be there, but three days of hectic back-to-back shifts and some time and distance from everything calm me down a little.

It's in the quiet moments, when I'm on the bus headed home, or alone in my apartment winding down for the evening, that the force of everything that happened on Friday hits me all over again.

Some kraken out there thinks I'm his mate.

It's absurd. Truly. What on Earth are the odds? He just happened to pick me out in all of Seattle, a metro of over three million people? It was only a coincidence he saw me at Second Cup?

He had the Bureau track me down, and I'm just supposed to be cool with it?

I try to hold on to all those reasons for acting the way I did, to justify the fact that I ran instead of hearing him out, that I protected myself over staying and finding out what he wanted to tell me.

Still, the more time that passes, the more the doubts creep in, and it's hard to stop myself from playing and replaying that scene at the Bureau.

I can't get Elias's face out of my mind.

Those blue, blue eyes, the scar on his cheek, the messy tousle of black hair, the way he looked at me when he first saw me...

I have to stop myself every time the thoughts go further than that—every time they veer toward doubt and regret and the inkling that maybe I jumped to conclusions before I should have.

Maybe I should have given Elias more of a chance.

Standing in my kitchen Monday night, washing the last of my dishes from dinner and looking out the small window over my sink into a dark, rainy night, all of it bubbles up to the surface.

It was raining just like this the night I arrived in Seattle, a little over three years ago.

I'd been fresh off a Greyhound, fresh off the worst relationship of my life and the riskiest decision I'd ever made, and I'd been terrified. It'd taken me months to just find my balance again, a whole year to stop looking over my shoulder every time I left the house, wondering if that would be the day my ex, Daniel, caught up with me. And even now, three years out, I have to be honest enough to admit all of that baggage is still coloring the way I live my life.

It's coloring the way I saw the kraken, too.

It was there, under the weight of Elias's hot, possessive stare, that another set of eyes came to mind. Light green instead of ocean blue, and always looking for a fault or some new way to ding my self-confidence. It was there, in the idea that some new man had come into my life thinking he could possess me, control me, treat me like an object that belonged to him.

I don't know Elias. I don't know what it actually means for a kraken to consider someone his mate. And even though I can recognize my history makes me somewhat less than objective in this situation, it doesn't negate the fact that I have some good reasons to be wary.

There's nothing on this planet that would tempt me back into a situation like the one I took such a gamble to leave, so why open myself up to the risk?

Those thoughts hound me out my door on Tuesday morning. The weather is gray and drizzly as I hop on the bus a couple blocks away from my apartment and head downtown to the bookstore. Twenty minutes before my shift starts, I get off at the stop down the street from Tandbroz and look left and right surreptitiously.

No krakens in sight.

The bookshop's only a half-block away, but there's one more important stop I need to make before I clock in.

It's Tuesday, and I need my chai latte fix.

There's another coffee shop, Driftwood Coffee Co, a few blocks over from Second Cup. It's not my favorite, and their chai really doesn't compare, but hopefully it's far enough out of the way that I won't accidentally run into anyone I would rather avoid.

Namely, the kraken.

He supposedly only saw me in the shop that one time, but I'm not taking any chances as I hoof it down the street.

The drizzle has picked up a little, but I've got my rain jacket and a good set of boots on, and I've never minded the rain. After growing up in Phoenix and going to college in Dallas before spending a few years in DC with Daniel, I never really expected how much I'd love the damp, cool climate and living near the ocean, but now I wouldn't trade it for anything.

Luckily, the line at Driftwood isn't too long, and my latte comes out quickly. I've just made it back outside, pulled my hood up over my hair, and rounded the corner to head back toward Tandbroz, when I stop dead in my tracks.

The kraken is staring back at me.

To be fair, Elias seems as surprised as I am as he holds his hands up in either surrender or an attempt to calm me.

"Are you following me?" I ask, hand tightening on my cup and heart rate ticking up a few notches.

"No," he assures me. "My office building is just up the street. I was... trying to avoid the part of downtown I saw you in before. I thought that might be best."

He seems sincere. Still, I'm not quite buying it.

"Where do you work?" I hope it's a fair question. I'd like to at least know the areas I should avoid in the future.

"Morgan-Blair Tower," he says, something hesitant flashing across his face.

Looking up the street, Morgan-Blair Tower rises from the pavement in a monolith of modern glass and steel. I've seen the building towering over the city a thousand times, known what its name is since the week I moved here, but standing here, now, with a kraken staring me down, it finally sinks in.

Morgan-Blair. The wheels in my mind are more than a little rusted and creaky as I try to reason it out, but clarity hits me like a slap to the face.

"Who... who are you?"

His expression is so uncomfortable that for a moment I

almost feel bad for him. At least until he answers the question.

"Elias Morgan," he says with a self-conscious shrug.

"No," I shoot back. "Absolutely not. Who *are* you?"

"I'm the CEO of Morgan-Blair Enterprises."

Another tilting of the world, a shift that makes my knees feel like jelly.

"And... Blair?"

He hesitates, but doesn't make me ask twice. "He's the man you met at the Bureau."

What the hell is going on?

"But, if he works there... what is he... how is he..." Elias still looks pained, but I hardly care as I take a step away from him, and then another. "Is all of this some kind of set up?"

"No," he says emphatically. "No, Lenora, it's not. Ewan Blair is my friend. He was my business partner for many years, but he's not a part of the company anymore."

"Then what is he?"

"He's the Director of the Paranormal Citizens Relations Bureau."

All the air whooshes from my lungs.

Director. Of a government Bureau. Sure, maybe it might make sense that Blair would be involved with his friend's case, but still... that's far, far more attention from a powerful person than I'm interested in having fixed on me. Ever.

And if Elias is some kind of wealthy businessman with government connections... my palms go clammy and my chest tightens.

The mantra I've been repeating to myself for the last three years plays again inside my pounding skull.

Lay low. Stay invisible. Survive.

It's what I've been telling myself since I snuck out of another fancy, opulent, high-rise building with only a few hundred dollars in my bank account, and all the jewelry from my jewelry box. The former had paid for a bus ticket across the country. The latter had tided me over once I'd pawned it, and had been enough for a security deposit and a couple month's rent on the studio apartment I'm still living in now.

All of it feels like it's hanging by a thread as I take the measure of the man in front of me. The *kraken* in front of me.

"And the two of you... what?" I ask. "Tracked me down? Found out where I work and invaded my life for what? Because you think you have some kind of claim on me?"

Elias's eyes flash, though whether it's with shame or annoyance, I can't tell and don't care.

I take another step back. "What gives you the right? What makes you think I'd be okay with that?"

I don't know where all of this courage is coming from. Normally, I get tongue-tied and stumble over my words when I'm nervous. That, or avoid the conversation altogether and fade into the background. With Elias, though, I don't hesitate for a minute before laying into him.

He thinks I'm his mate? Fine, let him see exactly what kind of mate he'd be getting.

"How did you find me?" I ask him.

His eyes dart back and forth over my face, studying my expression. "I followed you."

I'd suspected as much. Still, it's gratifying to hear him admit it.

"You stalked me."

Elias's jaw tightens. "I *followed* you. One block. Just from the coffee shop to the bookstore."

"No. You stayed long enough to realize I work at the store and wasn't just stopping to shop there. And you knew my name when we met. How did you find that out?"

This time, the shame in his face is clear as day. "I went to Blair and told him what I knew about you. The Bureau sent an investigator to the shop and they... they saw your nametag. Blair called and asked for you once they knew that much."

So, I was being surveilled. Figures.

Technically, a small, idiotic voice in the back of my mind reminds me, *Blair didn't lie.* He said the Bureau had investigators for cases like this.

I do my very best to ignore that voice. It doesn't change the fact that I was followed in the first place, or that some shady agent came into my workplace and got my information without me knowing.

"And you think that's okay?" I ask, still not pulling any punches. "You think that's an acceptable way to treat your supposed mate?"

"You *are* my mate, Lenora. Whether or not you accept it."

Elias's words are laced with enough possessive growl to have me retreating yet another step. It doesn't scare me as much as it did the day at the Bureau, especially not when he still looks so guilty, but that doesn't mean I'm going to stick around and give him any more time to lay whatever claim he thinks he has on me.

"Well, I don't. So I guess it's settled." With that, I finally turn and start walking away for real, leaving him behind on the sidewalk.

Or so I thought.

"Lenora," he says, keeping pace with me. "Wait."

"Nora." I don't know what makes me say it, don't know why I'm entertaining him for a single second longer, but the word slips out. At his confused look, I clarify. "Everyone calls me Nora."

I glance over at him, see something in his face shift and loosen, and it's almost enough to distract me. He still looks like a damn pirate, but a pirate with a warm, satisfied smile blooming over his face? It's not fair.

I look away.

"Nora," he says, that soft accent of his curling around the word. "I like it."

"I don't care if you like it."

I pick up my pace, making it clear enough that he can buzz right off. Still, a moment later, his hand touches my shoulder, halting me in my tracks.

Everything in me freezes. My blood, my breath, my bones. It all goes still as death. He must notice, because he draws his hand back immediately and takes a step away.

"Nora," he says. "I'm sorry, I didn't mean to—"

"Don't touch me." My voice is choked and barely audible. "Stop following me. Stay away from me."

He doesn't offer any further arguments, only nods and gives me more space as I turn and keep walking.

This time, he doesn't follow.

4

Elias

For the second time in less than a week, my mate is fleeing from me. Only this time, no part of me is tempted to follow her.

Gods, I fucked up.

Touching her wasn't even something I did consciously. All I wanted was a moment, just a moment to talk to her without her trying to flee, but the second I'd brushed her shoulder...

The look in Nora's eyes... fear, accusation, distress. Just the memory of it puts a black pit in the bottom of my stomach.

I crossed a line. While I don't know what made her react the way she did, it's not hard to guess the boundary I violated was a pretty damn big one.

Morning commuters, however, don't have a lot of time or patience for a kraken rooted to the sidewalk having a soul-consuming crisis, so the third time I'm jostled by a passerby I shake myself out of it and head toward the office.

It's only a block to the front doors of Morgan-Blair Tower, in the opposite direction Nora left toward the bookstore. Each step closer to the building puts another couple feet of distance between us, and I swear I can feel it with every cursed beat of my two hearts.

I didn't lie to Nora about any of it.

My role here. Blair's role. The fact that seeing her last week and this morning had indeed been nothing more than timing and happenstance. I'd been hoping that honesty might help ease some of her fears, even if it was not perhaps what she would have liked to hear.

If I have any chance of winning her, I owe her that much and more. Honesty, transparency, trust.

Well, if I *had* any chance of winning her. Those hopes seem to have dwindled near to extinction now.

The Tower's lobby is busy, and I nod a brief greeting to security before heading toward the elevators. The inside of Morgan-Blair Tower is sleek and modern, outfitted in dark gray concrete floors, three-story windows that let in the morning's watery gray light, and fixtures of black and silver metal. In the middle of the lobby, a large water wall stretches to the third floor mezzanine.

The image the building and company project to the world is one of modernity and strength, a sprawling conglomerate of shipping and manufacturing and a dozen other ventures that are the product of more than a century of careful planning and tending.

The image it projects to its employees and stakeholders, however, is rather different.

Each being who works for Morgan-Blair Enterprises holds company stock as a part of their compensation, and the vast, vast majority of those employees are paranormal creatures, who have always found a place here to make a good living.

It's been that way since the earliest days of my partnership with Blair.

The elevator dings, and I'm the last one off. My office is on the top floor, with brilliant views of Seattle and the Puget Sound. My office manager, Veronica, calls out a greeting as soon as I step out into the reception area, though her words die off as she catches my eye.

"Everything alright, Mr. Morgan?"

"Fine," I tell her, hoping my voice doesn't have an edge to it. "Can you hold my calls and meetings for the next hour?"

She nods, and I thank her before heading into my office, shutting the door behind me and crossing to the wall of windows opposite the door.

Even with as unbalanced as I feel, I'll never tire of this view.

Blair and I first set up operations in this part of the world over a hundred years ago. It had been humble, in the beginning, a venture we'd taken from England to New England, to the opportunity-rich west coast. Shipping yards and factories established, more than a century of carefully letting others be the face of the business so we could remain in the shadows. It all led up to the construction of this tower ten years ago, followed by the public revelation of our identities shortly after the passage of the Acts.

Even with all of that in mind, it's hard to dredge up much pride for it this morning.

Leaving the windows, I sink heavily into my chair, staring blankly at the assorted files and reports and papers waiting for my attention, not really seeing any of them.

My mind won't rest, and nor will my instincts, which apparently haven't gotten the loud and clear message I need to leave my mate alone.

What happened to Nora to make her react the way she did?

The memories of her fearful face, the sight of her retreating, and the shakiness of her voice swirl in my mind with Blair's warnings to tread lightly.

What isn't he telling me? Who is she?

Unable to let it go, and fully aware I'm likely crossing yet another line, I power up my computer and start searching.

Somewhat unsurprisingly, simply entering 'Nora Perry' doesn't bring up any useful results. Because of course it doesn't. That would be more mercy than I deserve.

My mind whirs. Maybe it's a false name. If she's got some kind of past she's trying to run from, it would make sense.

Thinking she'd be more likely to change her last name than her first, and knowing I'm out of luck anyway if I'm wrong, I do a few fruitless searches for 'Nora' and 'Lenora' paired with Seattle, criminal records, and a handful of other dead ends.

It's not until I input 'Nora, Congress' with the vague idea she might somehow be associated with someone in government, that a photo on the fifteenth or sixteenth page of search results captures my eye.

There. That's Nora.

Her hair is different, dyed a lighter shade of blond. She's younger and noticeably thinner, and she's wearing more makeup than she has been the times I've seen her, but that's her. I'm so busy studying her in the image that it takes a few seconds to realize who she's standing next to.

Daniel Sorenson. Son of one of the country's wealthiest industrialists, and a three-term congressman.

Stomach knotting, I click the link and read the accompanying article. The photo's caption lists her name as Nora Wheeler, and it also lists her as... Sorenson's girlfriend.

My two hearts beating fast in my chest, I do a little more searching and find a plethora of articles about a couple who, by all appearances, was in an elevated place in Washington,

DC society. Daniel Sorenson comes from old money, and if what's been written about him is true, he's on a fast track for a sparkling political career and a life firmly ensconced in privilege and power.

A life that apparently included Nora at some point.

All the photos and articles she's included in end abruptly about three years ago. After that, there's just... nothing. No articles about a breakup, nothing more than some passing references to Sorenson's newly single status and a handful of additional articles speculating on his status with other women he's appeared in public with during the years since.

There's not much left out there about Nora Wheeler, either, besides her associations with Sorenson. If she did once have a digital footprint, she's excised it completely. There are no old social media profiles, no college records I can find, not a single search result. Whatever the reasoning behind it, she's done a hell of a job making herself invisible these last few years.

Suspicion still prickling at the back of my neck, I spend the next fifteen minutes doing a deep-dive on Sorenson.

He won his third congressional election last year, and, surprise of surprises, he's recently been named to the House Committee which oversees paranormal affairs.

Blair must be having a godsdamned aneurysm over this.

Nora's the ex-girlfriend of a congressman—the ex who probably left him under some less than ideal circumstances if all the clues I'm gathering about her are adding up the way I think they are—and not just any congressman, but one who has sway over paranormal legislation.

Taking my hands off the keyboard, I sit back in my chair and rub my eyes with the heels of my palms.

I shouldn't know any of this.

Instincts or no, need to seek or no, I shouldn't have found any of this out until Nora was ready to tell me.

Just one more sin to add to my growing list of transgressions.

And still my chest aches with every breath I take. Even now, the burgeoning mating bond is reaching out, trying to find the one person in the world who can make it complete.

The same person who's forbidden me ever to speak to her again.

It's not Nora's fault. None of this is her fault. She didn't ask for this, she doesn't want this, and if what I'm beginning to suspect about her is true, she's probably afraid what all of this could mean for her. If she's hiding from Sorenson and has gone out of her way to be virtually invisible, the idea that all of this might lead him back to her must be terrifying.

No wonder she ran from me.

Knowing there's nothing I can do about it now, no way to speak to her or get close to her without breaking the explicit boundaries she's put in place between us, leaves me feeling unmoored, adrift, purposeless, with no way to fix it.

Choosing instead to focus on the day ahead of me and the responsibilities already stacked up on my desk, I rub a hand absently over the center of my chest in the place where it aches before settling in and getting to work.

5

Nora

"He did *what?*"

Sitting with Holly and Kenna around the coffee table in Holly's apartment, we've got three glasses of wine liberally poured as we recount our weeks. It's become a Thursday night ritual the last few months, and I'm endlessly thankful for the both of them tonight.

But, as luck would have it, this Thursday I'm the star of the show.

"Kept following me when I told him off," I say, cringing. "I also might have freaked out a little when he touched me and tried to stop me from leaving."

I've fully briefed Holly and Kenna on the Elias situation. Neither one seems as horrified as I was to learn there's some kraken out there who thinks I'm his mate, but neither of them has the same history that I do.

Still, after what I just said, they're both looking at me in concern.

Holly had her face in her phone, no doubt digitally stalking said kraken, but her eyes cut sharply to me. "Do we need to report this? Either to the Bureau, or I don't know, to the police or something?"

I shake my head. "No, it wasn't like that."

Honestly, he barely touched me. A hand on my shoulder. A light touch that had startled me, yes, but that didn't harm me. Did he cross a line? Absolutely. Do I think he meant to hurt me? No, I don't.

Even three days later, I'm not sure if I'm feeling embarrassed or entirely justified about how I reacted to it.

"What *was* it like?" Holly asks, not convinced.

Willowy, blond, and with piercing blue eyes that are way too preceptive, it's difficult not to squirm a little under Holly's focused gaze.

"I don't know," I mumble. "We were... kind of arguing in the middle of the sidewalk. I basically told him to fuck off, turned to walk away, and he touched my shoulder."

"Touched? Or grabbed?" Kenna asks, also going into protective mode.

Shorter than me or Holly, with a pinup figure and long, curly auburn hair, Kenna is chaos to Holly's cool control.

"Touched," I say. "Definitely touched. And he backed right off when he saw how much it upset me."

Neither of them looks like they're fully buying it.

"Do you think he's like Daniel?" Kenna asks.

Just the sound of my ex's name is like a bucket of cold water poured over my head. I've been asking myself that same question for the last three days, and I don't think I'm anywhere close to having an answer.

"I don't know," I say, taking a long sip of my wine. "I really don't know anything about him."

Kenna studies me thoughtfully, green eyes narrowed and hair piled in a messy bun on top of her head. She was the first friend I made after moving to the city, when she was also working at Tandbroz.

Her brash, confident attitude, endlessly extroverted personality, and warm kindness all but guaranteed she'd get her way in making the two of us friends once she'd decided it was something she wanted to do. Even after she left that job, she didn't leave me behind, bringing me into a fold of new friends that made being here in Seattle so, so much easier.

I eventually trusted her, and Holly, with the details about what actually brought me here, even if it was one of the hardest things I've ever had to do.

Well, maybe second hardest.

The hands-down hardest thing was my decision to flee DC. There really wasn't another option, but that doesn't mean I haven't lived with the consequences of it every single day since.

It would be too easy to let myself be sucked back into that place, like I always seem to when the subject comes up. Fear, paranoia, the knowledge I lost nearly every part of myself in that relationship and the doubt I have that I'll ever be able to put all those pieces back together.

"What if he's not?" Kenna prods gently. "What if he's a good guy? And, I mean, a kraken? You've got to be interested in what that would be like."

Out of the three of us, Kenna's the eternal optimist. She's also had the most experience dating paranormals, with the last couple of guys she's dated being a gargoyle and a demi-fae, respectively.

"Sure," I relent, cautiously. "Maybe I am a little curious—"

Kenna smirks at that. I ignore her.

"But, the whole 'you're my mate' thing? What am I supposed to do with that? I don't even know this guy, and he's probably already looking for a lifelong commitment."

Kenna makes a small, thoughtful noise as she considers that. "What do you think, Hol?"

Holly's been silent for the last few minutes, but pipes up when Kenna asks, holding her hands up in mock-surrender. "I don't think I'm the best person to be giving relationship advice right now, given how much of a cluster my own love life is."

"Sorry," I say, feeling horribly insensitive. "I don't mean to be such a downer. You don't need to be dealing with all my drama, too."

"It's alright," Holly says. "Just because I got dumped doesn't mean I'm the only person in the world with problems."

Dumped is an understatement. Her boyfriend of four years up and left out of the blue a couple of months ago, and I know she's still struggling to find her balance.

"And anyway," Holly continues. "Maybe Kenna's got the right idea about dating paranormals. I mean, they can't be worse than human guys, right?"

"Right," Kenna agrees. "And you would not believe some of the—"

"Hnng," I grunt, covering my ears. "Please. Nothing about your boyfriends' monster penises."

"Hey now, you might be dealing with a monster penis of your own pretty soon. It's only fair I get to share."

I can't help it, I laugh. It's the first genuine laugh I've had in a week and I'm grateful to know I've still got it in me. This week has been long and endless, and by some miracle I have a half-day shift tomorrow, and then a whole two days off before I start a few days of long shifts on Monday. Unfortunately, that will also probably give me a whole lot more free time to obsess about the kraken.

Leaning back against Holly's couch from where I'm seated

on the floor, I close my eyes and let out a long breath, thinking.

"What if Daniel somehow finds out?" I ask. "Elias seems… connected. High profile. Why do I feel like dating him would just be asking for trouble?"

"Let me ask a different question," Kenna says. "Why the fuck should you care if Daniel finds out? That prick has no claim on you, and it sounds like this kraken could probably use those connections of his to make sure Daniel gets his ass handed to him if he tries anything."

"Okay, fine," I concede. "But the whole mating thing? Wouldn't that just make him a possessive asshole?"

Kenna gives me a gentle smile. "It's not like that, I promise."

"How do you know? Did either of your last boyfriends think you were their mate?"

She shakes her head. "No, they didn't. But I got to meet some of their friends that were mated, and it seemed… nice. Like, this whole aura around them that just felt warm and fuzzy and calm, like they existed in this separate world made for just the two of them."

Holly sighs. "Well damn. Now I want a kraken mate."

I make a little noise of acknowledgment in the back of my throat, not sure what to say. Part of me can't believe any of those warm fuzzies are real in the slightest.

Belonging to someone stopped being a fantasy the day I met Daniel.

In hindsight, I should have been able to tell from the first date. The love-bombing, the gifts, the way he sweet-talked me and painted a picture of things that would never really be true.

God, how badly I wanted to believe it could be true.

But I was twenty-one. Not even old enough to really know myself, let alone know how to spot someone like that and stay far, far away.

By the time I realized it was a veneer for all the ugliness just underneath his surface, I was in so far over my head. Stuck in his condo in DC, no car, no degree, not working because he somehow always managed to twist things and convince me it was better for me to stay home and support his political career.

Completely at his disposal.

In the end, it wasn't too late to pull myself back out, but even now, six years after I first met him, I'm still paying the price for believing in him at all.

Shaking my head, I take another sip of wine and try to focus on the matter at hand.

"What would you guys do if you were me?"

Holly smiles sadly. "We can't tell you that, babe. I know you've got a lot of shit to deal with from your last relationship, and all the warm and wonderful things about mating aside… it's a lot."

Kenna looks a little less sure. "Would it hurt just to talk to him? It sounds like you really haven't given him a chance yet."

She's not wrong. Still…

I haven't even tried to date after Daniel, much less considered any kind of long-term commitment. In the back of my mind, I think part of me has just written it off entirely. I like my life in Seattle, and I'm more comfortable here than I've ever been anywhere.

But that doesn't mean I haven't been… stuck. Stagnated. Letting the baggage I've been carrying around keep me from truly moving forward.

All of it rattles around my brain—the reasons I should talk to Elias again and the reasons I should stay away—until it's muddled and messy and giving me the beginnings of a headache.

"I'll think about it," I say, not knowing how or if I'll ever be able to come to a decision, but also knowing it's not up to my friends to make my choice for me. "And by the way, I love you guys."

"We know," Kenna says with a bright, jaunty smile. "And we love you, too."

"Ms. Perry?"

The sound of a familiar voice has my head snapping up from where I'm sitting on a bench in a plaza just down the street from Tandbroz. My Friday shift ended fifteen minutes ago, and it's a blessedly sunny early October afternoon.

Mr. Blair from the Bureau approaches with two travel coffee cups in his hands, right on time.

I glance at the cups. "Don't tell me your investigators are invasive enough to know my coffee order."

He chuckles. "No. Well, I'm sure they could pull some strings to make it happen if they wanted to. But this is a tea that was given to me by a friend, and I thought it might be best to come with a peace offering."

He hands me a cup, and I gesture to the empty seat on the bench beside me. "Please, sit."

He does, and I take a long sip of the tea. It's delicious. Notes of cinnamon and cardamom mix with something lighter and almost floral I can't quite place. When he sees me smiling, Blair takes his own sip and settles back against the bench.

"A forest sprite who works for the Bureau makes it," he explains. "I've never tasted anything quite like it."

When he called earlier this afternoon and asked if I was open to meet up with him, I hadn't wanted to say yes. It had been on the tip of my tongue to refuse, but something small and needling in the back of my mind stopped me.

Maybe it was the conversation I had with Kenna and

Holly last night. Or maybe it's the way I haven't been able to shake the feeling of unease that slithers into my stomach every time the last image I have of Elias comes to mind—absolutely devastated and filled with regret as I walked away from him.

Whatever it was, it made me reluctantly agree to meet with Blair. In public, not at the Bureau, and definitely not if Elias was going to be a part of it.

I'm not sure whether I want to see the kraken again, and I'm definitely not ready to have it sprung on me with no warning.

"Mr. Blair..." I start, not sure what I want to ask.

"'Blair' is just fine," he tells me with another of his gentle smiles.

The softness of it doesn't quite match up with the rest of him. He's not as tall as Elias, but he's broader through the shoulders—more like a football player's build to the kraken's sleek swimmer's body. His hair is a thick, dark brown, neatly trimmed and styled with just a bit of gray around his temples. Like he was at the Bureau, he's wearing another suit today, dark gray, with a deep amber tie that almost matches the shade of his unnerving eyes.

"Blair," I say. "What did you want to meet with me about?"

He shrugs. "I just wanted to check in with you and see how you were doing after our last conversation."

"Really? And is that a routine duty for the Director of the Paranormal Citizens Relations Bureau?"

He cracks another smile, this one a bit more wry. "Did you look me up, then?"

"No. Mr. Morgan told me."

At that, his smile dies. "When?"

"I, uh, ran into him a couple of days ago. Almost literally."

"Did you? Because I specifically told him not to—"

"It was an accident," I say. "We were both trying to avoid each other and ended up running into each other anyway."

He studies me for a few long moments. "And how did that go?"

"Not great."

Blair looks troubled, but doesn't speak or ask any more questions, so I press on.

"Did Mr. Morgan ask you to meet with me?"

"No, he didn't. In fact, he'd probably be more than a little pissed off that I'm here talking to you."

"So why are you here?"

"Like I said, Ms. Perry—"

"Nora."

His smile starts to creep back in. "Nora. Like I said, I wanted to check up on you. And no, I don't do much case work, but this is an exception."

"Because you and Mr. Morgan are friends."

"Yes, Elias and I are friends. We were business partners for a long time, too, though I left Morgan-Blair over thirty years ago."

Hearing him say that so casually, when he barely looks over forty himself, is a serious mind-trip. I wonder how old Elias is.

Shaking off the thought, I glance back over at Blair. "How did you end up at the Bureau?"

"I started advocating for paranormals' interests even before I left the company," he says and then laughs a little. "The time seemed right, back then, in the 1990s. The world seemed like it was changing, modernizing."

"And it took this long for any changes to actually happen?"

He shakes his head. "I can't say a lot about it. Government confidentiality and all, but there's been decades of work that went into the Paranormal Acts."

It's not a stretch to imagine something like that would have taken a long time to come to fruition, especially with how carefully all those beings had to hide, or camouflage their identities, before being granted the protection to live freely as they are. Still, the mention of it stirs up the restless, unsettled energy in my chest that's still warning me to run away from all of this and never look back.

I take a deep breath and choose my next words carefully. "You seem like you're pretty connected in the government."

He nods.

"How much do you know about me?"

Blair glances over and fixes me with a hard, searching look before he answers. "Enough."

"Do you know about… Daniel?"

I don't elaborate, or give him any more than that, just testing the waters to see how far into my background they went digging.

"Yes."

I expect panic. I expect shame. Strangely, neither emotion comes. All I feel is… resigned. Of course the Bureau knows. If they somehow found out my real last name, it wouldn't have been a big lift to find out the rest of it. Or at least enough to infer what the rest of it might be.

Also strangely, I feel a faint but distinct pulse of relief. He knows. Blair knows, and the world hasn't come crashing down on me.

"And is Daniel… aware of any of this?"

A flare of hard emotion crosses his face, but he quickly hides it under his professional facade. "Of course not. The Bureau operates independently of politics. Though congress has oversight into our budget and high-level operations, we don't report on any individual cases to lawmakers."

I nod silently, mulling that over for a few seconds. "And have you told Mr. Morgan?"

"No. I wouldn't break your trust or the confidentiality of my office, even for my oldest friend. Though I'll warn you, he's smart and too obsessive for his own good. He may have found things out on his own."

"By following me?"

"No," he says emphatically. "Absolutely not. But you'd be shocked at what that kraken can sift up from the depths when he's got the scent of something."

"That's pretty invasive, you know. Almost as invasive as having someone follow me to my workplace."

Blair has the good grace to look chagrined. "You're not wrong."

Again, I wait for the anger, for the shame. It doesn't come.

Out of everything I could and should be upset about, this detail feels... more exhausting than anything.

It's been three years since I've seen or heard from Daniel, and while the thought of him finding me is still terrifying, the sheer weight of carrying the truth of what happened like my own secret shame isn't something I want to do anymore.

I tried my best to cover my tracks when I moved out here. I started using my mom's maiden name as my last name instead of Wheeler, even if all my IDs and documents still have my legal name on them. I wiped my social media profiles from existence, and I haven't opened up new ones for Nora Perry. Kenna and Holly have been my only confidants, and I trust them implicitly, but part of me has always known it isn't enough.

There are plenty of photos out there with me and Daniel in them, if someone got a hunch for where to look. He loved getting his picture taken, almost as much as he loved telling me exactly how I needed to look any time we went to another one of the stupid fundraisers or political events he seemed to be invited to every damned weekend in DC or back in Dallas.

Letting my hair go back to its natural light brown instead

of keeping it blond, and trading in all those expensive clothes for comfy jeans and thrifted sweaters had been as much a satisfying rebellion as any of the rest of it.

The possibility Elias might also have found some of those photos and put the details together on his own should make me angrier than it does. But, like it did when Blair mentioned it, a part of me is almost relieved he might know.

Sometimes all I want is for *someone* to know. Or everyone. Maybe the entire world.

If everyone knew what Daniel was like, the things he'd said and done while we were together, maybe it wouldn't feel like just my shame anymore.

Still, it feels like too much to sort through now. Not sure what else I want to say to Blair, I tip my head back to enjoy the beautiful day for a little while longer.

I enjoy coming here to eat my lunch when it's not raining, just to watch the world go by. When I first came to Seattle, it had been the place I'd come to pretend I wasn't so alone. Those first few months—before I'd met Holly and Kenna and a few other friends—had been the hardest of my life.

Still, when I'd sat here drinking my chai latte or eating a sandwich I'd bought with my own money, it hadn't felt so bad. I'd been able to sit in peace and enjoy the small life I'd made for myself.

It had been enough, then. Now, though, I'm not so sure.

"Do you think he'd want to speak to me again... Elias?" I ask.

Blair looks over at me, unable to keep the surprise from his face. "I'm certain he would."

The words are soft, reassuring, and combined with everything else I'm feeling, they make a lump of emotion settle itself in my throat.

"I don't know how to feel about the *mate* thing," I admit. "Doesn't that come with a certain amount of... obligation?"

The Director of the Paranormal Citizens Relations Bureau probably doesn't have it in his job description to play therapist to nervous krakens' mates, but Blair doesn't balk at the question.

"Not in the slightest. If I know Elias, he's ready to treasure you for the rest of eternity, but not if it wasn't what you wanted."

That lump in my throat grows even larger. I have to swallow painfully over it to answer him.

"And that's what you think he would do, treasure me?"

Blair chuckles, though there's something a bit sad about the sound of it. "Of course, Nora. And I would know, since krakens and dragons share a proclivity for guarding our treasures and keeping them close."

6

Elias

It's Friday afternoon, and I've got a wicked headache pulsing in my temples.

Part of it is from the tension I've been carrying there all week, the denied instinct that's making me restless and tense. That instinct would still have me seek Nora out, hold her close and keep her safe, despite the mess I've made of things.

It's getting harder to deny with each passing day. Like an itch directly in my prefrontal cortex, a damning temptation to throw my impulse control aside completely and act on what my nature commands. Find her. Claim her. Keep her.

I won't. I'm almost certain I won't. Still, the instinct persists.

The rest of my headache is coming from the visitors in my office.

The two men sitting on the other side of my desk are stony

faced. They represent a company that has been doing business with the ocean freight division of Morgan-Blair Enterprises for decades.

And, as it turns out, they weren't thrilled to learn what kind of company they were working with when the truth came out.

"We have ongoing concerns about the public perception of doing business with you." The company's CEO, Mr. Stanley Thoreson, is about seventy years old with the antiquated perceptions to match.

Although, at over three hundred years old myself, I suppose I'm not one to talk about being antiquated, but this fossil really puts himself into the stone age with the attitudes he has around paranormals.

"As such," he continues, folding his hands in front of him. "We're interested in renegotiating our contracts. As you're well aware, we spend millions with Morgan-Blair each year."

I'm aware. I'm also aware he wants to use his opinions as leverage to get a better deal for the thousands of shipments of particle board furniture his company ships across the Pacific each year. He's been angling for it since the day the news broke about Morgan-Blair's true affinity to the paranormal.

I look at his colleague. The other man is a few decades younger, maybe in his early forties, and if the corporate intel I have is correct, he's being groomed to step in as CEO whenever Thoreson retires. Or just disintegrates into a pile of bone dust. Whichever comes first.

Mr. Jason Rutelege, the colleague, is holding his cards close to the vest. Face carefully blank, he listens to the end of his boss's monologue before adding his own two cents.

"The contracts are well past due for a renegotiation," Rutelege says carefully when Thoreson is done. "We'd like to have our lawyers look at the terms and draw up a new proposal."

Thoreson cuts in. "What we'd like to see is for Morgan-Blair to come to the table first. We want to know what kind of recompense you can give to your loyal partners, ones who've been with you for decades, and have stuck with you through all of this. It really is—"

"Through all of what, Mr. Thoreson?" I ask, cutting him off.

During the entire discussion, he hasn't come right out and said it. I know well what he's referring to, but the old goat hasn't had the stones to own up to what he means.

And what he doesn't know? I've already got my lawyers looking into breaking the contract entirely.

The business we do with his company is a drop in the bucket, all things considered. It would mean shifting some other interests around, reassigning the team members who work on the account, but if it means cutting ties with a company whose values are so entirely opposed to the beings who work here, then so be it.

"Excuse me?" Thoreson asks, bristling at the interruption.

"It's a simple question," I tell him. "What exactly about Morgan-Blair Enterprises do you take issue with? What do you think is going to hurt your company's reputation?"

Thoreson opens and closes his mouth a couple of times like a trout on a riverbank, and Rutelege steps in to save his ass from answering.

"What Mr. Thoreson means—"

"I know what Mr. Thoreson means. But if he's adamant about it affecting our partnership, then the least he could do is own up to it."

Silence is my only answer as the two men glance at each other and shift uncomfortably in their seats.

It isn't the first time something like this has happened, and it won't be the last.

Attitudes about paranormal folk are still in flux. Most are

more than willing to accept us with open arms into the human world, but the detractors tend to be the emptiest, noisiest barrels. Though it's infuriating at times to navigate the complicated politics of it all, being able to advocate for all the beings who work at and have stock in Morgan-Blair is a privilege and responsibility I don't take lightly.

"Look, Mr. Morgan," Rutelege says. "The way we see it—"

Before he can finish, he's interrupted by a soft knock at the door. A welcome reprieve for whatever corporate half-speak he was about to offer as an excuse.

"Come in," I call out.

Veronica opens the door and sticks her head around the corner. "I apologize, Mr. Morgan, for interrupting."

"Not at all," I assure her.

"I have a visitor for you. One on your 'urgent' list."

"Who?" There are only a handful of people on that list, with the most recent inclusion being, perhaps idiotically...

"Nora Perry."

Standing immediately, I nod. "Please show her in."

Veronica disappears for a moment, and I'm about to dismiss my two guests when she reappears with Nora following close behind.

The restless, unsettled thing rattling around in my chest quiets and the lingering ache in my skull disappears the moment she walks through the door.

My mate, my kraken's instinct purrs. *Here. Safe.*

It's as unconscious and unstoppable as the beating of my two hearts or the drag of breath in and out of my lungs, but I make myself tamp it down as Nora glances uneasily around the room.

"Gentlemen," I say, gesturing toward the door. "I apologize, but I'm going to have to cut our meeting short."

They both stand, though not without some unhappy grumbles. Fine. They can deal with it. Rescheduling a meeting

I didn't want to have in the first place is no great sacrifice to make to have my mate so close.

After Veronica has shown them out and closed the door behind her, silence falls in the room.

Nora is standing near the corner of my desk, staring down at my three hundredth birthday present from Casimir. The wooden replica of a ship, an exact match of the one I sailed for nearly fifty years with Blair, though not under any country's flag.

And, as I watch, Nora reaches out to touch the cheeky little addition Cas saw fit to include below the ship.

A mass of wooden tentacles, a kraken come up from the deep to stalk the world above.

I clear my throat, a shot of discomfort moving through me. "I'm glad you're here."

Nora quickly draws her hand away and turns to face me, and we stare at each other for a few long moments. It's the first time I've seen her so still—not backing away from me, not fleeing—and I take full advantage of the opportunity to drink her in.

"Sorry," she says finally. "I didn't mean to interrupt anything."

"Don't apologize. You just saved me from a very, very irritating meeting."

"Did I?"

Am I imagining the ghost of a smile on her lips?

"Yes. Absolute waste of my time. I'd much rather have the chance to speak with you."

She nods, still not quite convinced. "About that... I... I wanted to see you and... apologize, I guess. Or just talk to you. You know, without losing it and trying to run away."

Despite her words, Nora looks like she still might want to run away. Her posture is stiff, expression guarded, and I wrack my brain trying to come up with any way I could make her more comfortable.

"What made you decide to come?" I ask gently.

The corners of her lips quirk up a bit more, and relief is an almost-palpable thing in my chest.

"Two of my friends made me realize I might have acted a little... hastily when we first met."

I chuckle. "I'll make sure to thank them if we ever meet."

"You can also thank Mr. Blair."

"Is that so?"

Blair talked to her? I make a mental note to pay him a visit so we can discuss the exact definition of what he meant by keeping me informed on their conversations.

"Yeah," Nora says with a shrug. "Just a few minutes ago, actually."

As if on cue, the cell in my pocket buzzes. When I pull it out and glance down, Blair's name is on the caller ID.

"Speak of the dragon," I mutter, silencing the call. "And what did the two of you discuss?"

Another shrug. "State secrets. Kraken mating habits. Tea."

"That's all?"

"Among other things."

Nora's still smiling, now with a bit of mischief in her, and I can't stop staring. She seems... relaxed, at ease, so much different from the last two times we've interacted that it's almost like looking at a different person.

In the sunlight streaming in from the wall of windows, her hazel eyes are shining. Her hair is in a high, bouncy ponytail today, and she's wearing a cozy tan sweater over light wash jeans. The makeup she has on compliments the fullness of her cheeks and the warmth of her eyes.

She's lovely. Even more so for her smile.

"What?" she asks, and it's clear she's caught me staring. "Do I have something on my face?"

I shake my head. "Forgive me. Would you like to sit

down?"

We cross to two chairs set in front of the windows, one of my favorite places to sit and think and enjoy the view of Seattle. Today, the sunny weather gives a clear view all the way to the Sound and the islands in the distance.

"So," she says after a few moments, looking over at me. "It seems like the last couple of times we... talked, there might have been more you wanted to say to me. About the whole... mates thing."

She sounds reticent, not sure of the words she should use or what she's allowed to say.

"I do." I wish I could let her know that anything she wants to say, any questions she has to ask me, none of it is off-limits. "But I also understand why all of this might be a lot for you, why you're no doubt feeling overwhelmed by it."

She gives me a hard, studying look. "Do you?"

There's something in that look which tells me she might already suspect I've done my homework on her, learned more than I rightfully should. I wonder what Blair told her. He's well aware of the lengths I'd go to know more about my mate, and the damned dragon probably took it upon himself to give her a warning.

"I want you to know you're in control here, Nora," I tell her.

Anything to do with Sorenson and her past doesn't matter, not right now, at least. Besides, all of it's just conjecture, a few scant details and my own imagination filling in the blanks. It's not mine to know or ask for until she feels ready to tell me about it herself. *If* she ever feels ready to tell me about it herself.

Nora's eyes widen, and her throat bobs in a harsh swallow. "What do you mean by that?"

"I mean that there's no pressure for you to do anything you don't want to, or to make any decisions you're not comfortable making. Anything that happens between us is entirely up to you."

"So…" she says, processing. "How does that work? Practically, I mean. Where do we go from here?"

"I want to take you on a date."

Her face scrunches up in adorable skepticism, apparently not convinced. How I'd like to run my thumb over the divot in her forehead and kiss the small, doubting frown off her lips.

"Just a date? Wouldn't it mean a whole lot more to you than that?"

Of course it would mean more. What she probably doesn't realize, though, is just how much more. If I had my way, our first date would end with us mated and bound, with Nora wrapped up in my tentacles, held open and bared for me, ready to take…

Stop. I have to stop.

"Just a date," I tell her. "I won't lie to you and pretend it's casual for me, but nor will I ask for anything more than you're willing to give. We do this at your pace, Nora. Whatever you're comfortable with."

"And if I decide I'm not comfortable with any of it? What happens then?"

My throat constricts, and every instinct in me calls out in protest, but I give her what I hope is a reassuring smile. "Then I respect your wishes. This doesn't have to go anywhere if you don't want it to."

She's not quite satisfied with that. "What would that mean for you? I don't really… I don't understand much about krakens or… mating."

What would it mean? A black stain on my soul that would follow me the rest of my life.

Still, that's neither her fault nor her responsibility. I wouldn't be the first kraken to be rejected by his mate, and though it's not something I'd ever want to live through, I could survive it.

"You let me worry about that," I tell her. "All I want is a date. If you decide this isn't something you'd like to pursue after that, I'll respect any decision you make."

Nora thinks about that for a few seconds before seeming to come to a decision.

"Alright. Alright, yeah, I think a date would be a good place to start. What did you have in mind? Drinks? Dinner?"

My mind is already racing, wondering how much might be too much. A private dinner at the top of the Space Needle? A weekend in Paris? Skipping it all and just eloping on the beaches of Bora Bora?

Gods, if she only knew. She'd run screaming from this office.

"Let me surprise you? Tomorrow night?"

"Yeah, tomorrow is good. And... nothing too elaborate," she says, glancing around my office. "It seems like your tastes might be a little more extravagant than mine."

"Nothing too elaborate," I agree, internally rearranging my expectations and giving myself a mental reality check.

Nora leans over the small table between us and grabs a notepad and a pen, scribbling something on it and tearing the sheet off before handing it to me.

"My number," she explains. "In case anything comes up."

It would take a damned apocalypse for anything to 'come up' that would keep me from our date. Still, I take the paper from her, fold it, and tuck it into the inside pocket of my suit jacket, just over my hearts.

Writing my own number down on the same pad of paper, I tear it off and give it to her. "And here's mine."

The act is so simple, so mundane. Two strangers getting to know each other, exchanging numbers, agreeing to test the waters and see if a relationship has any potential.

It makes a bubble of wry humor rise in my chest.

Not exactly the way I thought meeting and claiming my mate would go, but I'll take it. I'll take anything she's willing to give.

"I'll text you the details?" I ask, and she nods.

Nora stands from her chair. "Alright. That sounds good."

It's clear she means to leave, and even though I'd keep her here for the rest of the afternoon if I could, I stand as well. I follow a couple of steps behind as she crosses the office, and as she moves toward the door, I reach to open it for her. I settle my other hand unthinkingly on the center of her back and...

Shit.

Shit.

Just as she did the last time I touched her, Nora goes absolutely still.

Unlike last time, however, she doesn't move away. She leans minutely into the touch, turning to look up at me. Her lips are still curved into a delectable smile and there's a bright, teasing light in her eyes.

"You kind of have a thing about touching me, don't you?"

If she only knew.

Still, I don't remove my hand as I return her smile, and when she presses even closer into that touch, it's all I can do not to lean down and claim that sweet, full mouth of hers.

"Should I not?" I ask her.

"I... don't mind it."

Trying not to let that inflate my ego any more than strictly necessary, I lead her from my office and down the hall toward the elevators. I keep my hand on her back the entire time, and Nora makes no move to stop me from doing so.

A small victory, but after the absolute devastation of my last couple of attempts with her, it feels like triumph.

As we wait for the elevator, Nora looks around the space with sharp contemplation.

"So you're like, what? The boss of this entire place?"

I chuckle. "That's one way of putting it. I oversee the several divisions that make up Morgan-Blair Enterprises, but it's the talented teams within those divisions that keep the business running day in and day out."

"Ah," she says. "So you're more symbolic. A figurehead. Like the one on your ship."

"Ship?"

"On your desk. With the tentacles and the carved woman at the front of it."

Is Nora... teasing me?

It's such an unexpected delight that I bark out a startled laugh as the elevator arrives. "Careful, Lenora. Any more of that and I might just cancel our date."

"No," she says, absolutely certain. "You won't."

Clever little siren.

The nickname pops into my head unbidden, settling with a sense of permanence.

Nora's a siren made to tempt me, to draw me in with the song of her very being. I could be anywhere in any of the seven seas, and she'd be the light that always beckons me back to shore.

She steps into the elevator, and losing her warmth against my palm leaves me immediately unmoored.

Why didn't I ask her to go out tonight? Or better yet, right now. I'd cancel the rest of my plans for the day to have another five minutes with her.

Nora presses the button to take her down to the lobby, then takes a step back to stand in the middle of the elevator. She crosses her arms over her chest and looks at me thoughtfully.

"Tomorrow night?" she asks.

"Tomorrow night," I confirm.

"Alright then, kraken. It's a date."

The elevator doors close, and the last image I have of Nora

is a soft smile and the smallest glint of a challenge in her hazel eyes.

It's a date, indeed.

7

Nora

I'm going on a date with a kraken.

Standing in front of the closet in my studio apartment, I stare at my limited wardrobe selections. What do you wear on a date with a kraken?

Elias promised we wouldn't do anything too elaborate, but I'm taking that with a grain of salt. Too curious to resist, I spent an hour searching for him last night online.

The kraken is rich as hell.

There's not much written about him before congress passed the Paranormal Acts, but tons of magazine and newspaper articles published after paint him as a brilliant businessman.

Morgan-Blair is staffed mainly by paranormals, and if the articles are anything to go by, Elias and Blair worked for years in the shadows of the company to build it into what it is today. Successful, sprawling, and focused on giving each of its employees a stake in ownership. Over a hundred years' worth of work, though he didn't get to come forward and take credit for any of it until after the passage of the Acts.

Also according to the articles, he's over three hundred years old. He's lived lifetimes, seen times and places I can't even fathom, and now he wants... me? The idea is enough to make my head spin.

I try not to think about it too hard as I pick out a dark gray, long-sleeved knit dress, a pair of black tights, and a belt. Simple, somewhat casual, but also dressy enough if we end up somewhere fancy.

As I finish getting ready, I keep reminding myself to remain calm. Like Elias said, this is just a date. There's no pressure. If I decide it's not for me, if I decide *he's* not for me, that's it. I can walk away from all of this and never look back.

I have to trust he's being honest with me about that, otherwise none of this is going to work out.

Taking one last look in the mirror and deciding I've cleaned up as well as I'm going to, I take a few more calming deep breaths, grab my jacket, and head out the door.

It's a forty-five minute bus ride downtown, and although it's not raining yet, the sky is heavy with clouds as I get off at my stop and walk to the spot Elias texted me to meet him at. We're pretty close to Pike Place Market, just a couple blocks away from the water, and despite all my nerves, I find I'm getting unexpectedly excited to see him with each passing moment.

It feels... good, to be putting myself back out there. Scary, but good.

All the weird pressures about the mating thing aside, this is my first first date in years, and a small part of me is just proud of myself for doing it at all.

Rounding a street corner, I find Elias waiting just where

he said he would be, dressed in a soft-looking, deep green sweater, dark jeans, and a well-tailored coat.

God, he's handsome.

I've thought so since the day I saw him at the Bureau, but having the time to really get a look at him without panicking —well, without panicking *much*—drives that point home all the more clearly.

He looks way more put together tonight than he did the first time I saw him, and much less intimidating than he did all suited up as a CEO at his office, but even clean-shaven and with his hair styled a bit more casual, he still can't shake the whole pirate vibe. The scar and the wicked gleam in his blue eyes make that impossible.

"Hello," he says, and his smile is clear in his voice, all wrapped up in that deep, warm accent of his. It sounds vaguely British, but layered with other places and times I can't identify, something that's entirely unique to this kraken.

"Hi," I say nervously, tugging on my jacket.

Elias takes his time looking me up and down, and though I freeze for a moment under that inspection, it only lasts until I read the naked appreciation in his gaze. A few more of my nerves melt away, and a small, warm bloom of anticipation wells up in the bottom of my stomach.

"You look beautiful, Nora," Elias says as he offers me his arm. "Shall we?"

I nod and tuck my hand into the crook of his elbow. There's something endearing about the gesture, something old-fashioned and chivalrous that brings a small smile to my lips.

"Where are you taking me?" I ask him, too curious not to.

Elias gives my arm a squeeze. "It's not far. And you agreed to let me surprise you."

He's got me there, and it's only a few minutes later as he leads me from the street corner down a couple of blocks that we reach our destination.

"The aquarium?" I ask. "Is it still open this late?"

"Not usually," he explains, reaching for the door to open it for me. "But I called in a favor."

Of course he could call in a favor, but I'm not complaining as we step inside and a woman dressed in black slacks and a button-up is waiting to greet us.

"Hello Ms. Perry, Mr. Morgan," she says warmly. "And welcome."

"Denise is the aquarium's director," Elias explains. "I've been on the Board here for a few years and have worked closely with Denise on several conservation initiatives."

Denise laughs warmly. "That's certainly an understatement."

What she means by that, I'm not exactly sure, but a bit of color rises on Elias's cheeks and he clears his throat.

"Denise has been kind enough to allow us private use of the aquarium tonight."

"My absolute pleasure," Denise says. "And please take all the time you need. I'll let the two of you explore."

After she heads back into an office at the side of the lobby, I glance at Elias.

"Let me guess. By 'working with' Denise on conservation initiatives, does that mean you've donated a whole lot of money to those initiatives?"

The color on his handsome face deepens. "In simple terms, yes." He falls silent for a few moments, glancing around the space. "Does it bother you, my wealth?"

I can't help it, I snort. "No. It doesn't. It's just... a lot to take in, you know?"

He offers me his arm again. "I know. But luckily we have plenty of colorful fish to distract us tonight. You barely have to pay attention to me if you'd rather not."

That doesn't seem anywhere near possible given that I'm

already having a hard time keeping my eyes off him, but I take Elias's arm anyway and let him lead the way deeper into the building.

It turns out the fish *are* a nice distraction from any lingering nerves, and although we're the only ones here, after a few minutes it becomes easy enough to pretend this is just a normal date.

Even though I've lived in Seattle for three years, I've never been here before, and find myself fascinated by the displays and by Elias's running commentary. He tells me about not only the fish and crustaceans in the tanks around us, but the conservation programs aimed at preserving the diverse marine life in the Puget Sound and educating visitors and the community about the importance of that ecosystem.

I'm half taking in all the details, half just enjoying listening to him speak.

Elias is animated and passionate and earnest, a far cry from my first impression of him back at the Bureau. Still, there are moments where he stumbles over his words a bit, or seems a little uncertain if he should give me more space or keep his hand on my back, where it has a tendency to wander. In some ways, he seems almost as nervous as I am.

Which is... unexpectedly endearing. Seeing some of his nerves calms me down even more, helps me relax into the knowledge that all of this might be as strange and anxiety provoking for him as it is for me.

Watching him now, feeling and seeing the care he's taking with me, a thought strikes me suddenly, and brings a little bubble of warmth up into the center of my chest.

He's trying. Trying to make me comfortable, maybe trying to tamp down whatever kraken part of himself already considers me his.

After my conversation with Holly and Kenna, I did some research into the way mating and mating bonds work. If the articles I read and videos I watched are any indication, it can be a little... intense. There's not a lot out there on krakens—they seem pretty rare in the whole paranormal landscape—but for other species, it sounds like something that just reaches out and smacks them in the face. No warning. No preventing or getting around it. Just an instinctual draw to another person or being.

Sounds kind of miserable, to be honest. What if your mate turns out to be a person who's rude to restaurant servers, or who hates all the TV shows and movies you love? What if they end up being a huge bore, or have completely different life goals and ideologies?

Or is someone with a massively messy past and trust issues up to her ears?

"All of this sounds like a passion of yours," I say when we stop by a tidal pool display that's open to touch and explore. I crouch down and skim my hand over the water before glancing back up at him.

Elias is looking at me with a soft smile on his face, watching as I reach into the pool and run my fingers along a couple of sea stars.

"It is," he says. "I thought this might be a nice way to share a little more about myself."

Peeking out from a small rock cove in the pool, a long, red tentacle reaches out to meet my searching fingers. An octopus. Too curious to resist, I reach out and give it a gentle stroke. The bumpy, rubbery skin is strange under my fingers, but not unpleasant.

"Oh really?" I ask, glancing over my shoulder at him. "And you didn't just bring me here to get me comfortable with the idea of touching sea creature skin?"

The off-color joke slips out before I can stop it, and seems to surprise Elias as much as it surprises me.

His eyes widen, darting down to where my hand's still

sunken into the tide pool, stroking the octopus. "That's not—gods, I didn't mean for—"

He stops talking when I break out in giggles, snapping my dry hand over my mouth to stifle the sound.

"S-sorry," I stutter. "I couldn't resist."

His face is slack with surprise for a few moments, but when he finally smiles back at me, it's not just with humor.

No, there's a pulse of darker amusement there as well. A bit of that pirate's roguish promise, a sliver of undeniable hunger. Strangely, it doesn't frighten me in the slightest.

Quite the opposite, in fact.

Still, he's all innocence as he replies. "And what do you think? How does that skin feel beneath your fingertips, Nora?"

My palms twitch, fingers curling a little as I draw my hand back out of the water. "It's... alright, I guess."

He laughs softly, and I'm suddenly flushed again at the reminder of who exactly I'm on a date with. Is this what Elias would feel like when he shifted? How would that even work? The idea of going to bed with an octopus isn't exactly appealing, but a human man with some extra appendages that he could use to...

Elias's smirk only deepens, like he can follow the path my mind's going down, and I quickly straighten and dry my hands with a paper towel from the nearby dispenser.

"What's next?" I ask, a little more breathlessly than I intended.

"Dinner," he says, reaching for my hand and clasping it in his as he leads me on through the aquarium.

We walk through a short tunnel, and my breath catches as we step into a massive, domed room with glass-paneled walls and a ceiling looking out into a tank filled with fish and other marine life. In the center of the space, a table, two chairs, and a couple of pizza boxes and takeout containers.

"Nothing too elaborate," Elias says. "Just pizza."

Turning to face him with a wry smile, I shake my head. "I think all of this counts as elaborate."

He's absolutely unrepentant as he pulls out my chair for me. "I would apologize, but if you do end up wanting to date me, I fear you may have to get used to this. It's been a long, long time since I've had anyone to spoil."

"How long?" I ask, before I think better of it.

Are we already to the point of discussing our exes? Maybe not, and God, I hope he doesn't ask me about mine.

Elias's smile is a little sad when he answers. "A while."

For him, that could be decades. And who do krakens date, anyway? Other krakens? Other paranormals? Humans?

Opening up a pizza box, he elaborates. "The last time I had a serious relationship was maybe twenty, twenty-five years ago."

It would be the perfect opening to share something about my last relationship, to relate to him on some level deeper than the small-talk we've made so far, but I balk. I grab a piece of pizza and take a bite, and even though it's more delicious than any slice I've ever had, it doesn't take away the slight shame of chickening out.

"Bertrosa's," Elias says when he sees my reaction to the food. "The smallest little hole-in-the-wall place, but some of the best pizza I've had on this side of the Atlantic."

"And on the other side of the Atlantic?"

That launches a discussion of the merits of European cuisine over American, and a few small glimpses into the depth and breadth of life Elias has lived.

Outside of movies and TV, I've never seen any of the places he talks about.

Not London, where he was born in the early 1700s, or Paris or Rome. Not the various spots he's sailed around the Caribbean and through the Indian Ocean, details he gets strangely hesitant to dive into when I ask what he was doing in those parts of the world.

Maybe the pirate thing wasn't all that far off.

The idea is absurd, and yet, when I look at him I can still see it. The roguish glint in his eye, the accent that speaks of faraway lands and adventures. It also makes it all that much harder for me to believe he'd have any interest in me.

What do I offer in comparison?

When it comes to conversation, not much. And even though I'm well-aware I'm avoiding the openings Elias gives me to answer questions he asks about me, preferring to turn it back around to him, he doesn't press.

Despite how well the evening has gone so far, and despite how open and kind he's still being, I feel some of the nerves creep back in the longer we sit here.

Damn it, Nora.

This is what I didn't want to let happen. But every time a question comes up that might veer toward my past with Daniel, or to the small, scared life I've been leading for the past few of years, I just can't. Can't speak, can't elaborate, can't give anything but half-answers or non-answers that make me feel more and more self-conscious.

And that's not even mentioning the fact that Elias seems... great. Well spoken, well traveled, smart and witty.

"So," I say, still mulling over everything he's told me and feeling more confused and uncertain than ever. "Even after all the years you've lived and the places you've been, there hasn't been anyone else you considered as your... mate?"

The word still isn't easy to say out loud.

"No, Nora," he says softly. "There hasn't been. And there won't ever be."

My throat tightens.

There it is again, the reminder I'm not just some average woman on an average first date with an average, albeit extremely handsome, man. The reminder that none of this is casual for him, and that I'm in far, far deeper waters with Elias than I can even begin to comprehend.

It scares me. All of it scares me.

Not only because he's lived more life than I can imagine, and that he lives in a world so completely different from my own.

What scares me more than anything?

The way he still looks at me. Attention fixed solely on me, studying me, unable to completely hide the threads of possession I saw that day at the Bureau, even though I can tell he's trying to mask it.

Struck with the sudden need to get out of my chair, to fidget and move my legs, I stand from the table and cross the domed space to stand in front of the wall of glass, looking out into the tank. Various fish drift by, and the rippling movement of the water casts the entire room in a hypnotic blue glow.

"Tell me what you're thinking."

Elias's soft voice is the only warning I get that he's come to stand just behind me, and when I whirl around, he's right there. His brow is creased in concern, blue eyes searching and thoughtful as he waits for me to answer.

"I don't know how to feel about all of this."

"Which parts?" he asks gently.

My laugh is shaky as I try to think of where I should even begin. "Well, I suppose we could start with the whole *mates* thing and go from there."

"Would it be so bad?" he asks, voice low and soft. "Would it be so terrible to have a male devoted to you completely? One who wanted to take care of you and always ensure your safety, one who only wants to see to your peace and happiness?"

How can I make him understand?

Because that scares me, too, the idea of belonging to

anyone.

"What happens when caring for me turns into thinking you know what's best for me?" I ask. "Or what happens when you... I don't know. Get bored with me, realize I'm not what you wanted after all?"

Elias's eyes are soft, but somehow also impossibly knowing, like he could reach in and see every single secret I've kept tucked away.

"You pose hypotheticals without even knowing me, little siren."

"Little... siren?"

Those blue eyes darken nearly to black. "Yes, little siren. You're the temptation designed just for me, the lure keyed to my blood, the song beckoning me toward the shore."

"Into the rocks, you mean," I whisper, drawing on the scant mythology knowledge I possess.

"And I will crash gladly, Nora." His words are a low, dark caress, and when I don't flinch away from them, he leans closer and curls his hand around my jaw. "I'd smash myself to bits for you. I'd let myself be drawn to you, a thousand times and a thousand more, even if it meant my ruin."

"You don't mean that."

How could he? He doesn't even *know* me. He doesn't know all the ways I'm damaged, all the reasons it's so hard for me to trust him. To trust anyone, really.

"Don't I?" he asks. "And how would you know that?"

"Because I... I'm not..."

The hand curled around my cheek moves to the back of my neck, stroking lightly, fingers threading into my hair to grasp gently and tilt my face up.

Is he going to kiss me?

I'm half-convinced he is, but he only holds my gaze and strokes his thumb over and over the nape of my neck.

"Whatever you were about to say," Elias murmurs, "I

would ask that you never make any assumptions about how I see you and what I feel for you, little siren."

"How do you see me?"

Another stroke of his thumb, a pulse of gentle pressure that has me leaning closer to him.

"I see a woman who's strong and resilient. I see a woman who's braver than she might give herself credit for. I see you, Nora."

Without giving myself time to second guess, I lean in and lay my cheek against the soft fabric of his sweater. His breath catches for a moment, then leaves his chest in a long exhale when he brings his other hand to the center of my back and rubs in slow, soothing circles.

He must know. If not all of it... then at least some. Otherwise, how could he ever make that assumption? He doesn't know me, shouldn't be saying things like this, not so soon.

When I lean back and look into his eyes, it's gentle patience and sincerity looking back at me.

"We may have lived different lives," he says. "And we may not know much about each other yet, but all I would ask you for is time. And openness, if you're willing to allow it. Enough for us to give this a chance."

The request is... simple. And terrifying. Time and openness. Sharing things about myself that part of me would rather keep hidden forever.

"I... can try." It's as much as I can offer right now.

"That's all I need." With what appears to be a great deal of effort, Elias removes his hands from me and takes a step back, glancing once at his watch. "I'm afraid it's time for us to leave. I promised Denise we wouldn't impose on the aquarium's hospitality for too long."

Though it makes me a coward, I'm glad for the reprieve. I'm glad to have Elias tuck my arm back in his and lead me from the domed room back to the main entrance. I'm glad for the cool night air on my face, and the chance to hide from myself for just a little longer.

Still, with a handsome kraken on my arm and the earlier promise of the evening now dimmed, I can't help but be disappointed in myself, too.

Was it only a couple hours ago I felt excited for this date, hopeful, ready to take a step forward after so many years of standing still? How did I get from there to here, when Elias has been nothing but patient and understanding, careful with me, so willing to take everything at my own pace?

All those doubts and uncertainties, the endlessly frustrating conflict between the version of myself I wish I could be and the one that I am, follow me out of the aquarium and back down the sidewalk as we step out into the crisp Seattle night.

8

Elias

Leaving the aquarium with Nora's arm tucked into mine, my thoughts are scattered and every intention I had for this evening is laying broken like glass on the pavement around us.

How did I mess this up so spectacularly?

It's drizzling slightly as we head back toward downtown, and just before Nora reaches up to pull her hood over her head, I catch a glimpse of her face, expression tight and worried.

There have been moments over the last couple of hours when she seemed to relax. Well, almost relax. But any mention or reminder of who and what I am, of the bond that's growing more and more solidified in my chest with each moment I spend with her, sends her right back to square one.

I didn't even mean to delve into those topics tonight, but

once we'd gotten talking...

Gods, I should have shut my damned mouth.

This was supposed to be a date, a simple date, a chance to spend a little time with her—no pressure, no expectations.

There's something about Nora, though, that's scrambled my wits since the beginning.

Or perhaps it's just me, rusty and out of practice as I am, not giving her the space she needs or able to take things slowly. She gave me a chance, and all I did was overwhelm her.

I'd planned to see if she wanted to grab a drink somewhere after this, talk some more, but by the nervous energy radiating from her, it's probably not something she's even remotely interested in.

"Can I walk you to your car?"

Nora laughs a little, and I'm not sure why until she explains. "You can walk me to the bus stop, I guess."

Public transit is safe. I know it's safe. It's probably safer than getting in a car and driving.

Still, no part of me wants to walk her to the bus stop.

How far is it from here to wherever she lives? It's late. It's dark out. Will she have to transfer and take multiple lines? Will she have to wait outside in the dark and the cold?

"Would you let me drive you home?"

I'm convinced the question was a bridge too far when she turns to face me, looking me up and down with that familiar, worried little divot between her brows.

"Show me your driver's license," she says unexpectedly.

I'm not about to question it as I reach into my back pocket and pull out my wallet. Handing over the license, she squints at it for a moment before pulling out her phone.

"Mind if I send a pic to my friends? You know, just in case."

It makes my chest tighten painfully she would think that's

necessary, but I only nod. She snaps the photo and sends a text, then hands it back to me. As she does, she laughs softly again.

"What?"

Shaking her head, she tucks her phone away and smiles up at me before answering. "Your license says your eyes are blue."

"Is that not accurate?"

"Not quite. I don't know what I'd call them, but 'blue' doesn't seem like... enough."

Warmth diffuses through me, all the way from the slow smile that curls my lips to the two hearts beating in my chest, and further still, until I'm surprised my entire body isn't glowing with it.

"Come on," I tell her, taking her arm once more. "I'm parked nearby."

Opening the door to my Range Rover where it's parked down the street, I help her inside and close the door behind her before climbing in the driver's side.

"Where to?" I ask, starting the vehicle before typing the address she gives me into my phone's GPS.

Another pulse of relief as I see how far it is to her home. Not only for the additional time it affords us together, but because she won't have to make the long trip by bus.

Our conversation as we leave downtown and head for her neighborhood is light, slightly impersonal, but a welcome change of pace after the fraught end to our time at the aquarium. Nora seems to relax a little, too, now that she's not being forced to deal with topics far heavier than should be allowed on any first date.

She tells me about the work she does at Tandbroz as a shift manager, some of the new release books she's been enjoying, the drink she ordered the morning I saw her at Second Cup.

A job she likes, but doesn't love, if the tone of her voice is any indication. Epic fantasy and cozy romance. A hot chai latte.

I tuck each detail away, hoarding them like the avaricious creature I am. I'm greedy for this woman, for every little part of her, and I can't dredge up even the slightest sense of shame for treasuring anything and everything she's willing to give me.

The sky opens up with a deluge of rain mid-way through our drive, and I'm more thankful than ever she's trusted me enough to see her home safely.

When we finally make it to her neighborhood, Nora directs me down a tree-lined boulevard. It's a quiet street filled with older homes, and the one we're parked in front of has been converted into apartments. The area seems safe, though I can't help but squint out into the dark, rain-soaked night, looking for anything that seems out of the ordinary.

Inside the car, we're cocooned in soft, percussive sound and darkness as the rain continues to fall. In the engine's hum and the warmth from the car's heater, it's a small pocket of privacy made just for us. Nora's still settled back against her seat, looking at me with a question in her eyes, but not making any move to get out of the car.

I'm not going to rush her. I'd stay here all night if she wanted to, talking or just looking at her. It doesn't really matter.

"Thank you," she says finally. "For tonight. I'm sorry it got a little... heavy there, toward the end. But I had a nice time."

It's a lukewarm compliment, or at least it seems to be in the face of everything I'm feeling. *Nice* doesn't even begin to cover it. Not by a thousand leagues.

"No apologies," I tell her quietly. "I had a wonderful time with you. And I'd like to see you again, Nora. Although I think you already know that."

Saying I'd like to see her again is the understatement of the century. The millennia, probably.

When she doesn't reply, I dare to press a little more. "Is that something you might want as well?"

Nora looks up at me with big, uncertain eyes. "I... yeah, I think I do. But there are a few things about my life that make this... complicated."

She seems to consider what else she wants to say, and with no desire to rush her, I wait quietly and patiently.

"Mr. Blair mentioned that you have a knack for getting to the bottom of a problem. For knowing things."

I nod slowly, feeling the ax of the consequences I probably deserve for invading her privacy hanging over my head.

"And what do you know about me?"

It's no use lying to her, not when I'm so determined for there to be honesty between us. Though I'm not proud of myself, I fess up.

"I know you once were involved with Daniel Sorenson. And I know you used to go by the name Nora Wheeler."

"Is that all?"

"That's all. I now know a bit more about Sorenson than I ever would have cared to, but there's a lot more information available about him than there is about you."

Nora is quiet as she considers that. No force on Earth could compel me to speak again, to offer some other explanation or any excuses for my behavior, not until she has the chance to say what she needs to.

Outside, the rain continues to pelt the top of the car and the windshield, muffled sound that fills the spaces between us.

"That part of my life is over," she says finally. "But it's still something I struggle with every single day. Things with Daniel and I... they ended badly."

From the weight of the pain and exhaustion in her tone, I suspect that's another colossal understatement.

"He…" she starts, and then trails off, a flash of shame on her features. "He tried to find me. A few years ago. I left without telling him where I was going or giving him any way to contact me. But a friend from DC who did still have my number called and let me know that he… didn't take it well."

"And did he find you?" My tone is tight, strained, as I think about her being made to feel like she had to hide.

She shakes her head. "He didn't. I don't know if he ever even pieced it together that I'm in Seattle, or if he's still looking for me."

There's still a bit of shame lingering on her face, a haunted shadow in her eyes that has no place being there.

"None of that was your fault," I tell her.

Nora surprises me by laughing a little. "You don't know that."

"I do."

"How?"

"Because nobody has the right to make you feel unsafe. Nobody has the right to push past the boundaries you've set."

Even as I say the words, a deep sense of unease settles in my chest. Is that what I'd done to her at the beginning? Is that why she'd feared me so much when we'd first met?

"Sometimes I don't know how to separate it all," she says softly, not looking at me now, but staring out at the rivulets of rain running down the windshield. "I don't know how to put all of that fear aside and just… trust people."

There's something broken in those words, something that tugs at all the golden filaments reaching out from my chest toward her.

"I'm not demanding your trust, Nora. I would like it, yes, but I also intend to earn it. If you still have any reservations about me, or think that I'm someone who makes you unsafe, I want you to honor those feelings and make the choice you need to."

She looks back at me then, and everything she must be feeling is clear as day on her face. All the doubt, all the mistrust, every last thing that makes her so afraid of letting down her guard and letting me in.

"I... don't think you are."

"Good," I tell her gently. "If I ever give you a reason to doubt that, I hope you'll let me know."

Nora nods, though the troubled look doesn't leave her eyes. When she turns and reaches for the door handle beside her, I can't help but speak up.

"Can I walk you to your door?"

Finally, finally, that small smile of hers reappears. It starts with her lips, but goes all the way to her eyes before she nods. I get out of the driver's side, and something deep and ridiculously masculine purrs its approval when she waits for me to come around to her side and open the door.

Before today, I wouldn't have said chivalry was an intrinsic part of my nature. I've always been conscientious and polite with my lovers, but this is another matter entirely. Whether it's the bond doing something to my psyche, or just the soul-deep need I have to care for this woman who I suspect hasn't had anyone go out of their way to take care of her in a very long time, I'm not sure.

What I do know is that as I offer her my hand and help her out of the car, as we both dart through the rain to her front door, she's still smiling and looking so damned beautiful it hurts.

Standing in the glow of the porch light, with the rain falling beyond the small alcove outside the door, I'd do just about anything to stretch this moment out a little longer.

It's too much, too soon, and even I'm sane enough to recognize the need to give her space and breathing room. Nora needs to come to me, choose me, and making her feel stifled or pressured won't get me anywhere with her.

If it's forever I want, it's patience I need, even if my hasty, greedy nature wants me to reach out and snatch the treasure in front of me and hold her close.

With that in mind, I know I should say good night.

Nora hesitates, fiddling with her keys.

What's she waiting for? She can't be expecting... no, I wouldn't have that much good fortune handed to me this evening, not after I've barely started to make up for how poorly the beginning of our acquaintance has gone, not after I've—

Whatever other self-recriminations are about to run through my mind are stopped immediately by the grasp of Nora's hands on my shoulders, and the press of her soft, warm lips on my own.

They're wet with rain, and tasting just like I thought they would—like the cool bite of the ocean and the soft silk of flower petals.

And when she leans in closer, puts a hand on the back of my neck, and opens for me, I lose myself entirely.

9

Nora

When I got out of the car, I don't think I consciously intended to kiss Elias.

Or maybe I had, maybe part of me's been curious about what it would be like from the moment I saw him tonight. From the moment I saw him at the Bureau.

But physical attraction aside, it's the last half hour that's made the difference between scurrying into my apartment and being bold enough to lean into him and find out. It's the soft reassurance, the patience, the way he's stayed right with me and not pulled away for a moment, even when I was totally lost in my head.

Part of me's still humming with nerves as I reach up and put my hands on his shoulders, press my lips to his. It's a risk, one I'm pretty sure I can safely bet on, but still a risk, and my stomach is rioting with butterflies as I take it.

But maybe that's okay, too.

Maybe it's about time I took a risk.

I started it. I leaned in and took what I wanted, and though he goes absolutely still against me for a couple of seconds, Elias takes over almost immediately.

One of his hands cradles the back of my head, winding into my hair, and the other wraps firmly around my lower back, pulling me even closer to him. His tongue presses against my lips, and I open for him immediately, tasting his groan as he deepens the kiss. The hand in my hair tightens, angling my head back, and it's my turn to groan when he nips at my lip and teases me with gentle, wicked strokes of his tongue against mine.

Elias tastes like the crisp salt of seawater, blended with some dark, intoxicating spice I don't have a name for. His kiss is firm and unyielding, plundering, claiming, a blatant display of possession that should scare me.

It doesn't, though, not for a single second. Something Blair said to me rings through the back of my mind.

If I know Elias, he's already ready to treasure you for the rest of eternity.

That's precisely what this kiss is. A pirate taking the bounty he desires. A kraken hoarding a prized treasure close.

Walking me a few steps deeper into the alcove, Elias presses me up against the wall. His hand moves to my hip, squeezing tightly, and even through our layers of clothing I can feel the hard press of his body and the firm ridge of his erection.

Knowing that, feeling him already hot and hard against me, sparks something dark and dangerous low in my belly. I'm half-crazed with it as I cling to him, kissing him back with as much ferocity as he's claiming me.

What's happening to me?

I've never felt like this. Never been this starved for

someone else's touch.

It's like another person has stepped into my body and taken it over. Someone bold and eager and completely unrestrained by her past. I don't know who that woman is, but I'm not about to question it now. No, all I want to do is to be closer to him, wrap myself around him and drown in him until...

It's Elias who breaks the kiss, breathing heavily and leaning his forehead down against mine.

"Little siren," he says, voice raspy and hoarse. "I'm sorry. I didn't mean to—"

He really, really needs to stop apologizing. But instead of telling him that, I just kiss him again, cutting off his words and drawing a low growl from his chest. He doesn't pull away, though, but tightens his hold and makes no secret of the fact that he's enjoying this just as much as I am.

One of his hands comes up to cup my breast over my dress and I groan into his mouth. My thighs part slightly, tangling with his as he steps into me. I'm half-straddled over one of his thighs, pressing closer, shifting on him, chasing the friction of the firm muscle pressed against me and...

"Nora."

I lean back, some of the fog in my brain clearing. It leaves just enough space for a wave of self-consciousness to wash through me, staining my cheeks bright red.

My apology comes out in an embarrassing little squeak. "I'm sorry. I don't know what... don't know why I..."

Elias pulls me back to him, tucking my head into his chest, and his deep laugh rumbles against my ear. "No need to apologize. I just wasn't sure if things were moving a little too fast."

I nod against his coat. "Too fast. You're right."

Another laugh, accompanied by a finger under my chin, tipping my face up so he can press a few light kisses on my lips. He gives me just enough to tease, to tempt...

Only to have him pull away again.

It's an award-winning effort not to let out the whine of protest that's lodged itself in the back of my throat.

"Good night, Nora," he says, deep voice still tinged with humor.

My own voice is hoarse when I take an unsteady step back and smooth out my skirt where it's hitched up around my thighs. "Good night."

He doesn't leave right away. No, he reaches up and pushes back some of the damp hair that's fallen forward over my face, cups my cheek for a moment, and gives me another crooked, provoking smile before he turns and heads back out into the rain. I'm still standing there, kiss-drunk and wobbly, when he stops right in the middle of the sidewalk, getting drenched, and calls back over his shoulder.

"I do hope you consider a second date with me, little siren. Because if that's the only taste of you I ever get, I'm not sure I'll survive."

Fully unable to keep my knees solid enough to stay vertical, I slump against the alcove's wall and stay there until he climbs back into his car and drives away.

10

Nora

Five days later, I'm still floating somewhere near the ceiling as I arrange a display of fantasy paperbacks at Tandbroz.

I can't stop thinking about my date with Elias. In every quiet moment I'm not answering the phone or helping a customer or talking with a coworker, my mind wanders back to that exact same place.

And, unfortunately for me, the last couple of days in the store have been slow, so it's given me plenty of time to think and obsess and daydream.

About Elias, about how even though the date had it's rocky moments, it also had moments that have stuck with me for days. His patience, his kindness, the things he said about wanting to care for and protect me.

And that kiss... God. That kiss.

My face flames with the memory.

Did I embarrass myself with how much I wanted him, and how absolutely wild for him I got when he kissed me?

Elias seemed just as hungry as I was, just as eager, just as torn about ending our date and saying good night. With some time and hindsight, I'm glad he had enough sense to walk things back a little and slow us down, because I definitely wasn't capable of it in that moment.

Cheeks going even redder, and endlessly thankful I'm the only one in the shop right now, I shake off my distraction and get back to the box of books I'm supposed to be restocking.

As I do I can't help but pull my phone from my pocket and glance at it, feeling a tiny pang of disappointment when I see there are no new messages.

Elias and I have traded a few texts over the last couple of days, and made tentative plans to meet up this weekend.

Weird. Texting with my potential kraken mate is undeniably weird.

But also kind of wonderful, to have that fluttery feeling back in my chest, to flirt with him a little and feel embarrassingly like a teenager with a crush when I glance at my phone and see a message from him.

The rest of my worries haven't gone away, not for a single second, but they've taken up a lot less real estate in my brain the past few days. I'm thankful for the reprieve, no matter how long it lasts.

Even if that means I've been a somewhat less-than-stellar Tandbroz employee this week.

It's Thursday evening, and I'm working the closing shift alone. I usually don't, but my coworker Mirabel was sick today and Ana, the owner, is still trying to balance new motherhood with business ownership, and I was the only one available to close.

It's fine, really. Thursdays aren't our busiest days and I've got enough on my mind to keep me plenty distracted as I bounce back and forth around the shop getting some evening tasks done. I've got just a couple hours until I lock up and head home, and I'm already looking forward to my next three days off. A whole long weekend, and hopefully one that includes seeing my kraken again.

I'm so distracted by those thoughts as I straighten out a few shelves near the front of the store that I take a full five seconds to process the person who's just walked by the window. I see them out of the corner of my eye, and when something deep and instinctual pulls me to stop and turn to get a better look, I can't fully comprehend what I'm seeing.

A head of dark brown hair. The briefest glimpse of a profile and the outline of a body I know well.

Far too well.

My heart hammers in my ears and the entire world narrows to that one glimpse.

Everything else is darkness and static, and my brain goes completely, horribly blank. When I blink a moment later, the person has already passed by the window, but I'm still frozen in place.

It isn't. It can't be. There's no way it can be…

Daniel.

A deep well of black, clawing fear opens up in my chest.

It's not him. It's can't be him.

He's in DC. He doesn't know where I am or where I work. There's no way…

Finally shaken out of my paralysis, I duck behind a shelf and move slowly and steadily toward the front window, doing my best to stay out of view of the street as I peer into the Seattle night.

There are plenty of people walking the downtown sidewalks, and the man I saw is already gone, but that doesn't stop the panic. It doesn't erase the lurching in my stomach or the soul-deep certainty I just saw my worst nightmare walk by.

And I'm here alone. Completely vulnerable if he comes back.

Running back behind the front counter, I crouch down on the floor and try to think. What do I do? Who can I call?

The police aren't an option. If that person really was Daniel, he did nothing illegal by just walking down a public street. *I* left *him*. There was never any law enforcement involved, no restraining orders, nothing in our relationship that would have escalated to that level, other than on that very last night and...

No, the police won't be any help. Especially when I'm well aware of the different set of rules for wealthy, important people dealing with law enforcement.

Do I call Ana? What do I say to her?

Sorry, I know I said I was alright closing tonight, but I think I just saw my nightmare of an ex walk by and now I need to go home. Do I know it was him? No. Have I ever said a single thing to make you think I have a nightmare ex to be concerned about? No.

Holly or Kenna? No, neither of them should be involved in this.

Mind still racing, body still numb, I pull my phone out of my pocket and hit 'call' before I can really think it through.

"Hello?" Elias answers on the second ring. "Nora?"

"Hi," I say, trying to keep the trembling out of my voice. "I'm sorry to call you out of the blue."

"What's wrong?"

Well, so much for playing it cool. His voice is clipped and concerned, and I can almost imagine the furrows on his forehead and the way his ocean-blue eyes would be narrowed. It snaps a bit of rationality back into me, knowing I'm burdening someone else with my problems.

"It's probably nothing, but..." I trail off, suddenly feeling so, so stupid for blowing this out of proportion.

"Nora," Elias's deep voice prompts. "Tell me."

"I thought I saw Daniel. Outside the shop. It was just for a second, and I'm sure I'm imagining things... but I could have sworn it was him."

Elias's harsh curse is muffled, like he tried to pull the phone away from his mouth before he said it.

"I'm not in the country," he says, voice clear again.

"Oh." My cheeks heat with embarrassment. "I'm so sorry for bothering you. It's fine, really. It's nothing. I can—"

"I'm going to have Travis come and pick you up. He'll bring you to my house."

"Who's Travis?" I ask in a small voice.

"He works for me. He coordinates my private security."

Elias's steady, even words wrap around me through the phone, easing some of my lingering panic and making me clutch my cell even more tightly to the side of my face.

"Oh," I say again, still feeling foolish despite that reassurance. "That really isn't necessary."

"It is. If Daniel's in the neighborhood, he could come into the shop or find you after work."

My stomach clenches. He's got a point. Still, even though I called him for help, some part of me instinctively wants to deny actually accepting it.

"I have to work for a couple more hours. I'm here alone and I'm closing the store tonight."

"That's fine. Travis can stay and wait in the store while you finish up."

I pause before responding. Now that the initial adrenaline has faded and I've got a competent, very concerned kraken on the phone, I feel more idiotic than ever.

I shouldn't be bothering him with this. In all likelihood, I saw someone who only looks like Daniel. He's just your average white dude, and I'm sure there's a thousand people who look like him in Seattle alone. All of this is probably my own unresolved anxiety manifesting itself and making me someone else's problem.

Elias's voice reaches me again, low and gentle through the speaker. "Why did you call me, little siren?"

"Because I..."

Why *did* I call him?

On the other end of the line, he silently waits for me to answer, patient as ever.

"Because I knew I could count on you to help me," I whisper.

Elias lets out a short, harsh breath. "Always, Nora. You can always count on me to help you. Now, I'm going to hang up and call Travis. He should be there in fifteen minutes. In the meantime, I want you to keep your phone on you in case you need to call for help. Do you think you can lock the front door just until Travis gets there?"

"Yes. Yes, I think I can do that." Having a set of clear, concrete instructions makes my heart rate slow even further.

"I'll give him your phone number and let him know he needs to stay until you're finished working. Is that alright with you?"

"Yes," I say again. "And I'm sorry. I'm sure all of this is nothing. I'm sure I'm just overreacting and—"

"Nora," he interrupts, still gently, but with enough firm command in his voice for me to stop my stream of babbling apologies.

"Yeah?"

"Everything is going to be alright. Travis will be there soon. Keep your phone in your hand until he gets there, and know that I'll be home as soon as I can."

Some part of me still wants to argue. No one has looked out for me or cared for me like this in years—or ever, maybe—and I don't know how to accept it now that it's being offered.

"Call me if you need anything else, little siren," Elias

continues. "Alright?"

"Alright," I whisper, deciding to trust the help he's offering—deciding to trust *him*. "I will."

11

Elias

The moment my front door closes behind me, I sense my mate is nearby.

Nora is here, in my home, safe and protected, and it's enough to make my hearts feel like they're cracked wide open in my chest.

I should have never left the city.

Even though I was wheels-up and taking off from Montreal just an hour after speaking with Nora, it still took me six excruciating hours after that to get back to Seattle.

Fortunately, I didn't spend my time in the air completely idle. As soon as I got off the phone with Nora, I arranged for Travis to wait with her at work while another one of the security contractors we work with did a sweep of the neighborhood. After that, I'd spoken to Blair. And it only took me twenty seconds of that phone call for an unpleasant truth about Daniel Sorenson to come to light.

The bastard is in Seattle.

Not only in Seattle, but he was at the godsdamned Bureau meeting with Blair just a couple of hours before Nora saw him downtown.

The visit was unannounced, and held under the guise of fact-finding for the brand new congressional Paranormal Oversight Committee. Blair tried to call me right after, but I'd been in meetings with one of Morgan-Blair's Canadian partners and missed the call.

All of it smells foul.

Sorenson just so happens to show up in the city where his ex is living, the one who left him high and dry, the one who only a couple of weeks ago got herself onto the radar of the same government agency he's visiting? It's one too many coincidences to be pure happenstance.

I also can't escape another terrible truth.

Nora's wrapped up with the Bureau because of me. If that's how he found her…

Guilt clogging my throat, I set my things aside in the foyer and make my way to where a light is still shining in the kitchen.

Both Travis and Marta, my housekeeper, are waiting in the kitchen when I arrive.

They've both worked with me for years. Travis is a demi-fae with some of the keenest hunter's instincts I've ever encountered. Marta's a half-nymph, half-orc and has a remarkable talent for making people feel comfortable and at ease. Both of them are looking at me with concern as I enter the room.

"Where is she?" I ask.

Marta answers. "In the guest bedroom at the back of the house, the one overlooking the Sound."

I nod, pleased with that. It's the best room in the house.

Well, aside from my own bedroom, and as much as I'd rather Nora be there, I'm glad at least she'll be able to see the amazing view when she wakes up.

"And she's alright?"

Travis nods. "No sign of Sorenson anywhere downtown. I brought her here straight after she was done working and sent a team to do a sweep of her neighborhood as well."

"And I made sure she had the necessary toiletries and a few things to wear, per your instructions," Marta chimes in, smiling softly. "She's a very kind woman, your Nora."

My Nora. That's not quite true, but I don't have it in me to correct her.

Not in the mood for more small talk, I thank them both for their help tonight and head toward my bedroom. On the way there, I pass by Nora's door, and everything in me aches to stop, knock, see her, but it's late, far too late to disturb her.

Still, the urge doesn't give me a moment of peace as I hop in the shower. It doesn't abate for a single second as I pull on a pair of sweats and a t-shirt, or when I sit down on the edge of my empty bed and massage my aching temples.

Her siren song calls to me now more strongly than ever. Having her so close, knowing she's here in this place that belongs to me, it calls to something primal and powerful lurking in my soul.

I should keep my distance. I should crawl into bed and surrender to the tendrils of exhaustion that are pulling at my mind and body even now. I should leave her well enough alone, there will be time to talk in the morning.

All those thoughts circle pointlessly in the back of my mind, discarded and ignored, as I walk from my bedroom to hers. Just a look. That's all I'm going to allow myself. A look to reassure myself she's truly here and unharmed.

Opening her door with careful ease, I peer inside.

"Elias?"

Nora's voice pierces the quiet darkness, and it only takes a second for me to find her where she's sitting silhouetted in one of the chairs in front of the windows. She stands, turning to face me fully.

"I'm sorry," I say, wincing. "I shouldn't have disturbed you. I only wanted to make sure you were—"

My words cut off as she runs across the room toward me, and any rational thoughts I might have been holding onto disappear completely when she throws her arms around my neck, pressing herself to me. Wrapping her into an embrace, I hold her even closer, tucking her head into the space between my shoulder and jaw, letting out a ragged breath at the feel of her there.

Mate. My mate. Safe and in my arms. If having her in my home was a powerful, primal thing, then this is something else entirely.

It takes me a few seconds to concentrate on anything other than that instinct and on Nora's body pressed up against me, but when I do, I realize what she's wearing. A pair of shorts and a thin cotton tank top that leave her arms and legs bare.

I want to groan out loud.

Though we're both technically clothed, it feels impossibly intimate, holding her like this. Just a couple of layers between us do nothing to mute the delicious warmth of her skin and the sea salt of her scent.

"How did you get here so fast? Where were you?"

"Montreal," I say into her hair. "I headed for the airstrip right after you called me."

Nora's body goes stiff, and she tries to pull away. "I'm sorry. I shouldn't have made such a—"

"None of that," I murmur. "No apologies."

"But, I—"

My mouth finds hers, not sure what else I can do or say to make her believe me.

It might be a mistake to assume she'd even want to kiss me after everything she's been through today, but as soon as our lips meet she comes to warm, vibrant life in my arms. I swallow her small groan and tangle my hands into her hair.

Gods above, I needed this.

It seems that she may have, too, as she presses closer, meeting each one of my urgent kisses with her own. She tastes like toothpaste and her own unique salt and floral essence, and with every passing moment I sink further and further into her.

If I'm not careful, I could devour her whole. And Nora is just as eager, hands fisted in the soft fabric of my shirt. She tugs it upward, darting her fingers beneath to skim along my bare skin.

Reluctantly, I pull back from her. Not far enough to put any real space between us, but just enough to look into her bright, slightly glazed eyes.

"Nora," I half-whisper, half-groan.

She lays her forehead on my chest, still breathing hard.

"It's late," I murmur. "You should get some rest."

And indeed, it's a little past two in the morning. With the flight and the time changes, I'm just starting to feel the effects of my day of travel, and I imagine she must be exhausted after the day she's had as well.

"Would you stay?" she asks, voice barely above a whisper.

She... wants me here?

"Stay with you? In your bed?"

Nora nods. "Yes... I mean, you don't have to. If you'd rather—"

"There's nowhere else I'd rather be."

I take her hand and lead her to the bed, pulling back the covers and sliding in after her before settling on my back, giving her plenty of space.

Nora, the unimaginable treasure that she is, curls immediately against me. She lays her head on my shoulder, wraps an arm around my waist and glances up at me, something shy and questioning in her eyes.

"Is this alright?"

Gods, I can't help it, I laugh. When her brow furrows, I lean down and kiss it.

"It's more than alright."

Nora's answering smile lights up every part of me, and I kiss her forehead again.

"Sleep. I'll still be here when you wake up. You're not alone, little siren."

12

Nora

There's a kraken in my bed.

Well, technically it's *his* bed, but the point still stands as I blink awake and find myself sprawled across Elias's chest.

Did I really ask him to stay last night? Did he really accept?

The answer is obvious as he stirs beneath me, grumbling a little in his sleep. He has an arm banded around my back and when I lean back to get a better look at him, it tightens, keeping me in place.

I can't help my smile, just like I can't help taking a few long minutes to lie here and admire the impossibly attractive kraken I'm on top of.

It's... cute. Seeing him like this—sleep-tousled and a little grumpy about being woken up—is undeniably adorable. Which is one adjective I never thought I'd assign to this kraken, but here we are.

Some small, dim part of my brain has a moment of pause. Should this feel as natural as it does? Should I be more shy about this? More panicked?

Yesterday was an absolute roller coaster of emotions, and yet somehow I'm not feeling any of that right now. No, I'm only feeling calm and safe and very, very into the handsome man beneath me.

It's... strange. Feeling this way, *trusting* him enough to feel this way.

He came home for me. He helped me last night without a single moment of hesitation. I called, and he came. Simple as that.

When's the last time I had someone in my life who would drop everything for me?

Holly and Kenna are good friends, but I'd never imagine imposing on them that way. And family? My mom still lives in Phoenix, and we're not close. My dad fucked off to god knows where when I was just a baby and has never tried to contact us since.

I grew up used to being self sufficient, and maybe that's what Daniel had seen in me, someone desperate to be cared for, to have someone I could rely on, to feel like I wasn't alone. That need had turned out to be the thing he twisted and exploited for his own gain.

What if I'm falling into the same trap now?

Elias is still breathing deeply and evenly, and as I study him, I can't believe that worry is true. This feels... different. There was no expectation last night, no guilt, no exasperation at being inconvenienced by one of my problems.

I only had to ask, and there he was.

A small thread of guilt tugs at the back of my mind. Elias believes I'm his mate. He's already made it clear he wants a relationship with me, maybe even wants forever with me, and I'm still making up my mind.

Did I take advantage of him? Should I have left him alone and dealt with it on my own?

I'm still studying Elias's sleeping face when he startles me by speaking, eyes still closed.

"Don't tell me you're a morning person."

Lowering myself back onto him, I press a kiss on his jaw before answering. "And if I said I am?"

The rumble in his chest is more of a growl this time, and it's the only warning I get before he surges up and flips our position so I'm sprawled out on the bed beneath him. He leans down and runs his lips over my throat, morning stubble slightly scratchy, kissing and teasing until I'm squirming under him.

"If you are," he says, teeth grazing over the ultra-sensitive spot just below my ear, "then this will never work, little siren. I draw the line at being woken up at the crack of dawn."

"It's almost nine," I protest, giggling.

"Too early. I need you in bed at least until noon."

"Do I look like I'm going anywhere?"

Elias pulls back to meet my eyes, something dark and promising sparkling in that deep blue. "No, Nora. You're not going anywhere."

When he kisses me this time, there's nothing teasing about it. There's nothing but open, carnal want, a claiming that leaves me breathless and panting. Instantly, I'm ravenous, clinging to him and pulling myself close, closer, not nearly close enough.

He responds in kind, deepening the kiss and pressing the length of his body down on mine. He's heavy, so deliciously solid as he dips me into the mattress, kissing me with a hunger that makes my toes curl and my belly clench with need. I spread my thighs for him instinctively, making room so he can settle between them.

The hard line of his cock presses into me through the sweats he's wearing. I break the kiss for a moment to glance down and... oh.

Elias stills when he sees where I'm looking, and when I finally pull my gaze from the truly impressive erection outlined by the light gray fabric, that devious smirk is back on his face. His eyes are bright, shining in the morning light streaming in through the windows, and he presses his hips into me again in an act of deliberate provocation.

God, it feels good. Having his big body on top of me, hearing his ragged breath, and feeling the tense shift of muscles where my hands are pressed to his shoulders... all of it makes me feel warm and powerful.

Having this kraken in my bed, wanting me, is an unexpectedly heady thing.

Elias thrusts against me again, groaning a little when I meet the insistent press of his cock with my hips. Still, when he drops his head to lean against my chest, there's something hesitant about the rasp of his breath and the creases in his forehead.

A sudden realization strikes me. "Would you rather be... shifted for this?"

His eyes are two blue flames when he glances up at me, dancing with sensual promise at the idea. "Would you like me to be shifted for this?"

Would I? I'd be a filthy, filthy liar if I denied that I'd skimmed some kraken porn videos in the days since our first date.

Well... maybe more than skimmed. And maybe there were a few scenes that made my blood race and damp heat pool between my legs. Maybe there were a few tangles of limbs and tentacles that had me reaching a hand down to stroke my clit, desperate for relief...

Still, am I prepared for what that would all entail?

"I don't know," I say, as honest as I can be. "I'm not sure I'm ready for that."

For just a moment, something like disappointment flashes across his face.

My heart sinks. I pretty much just told him I'd rather him not be his true self with me, didn't I? I open my mouth to apologize, to reconsider. Maybe I *can* be ready for this. If it makes him more comfortable, maybe it's alright if he...

I don't get the chance to take the words back before he's kissing me again.

"We have all the time in the world to explore that side of our relationship. This morning, all I want is your comfort. And your pleasure."

"What about—"

"So many thoughts in that head of yours," he murmurs, kissing the words from my lips. "So many worries. What would happen if you let me help you forget them for a while?"

"Yes," I say breathlessly. "Please."

"Then just relax, little siren."

My core tightens, but not in fear or discomfort. No, it's something else entirely that has me feeling restless and boneless all at the same time. That feeling only grows as Elias moves down over me, kissing from my jaw to my neck to the exposed skin above the neckline of the tanktop his extraordinarily helpful housekeeper had waiting for me when I arrived last night.

His teeth catch on the fabric, another low growl sounding in the back of his throat.

"I'm going to have to thank Marta for this," he murmurs, drawing the shirt down low over the tops of my breasts. "And for these."

His hand moves under the covers to skim up the bare skin of my thigh, toying with the leg of my shorts.

"She left me a nightgown, too," I say with a laugh. "A long

one with a ruffle around the neck. Should I have worn that instead?"

A quick nip at the curve of my breast tells me just what he thinks of that idea.

"I'd rather have you in nothing at all." He tugs the loose tank down even further with his teeth to expose my breasts.

Elias draws a nipple into his mouth, and all the rest of my laughter flees, replaced by aching, urgent need. I tangle my fingers into his hair, pulling him close as he lavishes attention on one breast and then the other. Gentle swirls of his tongue and long, slow draws on each aching peak. Little nips that make me arch into him.

All the while, his hand is inching higher, playing with the hem of my shorts. His clever fingers find the edge of the panties beneath and dip just inside. My hips rise immediately into his touch, and a strangled groan works its way out of my chest. It's enough to have him pausing and pulling back slightly, his roguish face filled with heat and taunting amusement as his fingers continue to explore.

"So responsive," he murmurs. "Are you enjoying this, little siren?"

To punctuate his words, he leans in and nips at my lips, swallowing the needy sound I make in reply to his question.

"Is that a yes?"

He knows it is, but I nod anyway, hips still rising to meet the fingers that are toying with me over the fabric now. It's deliberate, a slow build meant to tease me.

"Can I touch you, Nora?"

I nod again, but it's not quite enough for him.

"Words, little siren. I'd like to hear the words."

"Yes," I say, cheeks heating with a mixture of anticipation and slight embarrassment. "Yes. I want you to touch me."

"That's what I thought."

There's laughter in his voice, a thread of amusement that

pokes and prods at sensitive places I didn't even know I had. A challenge, the absolute confidence of a man, a *kraken*, who knows he's got his treasure right where he wants her.

And I'm not complaining.

Wherever that challenge comes from, whatever dark corner of my psyche it reaches in and strokes, I'm too far gone to examine it now. I'm too far gone to do anything but surrender to this kraken and the promise of his touch.

Elias's big hands skim over my hips and thighs, tracing the shape of me through the fabric of my shorts.

"Up," he commands, squeezing my hip.

I obey immediately, lifting my ass off the bed. He slides my shorts and panties off in one smooth movement, baring me from the waist down, before reaching up to deal with my rumpled tanktop. He pushes the covers back, too, until there's nothing between me and him but the light of day.

Sitting back on his heels, he takes a few long, silent seconds to look down at me, and I want to squirm under his inspection. That, or reach down and grab my shorts back, pull the sheets up, anything to cover myself and…

"Fuck, Nora," he breathes, interrupting my self-conscious inner monologue. "Just… fuck."

"Good 'fuck' or bad 'fuck'?"

The noise he makes is somewhere between disbelief and aggravation as he leans back over me to claim my mouth in a hard, demanding kiss.

"You have to ask me that?" To emphasize his point, he rolls his hips against mine. His cock notches against my bared pussy and I can't help but press right back up into him. The growl it elicits reverberates through every part of me.

"Little siren," he says sternly, pulling his hips away and leaving me wanting. "This is for you, remember? Now, how do you want to come? On my fingers, or against my lips?"

Holy shit. If polite, caring, considerate Elias was tempting, then demanding, bossy Elias is downright devastating.

"Both," I gasp, and the feral gleam in his eyes makes everything in me clench. My pussy, my toes, something aching and dangerous near the center of my chest.

"Greedy girl," he murmurs appreciatively.

Elias maps a path down my body with lips and teeth and touch, skimming down my neck to lay kisses on my collarbone and stopping to tease my nipples into stiff, flushed peaks. The entire way, he murmurs into my skin. Some of it I can hear—endearments and soft reverence and more blush-inducing praise—but some of it seems meant just for him. A steady stream of reassurance that melts the last of my hesitance away.

Every single place he touches hums with awareness, with an electric, urgent energy that has me bowing off the bed, clutching at his hair and straining to get closer, closer...

He chuckles when he reaches my navel, biting the skin just above it with enough surprising sting to make me gasp.

"Relax, little siren," he tells me. "And enjoy."

I want to laugh out loud. What he's asking is impossible. Not the enjoyment part, of course, but relax? How on earth am I supposed to relax when I've got the sexiest man I've even been with on top of me, worshiping me, sliding lower until he...

At the first brush of his lips against my pussy, all those thoughts evaporate. There's nothing in my head at all—nothing but need and pleasure and *Elias*—as he leans down and runs his tongue along the length of my slit before dipping just inside. Learning me, teasing me, dark eyes flashing up to watch the play of devastating pleasure over my face.

"So wet for me," he murmurs, sinking two long fingers into my pussy. "You love this, don't you Nora?"

"Yes!" I cry out, pulsing my hips involuntarily and fucking against his hand.

That damned chuckle of his vibrates against my clit as he catches it between his lips and sucks, lighting up every nerve ending and drawing another tortured moan from my lips.

Elias works me fast and slow, alternating between deep thrusts of his fingers and long, slow draws and circling licks against my clit. His focus is entirely on me, watching my reactions, feeling how I shudder and press against him, learning how to make me lose my mind.

It's almost too much, that focus, knowing all that attention is fixed on me. It makes me feel seen in a way that I haven't in a very, very long time.

It's terrifying, and wonderful, and I barely have the mental faculties to process it because he's absolutely relentless in the pleasure he's giving me.

When I cry out and clutch even tighter to his hair—probably a little too tight, not that he's complaining—he ratchets up that demanding pace, pushing me higher, closer, right to the edge.

I tumble over with his name on my lips and heat coursing through every inch of me. Even then, he doesn't back off for a moment, keeps working me through each spasm, devouring me completely.

It's only after I've slumped back to the bed, boneless and exhausted, and make a protesting little noise in the back of my throat when his lips brush up against my too-sensitive clit that he relents. Moving up the bed, he hovers over me.

"Gods above, Nora," he breathes, kissing me and feeding me the taste of myself.

His hips settle against mine, cock still hard and insistent under the soft fabric of his pants. I trace my fingers under his waistband, reveling in the feel of his hot skin and the firm muscles of his ass and hips. All of that power, all of that strength, just waiting to be unleashed.

Only... that's not all I feel.

There, just at the side of his hip, his skin has changed. It's deepened to a dark blue-gray. It has a different texture as well, covered in striations and bumps, and it's slightly slippery.

Kraken skin.

Elias notices it at the same time I reach down to touch, and he jerks away like my fingertips have burned him. Cursing softly, he rolls off of me and settles on his back on the bed.

"Fuck, Nora," he says. "I'm sorry."

Confused, I prop myself up on an elbow and look at him. "About what?"

He lets out a long, shaky breath. "You said you weren't comfortable with me shifting. And I... I didn't mean for that to happen."

"This?" I ask, reaching back down to stroke the patch of kraken skin that's already receding.

At my touch, he leans instinctively closer, even as a frustrated growl rumbles in his chest.

"Yes," he says, moving my hand away again. "I usually have better control of the shift."

He still looks irritated and disappointed with himself, but an improbable laugh bubbles up in my chest.

"So," I say, laying back down on top of him. "What you're telling me is that I'm bad for your sense of control?"

All that irritation disappears. "You're devastating for my control, Lenora Perry."

"Good. I think I like that."

Elias's grin is crooked, his eyes dancing in the morning light. "Little siren. You're going to be the absolute unraveling of me, aren't you?"

"Maybe." I snuggle closer to him. "But maybe you'll like being unraveled."

Another low, warm laugh. "Yes. I think I will."

13

Elias

When Nora and I finally get ourselves out of bed and I return to my room to get dressed for the day, it's with a mixture of shame and desire and disappointment in myself.

I've never shifted unconsciously. Never even so much as half-shifted.

I have no excuse for it, no reason other than how lost in Nora I was. Having her respond to me, feeling how eager she was, how wet, how wanting as I slid between her thighs…

In my three hundred years, I've known nothing sweeter than Nora. I could have stayed there for hours, days, the rest of my life, wringing drop after drop of pleasure from her until she was delirious with it.

It's truly no wonder I started to shift without meaning to. Regardless, I can't forget myself like that again. It was there, in her eyes, the hesitance to see me in my shifted form.

I would be lying to myself if I pretended that reluctance didn't sting.

All my life, I've dreamt of having a mate. Any creature with this instinct does. That fate might unite you with a partner perfectly suited, that the other piece of your soul might one day walk into your life, is a tempting, tormenting thing.

How many monsters have I seen find their mate? How many have I watched sink into that blissful peace and belonging with their fated ones?

Too many to count. And for each one, I felt a mixture of elation and painful, hollow longing for the same. I'd nearly given up hope I'd ever be blessed with a mate, and even now that I have, it's hard not to let a small thread of disappointment creep in.

Not because of who Nora is. Of course not. But simply because I'd always hoped my mate would accept me as I am, that they'd see me and be just as enamored with me as I was with them. What freedom, to be known completely and welcomed with open arms.

It's a foolish hope, a fanciful one, but it's sunk its claws soul-deep into me and won't let go.

What I'd give for Nora to see and love every part of me.

Shaking off the pointless angst, I finish dressing and walk back down the hall to the guest room, knocking softly. Nora answers the door a few seconds later, looking rested and relaxed, a winning smile on her face.

And just like that, my own worries and wants seem like nothing.

She's lovely. Achingly lovely with her hair pulled back from her face and wearing some of the clothes Marta picked up yesterday. I'd had to guess Nora's size, and make sure Marta bought a wide range of options so Nora would have something she liked, and the outfit she's chosen suits her perfectly. A thick gray sweater for the cool fall day and a pair of soft black leggings that hug her luscious thighs.

It was probably too much—buying all of this for her—but I don't regret it for a moment.

"You didn't have to do all this, you know," Nora says, thoughts apparently following the same path as my own as she steps out into the hallway. "I could have just put on what I was wearing yesterday."

"You remember what I said about having someone to spoil," I remind her, holding out an arm for her.

She seems a little bemused by the offer, but slips her arm through mine. It's not a modern gesture, but I can't help it. I came of age in a time where it was what one did for the woman they were courting. Escorted her, kept her close, and I'd do nothing less for Nora.

I watch her closely from the corner of my eye as we make our way from the wing where the bedrooms are toward the kitchen at the center of the house.

It's not lost on me that the fact my house has *wings* might be a little off-putting to her. The whole thing is a modern construction I had built just a few years ago on a tract of private estate an hour outside of Seattle. There are neighbors not too far away, but it's as remote as I could get while staying close to the city.

I've also got a condo in the city for times when it's necessary to put in longer hours at Morgan-Blair and I can't justify the commute, but I don't really see a reason to mention that to Nora right now. With her history, it's not a huge stretch to guess that wealth and power are far more of a deterrent than an attraction in a partner.

Nora doesn't seem phased by the house as we make our way to the kitchen, and some of the tension in my chest relaxes.

I'd arranged for a private chef I hire occasionally to come

by this morning, and she's laid out an impressive breakfast spread for us on the kitchen island. Muffins and fresh fruit, a tray of crispy bacon and steaming scrambled eggs. Nora just shakes her head as she takes it all in, still a little wry and bemused, but grabs a plate and loads up without hesitation before settling down onto a stool at the island.

And… gods. That senseless, primal thing in my chest roars back to life.

My mate is here being fed and cared for.

The notion is antiquated, and my rational brain can differentiate between modern expectations and my own need to care for Nora, but that doesn't mean I'm not still pleased as hell to have her here and spoil her a little.

"Anything else you need?" I ask her, settling onto a stool on the opposite side of the island.

Another winning smile, followed by a deep sip of coffee, and she shakes her head. "Nothing. All of this is amazing. Too much, really, but amazing. Thank you, Elias."

Even though her words soothe and stroke the monster in me as we dig into our breakfast, the sentiment within them tugs at something guilty and sour in the pit of my stomach.

We haven't really talked about what happened yesterday, and as much as I'd like to sink into the fantasy of having Nora here and pretending this is any normal morning, I know better.

"It's no problem at all," I assure her, swallowing past that guilt. "After everything that happened yesterday, I'm still so glad you called me."

"About that," she says, brow furrowing. "I'm sure I was just overreacting. Now that I've had some time and space to think about it, I feel stupid. Really, I should have…"

She looks up, words trailing off at whatever she sees on my face. No part of me wants to ruin this moment, but Nora deserves the truth.

"Daniel is in Seattle."

Nora takes the news with a remarkable amount of calm. She sets her coffee down, braces her hands on the counter, and takes a deep, steadying breath.

"How do you know?"

I give her a brief recap of the conversation I had with Blair while I was flying home last night.

"So he's... what?" she asks when I'm finished. "Poking his nose into the Bureau's business? Did Blair say if he's accessed any records, or learned anything about me?"

I shake my head. "Bureau business and information about individual cases is still confidential, no matter what any government official might want or ask for. It's not in anyone's right, even a sitting congressman's, to ask for that information."

Nora seems to have lost her appetite as she pushes her plate a few inches away and rests her elbows on the counter. Her head follows, cradled in her hands as she presses the heels of her palms against her eyes.

"I'm really sorry for all of this, you know," she says softly.

I'm at her side a moment later, a finger tucked gently under her chin as I turn her face up toward me. She swivels her stool so she's facing me, eyes still clouded with concern.

"I'll tell you again, little siren, there's no need to apologize."

Like I already knew she would, Nora can't accept that without a fight.

She shakes her head. "But—"

"Will you do something for me?" I ask, ready to combat any lingering guilt she's feeling.

It's guilt I can understand, guilt born out of the fact that she's nowhere near ready to accept me as her mate and likely feels uncomfortable with the inequity in the situation. The hesitance and regret in her eyes says it all.

"When I tell you something, will you believe I'm telling the truth?"

Nora nods. "I already believe you're telling the truth."

"Good. And so will you also believe I'm not doing any of this for any other reason than I want to? No expectations. Nothing owed in return."

She nods again, though a little more slowly this time.

"Alright," I tell her, leaning in to place a kiss in the center of her forehead. "Then no more apologies."

Nora leans in to the kiss, then surprises me by wrapping her arms around my waist and laying her cheek against my chest.

"Do you have to work today?" I ask, stroking her hair. "And if you do, is there anyone who can cover your shift, just until we know Sorenson is dealt with?"

She doesn't ask what *dealt with* means, and I'm not entirely sure either. Truthfully, there's little to nothing I can actually do to deal with him right now, short of committing some sort of crime. I have my suspicions and my gut feelings about the situation, but no proof.

As far as anyone knows, he's here in an official government capacity. He has every right to visit the Bureau, every right to walk down a public street, and as long as he keeps his distance and doesn't approach Nora, there's not a damned thing I can think of to do about him being in the area.

Other than to keep Nora safe. To keep her with me. Not that I have any idea if she'll even allow it.

Nora shakes her head slightly where it's still resting on my chest. "I'm off until Monday."

"That makes two of us."

It's not exactly the truth. I didn't have any plans of taking today off, and in my normally hectic life, it's not at all unusual for me to spend my weekends doing at least a bit of work. But for Nora? Taking some time away from a company I know is well set to take care of itself for a few days is no burden at all.

"Really?" she asks, looking up at me and arching a brow like she can see right through my fib. "And is that something a big, powerful CEO gets to do? Just play hooky from work whenever you want?"

"Yes," I tell her, leaning in to catch her mouth in a quick kiss. "It is. And I plan to abuse that power fully. What would you like to do today?"

For just a moment, doubt creeps in. Perhaps she'd rather spend the day alone, somewhere else. Perhaps I presume too much.

All that doubt, however, melts away a moment later when Nora's smile reappears.

She glances at the wall of kitchen windows looking out over the yard. Already, the morning clouds are breaking up with what looks to be another glorious day of autumn sun.

"I don't know about you," she says, standing from her seat and reaching casually—so casually, like she's done it a thousand times—to loop her arms around my neck. "But I could use some fresh air somewhere away from Seattle."

14

Nora

Daniel is in Seattle.

First and foremost, I'm relieved to know I wasn't actually seeing things last night. He *did* walk down the street outside the shop. I'm not anxiety-ridden to the point of seeing things that aren't actually there.

Well, probably. I guess it's still possible it could have been his Seattle doppelgänger, but I'm choosing to believe I was right.

Beyond that relief, I'm torn.

Even as we finish breakfast, and even as Elias leads me outside to where his SUV's parked in the driveway, I can't quite make myself calm down.

I want to be rational about this. I want to be reasonable. Daniel being in the city for business with the Bureau makes sense. There's absolutely no reason to think he's here because he knows I'm here, or that I'm in any danger at all.

I just wish it wasn't happening.

Still, I manage to logic myself out of panic-spiraling as we pull out of Elias's driveway and start heading north. The further we get away from the city, the more I relax.

The day is beautiful and bright. I have a handsome kraken beside me who only wants to spend time with me, who gave me the best orgasm of my life this morning, and who's shown me over the last twenty-four hours that he's not going anywhere, even when I'm a mess.

And, even beyond that, fuck Daniel.

Today, I don't care about what happened between us or how it ended. I have my own life. I have a whole day with Elias to spend just how I want, and I'm determined not to let Daniel ruin it.

Elias is surprising me again today, and I'm more than willing to let him.

The road opens up wide before us, and I take in the passing scenery eagerly. Despite living here for three years, I haven't gotten out of Seattle all that much. Partly because I don't have a car and partly because between my limited funds and my busy work schedule, there just hasn't been the opportunity. It makes today feel all that much more like a treat.

We chat as we drive, not diving into any deep waters or fraught topics. Elias has one hand on the wheel, the other holding mine on the center console, and I can't stop myself from looking over at him again and again. It brightens my mood even further, enough that by the time he turns off the road, I've almost found my even keel again.

When he pulls the vehicle into line at the ferry terminal in Mukilteo, I perk up in my seat. "Where are we going?"

Elias smiles at me, looking pleased by my reaction. "Whidbey Island. There are a few spots I thought we could visit."

Once we're parked on the ferry, we leave the vehicle and go to stand at the side of the boat, watching the mainland coastline recede. I'm leaned up against the railing, and when he comes to stand behind me, hands braced on either side of me as he makes a protective cage of his body, he hesitates for a moment.

I crane my neck back to look up at him, finding him staring down at me with a slightly sheepish expression on his handsome face.

"Is this alright?" he asks, voice low and soft and just for me.

I laugh. "You have to ask, after everything we did this morning?"

A satisfied rumble kicks up in his chest and he leans in, kissing the tip of my nose before fitting his body more closely to mine.

"Have you been?" he asks, nodding toward the island.

I shake my head. "No, I haven't gotten out of the city all that much since I moved here."

When he answers, I can hear the smile in his voice. "Well, then, just all the more places I might have the privilege of sharing with you."

I smile, too, closing my eyes and reveling in the feel of the salt air and the breeze on my face. When I open them again, I can sense Elias's gaze on me, and throw him a questioning look over my shoulder.

"What?"

He shakes his head, chagrined. "Something that reminded me of the first day I, uh, saw you."

"When you stalked me, you mean."

Elias's eyes sparkle. "Such sass."

I open my mouth to offer him some more, but he catches my chin between his finger and thumb, and turns my face toward his, nipping lightly at my bottom lip.

"Such delicious sass," he murmurs.

Knowing I could get far, far too caught up in that kiss, I pull away and roll my eyes. "Save it. Tell me what you were thinking."

"When you left the coffee shop, you looked up at the clouds and smiled. It was raining a little that morning, and it made me wonder why you looked so happy about that."

He noticed that?

"I grew up in Phoenix," I explain. "Then went to college in Dallas for a couple of years before moving to DC with... anyway, I like how cool and wet it is here."

Elias's arms tighten a fraction around me.

"I like the rain. And being so close to the ocean. I didn't really realize it until I moved here, but the longer I stay, the more it feels like the place I'm supposed to be."

A tender press of lips against my temple. "I'm glad to hear you've found somewhere that feels like home."

"Me, too."

The rest of the ferry ride passes quickly, and from our place at the railing we talk, blissfully, about nothing important at all. Coffee shops, restaurants, our favorite Seattle haunts.

When the ferry docks, Elias drives us off and onto the island.

"I thought we'd head to one of my favorite parks on the island," he says, navigating away from the terminal. "Get out and do some hiking."

"That sounds great."

And it does, it really, really does.

I have nothing I need to do today. Nothing to worry about, not right in this moment. I'm here, I'm safe, and I'm choosing to leave the rest behind for a little while.

The park we pull up at a half-hour later is beautiful. A

nature preserve with plenty of walking trails and views of the Sound, quiet forest paths lined with towering trees and sprawling, vibrant ferns. Everything is lush and green after this morning's rain, and when Elias takes my hand and walks beside me down the path, it feels like the most natural thing in the world.

The winding trail takes us to a quiet beach where we stroll for a while along the shore. The views of the Sound are incredible, and in the middle of the day on a weekday, there's only a few other people on the beach. The sun is still shining, and with the cool breeze off the water, the pebbles crunching and sliding beneath my feet, and the handsome man at my side, I don't know the last time I've felt this peaceful or content.

Stopping to sit for a few minutes on the dry, sun-bleached trunk of a tree that's washed ashore, we both bask in the sunshine and sea air.

"Did you choose to live in Seattle because it's on the ocean?" I ask him, looking out at the islands in the distance.

Beside me, Elias nods. "Partly, yes. I don't think I could live anywhere without easy access to an ocean. Well, at least not comfortably."

"What made you pick here?"

"The business, mostly. There was a lot of opportunity in this part of the world back around the turn of the last century. Blair and I couldn't pass it up."

It's still disconcerting, hearing him talk about a date more than a hundred years ago and knowing he was alive then, but I do my best not to show it.

"What was it like here, back then?"

Elias's wry smile lets me know he sees right through my forced casualness. "We don't have to talk about it now, if it bothers you. The age difference between us, I mean."

Well, at least he was the one to bring it up.

Getting up from my perch on the log, I stand in front of him, right between his legs where he's still seated. Bracing both hands on his shoulders, I narrow my eyes slightly as I study him. Elias sits stock-still under my inspection.

"How old are you, exactly?"

He winces. "I was born in the early 1700s. The year is up for debate, but let's just say 1710."

I mentally spin out for a moment, trying to fathom that number.

"And..." I say slowly. "When you look at me, do you see... I don't know, like, a child? I mean, not an actual child, obviously, but I'm so much—"

"Absolutely not a child," he growls, leaning forward to brace his hands on my hips. "And despite my age, I don't believe you and I are all that different."

"Really? I find that hard to believe."

Elias thinks for a moment. "I'm not exactly sure why, or how, but I haven't grown... *odd* with age, the way some creatures do. Maybe it's stunted development, or just a pause at the age of maturity, but I could swear I still feel thirty-five, maybe forty, despite the years I've lived."

"I'm twenty-seven," I volunteer, and then frown. "I mean, if you didn't already know that."

"I didn't," he assures me.

There are other questions swirling in my mind, other considerations for the stark practicalities of any relationship between us. There are things I've read about mating bonds, things that are more magick than science, certain conditions that might make all of those considerations nothing...

That's a question for another time, though.

Instead, I tilt my head and narrow my eyes even further. "Forty, huh? So, that still makes you kind of a creep."

His hands tighten on my hips. "Am I too old for you, little siren?"

I can't help it. I respond immediately to that touch. "No. Not too old."

My whole body sways into him and he wraps his arms around me, pulling me into an embrace. Elias's body is warm, the wall of his chest firm beneath my cheek and the beat of his heart pounding against me.

"In all the years I've lived," he murmurs into my hair, "I've dreamed of you, Nora. I didn't know your face or your name, but I knew *you*. And I can't tell you how glad I am I've found you."

Elias's words are... big. Deep and important and permanent, they contain questions I can't answer and promises I'm not capable of making. Still, I can't let the moment go without acknowledging them. I can't let *him* go without letting him know I hear and see him, that I'm here, even if I'm not ready to offer my own words in return.

"I don't know how you waited so long," I whisper.

His hand strokes a soothing path up and down my back. "I would have waited a thousand years for you, little siren. Gladly."

Searching for a new topic, anything to dispel the huge, overwhelming feelings rising from the bottom of my belly, I reach up and touch the line of his scar where it bisects his cheek. "What happened here?"

He lets out a long breath, and I almost think the question was pushing too far when a small, wry smile turns up the corners of his lips.

"It's not a story I'm proud of."

"Oh. You don't have to tell me if you're not—"

He silences my protest with a light kiss. "I want you to know every part of me, Nora. Including the shadows."

Elias takes my hand and leads me from the beached tree trunk. We wander slowly down the shore and he takes a minute or two to gather his thoughts before he finally starts speaking, telling me the truth about who he was centuries ago.

A pirate. He was an honest-to-god pirate.

I freaking *knew* it.

Stopping in the middle of the beach, I just stare at him for a few seconds, open-mouthed.

"Was it..." I say finally, still trying to process. "Was it like Pirates of the Caribbean?"

His booming laugh echoes down the shore. It's loud enough that an older couple a few dozen yards away turns to look, startled, and I have to cover my mouth to keep from bursting out in laughter.

God, he's gorgeous when he smiles.

And when that smile turns into a smirk, a raised eyebrow, and a kiss stolen from my smiling lips, he looks every inch the pirate he once was.

"No," he says emphatically. "No, little siren, it wasn't. It was a lot less *Hollywood*, and a lot more long, tedious days at sea and the endless work of keeping a ship and crew running smoothly and not tempted to mutiny."

"Did that happen?" I ask, far too intrigued by this. "Did you ever have to, like, sword fight people? Or, I don't know, shoot canons?"

Elias smiles again, but there's a thread of sadness in it this time. "Occasionally, yes. And that's what led to Blair and I giving up that life for good."

For the next half-hour, he tells me more about those days. The places they sailed, the treasures they found or stole. When he gets to the part about his own role as the kraken threat come up from the depths to scare human pirates into giving up their bounty, a bit of color blooms high on his cheekbones.

"I'm sure you were very fearsome," I say mildly, patting his cheek.

He catches my hand in his and nips gently at my

fingertips. "I was, I can assure you. Still am, when I want to be."

The idea of that is... more intriguing than I thought it would be. What would Elias look like as that monster? What would it be like to peer into the depths of the ocean and see the shadow of massive tentacles rising from the deep?

I have to shake my head to clear away the image and the brief pulse of strange, improbable excitement it puts into the bottom of my belly.

Returning to our stroll down the beach, he tells me about meeting and inviting Blair aboard his ship, and all the misadventures they got into. As his story winds down, however, lines of tension appear on his forehead.

"Things came to a rather abrupt end after Blair met a woman," Elias says. "He was ready to leave the ship, the sea, the crew, and set off with her on a new adventure."

"She must have been amazing, if he wanted to give all of that up."

"She was," he says, the weight of centuries' worth of guilt in his voice. "Her name was Lizzy. And Blair loved her."

"What happened to her?"

He gazes out at the sea, studying the gently rolling waves and the islands in the distance. "She was killed. And it was our fault, the both of us."

In a softer, sadder tone than I've ever heard from him, he tells me a story about a vibrant, lively young woman with raven black hair and an adventurous spirit who joined them for a journey back to England, only to be killed when they were attacked by a pair of French ships.

"He thought she was his mate," Elias says, still looking out at the water. I'm not sure it's this ocean he's seeing, not sure where exactly it is his memory's taken him, but I reach over and squeeze his hand gently to offer whatever support I can. He squeezes back, though the sadness doesn't leave him. "All these decades and centuries later, Blair has never spoken her name aloud again, and I know there's some part of him that will never forgive himself, or me, for what happened."

"Even after all this time?"

He nods. "It will always be there, that guilt. And that grief."

We walk in silence for a little while, the sounds of the waves breaking and gulls calling filling the space between us.

"I'm sorry, Nora," he says quietly a few minutes later. "I shouldn't have dumped all of that on you. Not when this day was supposed to be—"

"It's alright. Really. I'm glad you told me."

He seems unconvinced, and I reach up and cup his face, fingers lingering over the line of his scar. "It is," I assure him. "I mean, *all* of this is a little strange. At least for me. So it kind of feels like normal second date rules don't apply. I want to get to know you, so whatever you want to tell me, you can."

Elias lets out a tense breath. "That means a lot to me, Nora."

My stomach chooses that moment to grumble its protest at not having anything since breakfast back at Elias's house. It breaks some of the tension of the moment, and even draws a chuckle from Elias.

"Come on," he says, taking my hand again. "I know a spot we can get a late lunch."

15

Elias

Sitting in the car outside the diner after we've finished lunch, I can't stop staring at my mate in the late afternoon sunshine.

Cheeks a little pink from our time outdoors, smiling over at me, relaxed even after our mess of a conversation at the beach, she's never looked so beautiful.

I may just have to accept the fact that my best laid plans always seem to crumble where Nora's concerned. Part of me still expects her to run every time I open my mouth and share more than I should, and feeling the weight of her acceptance, having her still here and smiling despite it all, it humbles me.

"Where to?" I ask her, finally starting the vehicle and pulling out of the diner's lot to head back up the road toward the ferry. We'll be in time to catch the four o'clock, but where we go from there, I'm not at all certain.

"What do you mean?" she asks.

"Well," I say slowly, navigating my next few words carefully. "If you'd like to stay at my place until we know what's going on with Sorenson, that's perfectly fine."

Perfectly fine. What bullshit. More like preferred, wonderful, the only thing I want in this wide world.

She looks torn, but eventually shakes her head. "I should go back to my place. If there's no reason to think Daniel's in town for anything other than government business... I'm probably overreacting about the whole thing."

I don't think she is, and I tell her as much, but she decides to be adamant about it.

"We've only been on two dates," she says with a laugh. "It's not like I can just move into your house."

Why can't you? I want to ask, but she's right. I'm the unreasonable one.

The ferry ride and the drive back into the city are comfortable. We talk about everything and nothing. Movies and music and TV shows we enjoy. Trips we've been on and places we still want to go. It's normal conversation, getting to know each other conversation, and it's all wonderfully mundane, the type of ease between two people finding out they have a lot more in common than they realized.

When I turn down her street and park in front of her apartment, absolutely no part of me wants it to end.

Nora fidgets slightly in her seat, like she's not ready to say goodbye, either. "You could... come in for a few minutes."

A shot of heat spreads through my veins.

This morning was just a taste, the smallest drop in the vast ocean of what I want from my little siren. And even though today was wonderful, I hadn't expected anything more.

That is, until I look over and see the unmistakable interest in Nora's eyes, the promise and temptation. If I had any reservations before, they evaporate on the spot.

Again, Nora waits for me to exit the car and come around to open her door, giving me a knowing grin as she takes my hand and hops down.

"You're kind of old-fashioned, aren't you?"

"I don't know what you mean," I tell her, even as I take her arm in mine and walk up the sidewalk to the front door.

"This," she says, squeezing my arm. "And the car door thing. Plus the way you pulled my chair out when we had dinner at the aquarium, and put your hand on my back when you walked me to the elevator at your office."

"You've been making a study of me, little siren?"

"I'm just a very observant person," she retorts. "And I'm not saying I dislike it, either. Especially since I know you're not so polite all the time."

I lean down to kiss the sensitive spot just below her ear, enjoying her shiver. "No. Despite my antiquated manners, most of the things I think about you aren't *polite* in the slightest."

As she reaches for her keys to unlock the exterior door, I crowd in behind her, pressing up against her and running my lips over the back of her neck. She fumbles with the lock, and I chuckle into her hair.

"Need some help with that?"

Her answer is tart, as is the adorable little glare she throws over her shoulder at me. "No. Not if you would stop distracting me."

"Ah, little siren, but I enjoy distracting you far, far too much."

Another shiver, and although she finally gets the door open, we take our sweet time climbing the narrow set of stairs to the second floor.

She's just as much a tease as I am, bumping into me, craning her neck up and back to nip at my lips and feed me more of her sass as we make our way to her door.

That lick of flame in my blood has been kindled into an inferno by the time we reach her floor, and by the way Nora's own teasing has grown darker and more insistent, she's feeling her own little fire. The press of her body and the taste of her sweet lips are almost enough to make me lose myself completely, push her against the wall and drop to my knees in front of her right here in the damned hallway.

As soon as we're in sight of her door, though, the warm, wanting woman in my arms goes utterly still.

When I look down at Nora, all her playful desire has disappeared. She's staring at her apartment door, bone pale and slack-jawed with horror.

16

Nora

He found me.

Daniel.

As soon as I see the handwriting on the note stuck to my door, I know.

How many times did that same handwriting stare up at me from notes left on the kitchen counter or the nightstand or the bathroom mirror?

In the beginning, they'd been love notes. Little compliments or endearments, cards tucked into bouquets of flowers. Sweet, so sweet, more thoughtful than anything a guy had done for me before. Proof I was special to him, proof I was important.

Or so I'd thought.

By the time we'd moved in together, the notes he'd left me were decidedly less sweet. Reminders about a chore I hadn't done or a promise that we'd 'discuss' something I'd said or done to disappoint him when he got home. Instructions to wear a particular piece of clothing or jewelry to an event, cutting commentary about how I needed to impress him this time.

I'd grown to dread seeing those notes, wondering what sin I'd committed and what his reaction to it would be.

Seeing one now, taped to the door of the small, safe place I've created for myself, shatters something in me.

"Nora?" Elias asks.

I've almost forgotten he's still standing behind me, and for a few seconds I can't find my voice to answer him.

"The note," I finally croak. "It's... it's from..."

Without waiting for any further explanation, he snatches it from the door. As he reads, his jaw grows tight and his eyes darken ominously.

I'm sorry I missed you, Nora. I hope you're doing well.

Innocent, innocuous. Threatening as hell. He knows where I am, left a note on my fucking door.

"Keys," Elias says, holding out his open palm.

I hand them over without a word, completely numb.

Seeing my expression, he takes me gently by the shoulders. "Look at me, Nora."

I do, and find all the hardness gone from his eyes, nothing but gentle reassurance as he reaches into my coat pocket and pulls out my phone, handing it to me.

"I'm going inside to make sure nobody's there, alright?"

I nod.

"If anything's wrong, if you hear me call out to you, I want you to run. Understand?"

Another nod.

"If that happens, I want you to have your phone ready to call for help."

"Alright," I whisper, hand clenched painfully around the

phone.

Elias kisses my cheek and turns to unlock the door without another word. He disappears inside, and the only thought that sticks in my brain is that this isn't how I wanted him to see my place for the first time. It's ridiculous to focus on that, all things considered, but I'd been so excited to invite him up, humming with anticipation to let us inside, pull him down on the couch and...

Stupid. Stupid. Stupid.

Why did I think I could have this? Why did I think I was safe? How could I let my guard down like this and forget—

"There's no one here."

Elias is back, keys still in hand, and he sets them into mine before putting a hand in the middle of my back, ushering me inside and locking the door behind us. Gently, he rests both hands on my shoulders and squeezes in reassurance.

"Are you alright?"

All I can manage is a shaky nod and an even shakier breath. Elias looks troubled, but doesn't press for more. He just pulls me into a hug, and when I lay my head against his chest and hear the steady beat of his heart, my own slows down to match it.

I don't know how long we stay that way, but when he pulls back and brings a hand up to smooth some of the hair away from my face, there's one single thought that flashes through my mind, front and center and unexpected.

I'm so glad he's here right now. I'm glad I'm not alone.

"Stay here for a minute?" he asks, and I nod.

Elias disappears into the kitchen, and even though it's still a comfort to have him in my apartment, I can't help the pulse of unease that moves through me. Memories I don't want to deal with right now bubble up to the surface—memories of not having control, of feeling someone pull on my strings like a marionette.

It's how I felt for years when I was with Daniel, and it comes rushing back with a ferocity that steals my breath.

Elias mumbles a curse when he comes back into the room. Setting the glass of water he's carrying aside, he wraps me up in another hug.

"I'm sorry," I rasp against the soft fabric of his sweater.

He pulls back. "Sorry for what, Nora?"

I can't bear to look at him. Resting my forehead against his chest, I take a deep breath.

"For all of this. You didn't ask to be involved in something like this."

He doesn't correct me, doesn't remind me he's already said I don't need to apologize. No, all he does is let me take the comfort I need from him, silently offering me the strength I can't find right now. When he speaks again, his voice is low and hoarse with concern.

"I don't think you should stay here. Not tonight."

I nod. "I know."

"If you don't feel comfortable coming back to my house, can I pay for you to stay in a hotel? Or I have a condo downtown, just a couple of blocks away from my office, if you'd prefer to stay there."

The offer is generous, too generous, and I should probably take him up on it.

Still, that's not where I want to be, not tonight. I don't want to be in the city with all the noise and the people and the lights. I just want to be somewhere quiet and remote, somewhere hidden where Daniel can't find me.

Somewhere with Elias.

"Can I come back to your place?"

Elias's arms tighten around me. "Of course, Nora. Of course you're welcome to stay with me."

17

Elias

The first part of the drive from Nora's apartment to my home is absolutely silent. I've got one hand white-knuckled on the wheel, the other clasped around hers, and although she didn't pull her hand away when I reached over, she's not talking. Every so often I glance over to see her staring firmly ahead at the highway, expression giving away nothing.

We left her apartment in a rush, just enough time for her to pack a bag with clothes and everything else she'll need for a few days away from home.

In the silence, I don't know how to read her, or what might help ease some of the tension creasing her forehead and bracketing her mouth, so I just keep my hand in hers.

"He used to leave me notes all the time."

Nora's voice is barely audible in the quiet of the car. I glance over at her again, and am about to tell her she doesn't need to share this with me if she doesn't want to, but something in the hard set of her features makes me hold my tongue.

"Daniel, I mean. He used to leave them for me all the time."

Just the sound of his name sends a flare of anger through me. I clench the steering wheel even harder and stay silent, waiting for her to continue.

"It was really sweet, at first, when we were just dating. Love notes. Notes in flowers. Scribbled on the backs of receipts. It made me feel special. I didn't see what it all was, what *he* was, until later."

"Nora," I whisper, not sure what I can say to make any of this better, but unwilling to let her admissions go unacknowledged.

She shakes her head and continues speaking. I shut my mouth, giving her the space to say exactly what she needs to.

"Everything changed after I dropped out of college and moved to DC with him." Her tone turns sour and mocking. "'Don't forget to have dinner ready tonight, Nora.' 'Don't forget to smile at the press event this afternoon.' 'Remember how poorly the last gala went? Try to do better tonight. It's important for my next election.'"

Right then, I know. Daniel Sorenson is not getting out of this unscathed. Wherever the bastard is and whatever he thinks he's going to accomplish by further traumatizing the woman he's already fucked over so thoroughly, he's not getting out of this without consequences.

"Even the morning of the day I left," Nora continues, voice raspy and strained, "there was a note taped to the mirror in the bathroom, reminding me about a dinner with his parents that evening and telling me the exact dress he wanted me to wear."

She shakes her head, disgusted. "I always hated his parents. They thought I was trash. And maybe to them, I was."

I can't help but interrupt. "You're not—"

"I know," she says, cutting me off in a tone that's gentler than I expected, and when I glance over at her, she squeezes my hand.

My chest tightens in response. *She's* comforting *me*. Even now. I give myself a mental slap and double down on my efforts to keep my own damn feelings out of this.

"I know I'm not trash," Nora continues. "But I wasn't a part of their world, either, and I think that's why I tried so hard in the beginning to fit in, and why I excused a bunch of giant red flags I shouldn't have.

"That night, though..." she trails off, eyes fixed out on the dark highway again. "That night I was just so tired of it. I didn't want to get dressed up and go to another horrible dinner so his mom could make little digs at me and his dad could say the most inappropriate shit. I was just... tired.

"I told Daniel that when he got home. I'd deliberately put off getting ready and getting dressed, even though we were supposed to leave right after he got back from the office. I was just sitting on the couch in my sweats and no makeup, ready to make my damn point about not going, for once, tell him I could choose not to participate when I didn't want to, and he...

"He didn't hit me. But I thought he was going to." Her voice is even softer now, hardly above a whisper. "The fucking selfish asshole that he was, he couldn't understand why I was being so difficult. He gave me *everything*, he said, and I couldn't suck it up for a few hours and look nice, stay quiet, and deal with his parents' bullshit? When I still didn't do what he wanted, he got me by the shoulders and he shook me, not hard enough to do any damage... but it was enough."

Nora's hand is cold and clammy in mine, and her expression is hard when she finally looks back over at me.

"I guess it startled him, too, because he went to dinner with his parents without me. Even before it happened, I'd been thinking about leaving, but all of it... it was my breaking point, I guess. I left that night, right after he was out of the condo. Took everything I had that was worth something and bought a bus ticket with the bit I had left in my bank account."

"And you ended up in Seattle," I say softly.

"And I ended up in Seattle."

Gods above, the courage it must have taken.

The idea of Nora on a Greyhound in the middle of the night, headed away from her home and her life, however intolerable that life might have been, makes me feel physically ill. It's an ache in my chest that demands retribution on her behalf, some sort of reckoning for the person who caused it.

I'm not a violent creature by nature, and I don't intend to do anything that would get me arrested and take me away from my mate, but my mind is already spinning. What weaknesses does a man like Sorenson have? What sort of below-board deals or shady business interests or damning secrets might be there below the surface, just waiting to be brought to light?

As much as I'd like to beat him to a pulp like he might deserve, the idea of using the considerable resources at my disposal to ruin his life entirely has its merits as well.

"I left *him* a note," Nora says with a brittle humor in her voice, shaking me out of those dark thoughts. "Saying that I wasn't coming back, telling him to fuck off, essentially."

"Good," I say gruffly, and she squeezes my hand again.

For a moment, I can feel all those threads of understanding between us, the bond I've been doing my best to ignore. Only right now, I'm not strong enough to deny it.

I'm here, I want to tell her, *right here. You're safe with me. You never have to worry that I'll stifle you or change a single thing about you. You never have to be anyone with me other than exactly the woman you are.*

None of it is anything I can tell her, not now, not when all of this is still so new and she truly has no reason to believe it or trust me. So I tuck it away, keep it for later, and hold her hand tightly all the way back to my home.

Pulling into the garage, I grab her bag from the backseat and let us both inside. The house is quiet, dark, and when she tenses a little beside me, I hurry to reassure her.

"I called Travis while you were packing. He double-checked the security systems and had his team do a sweep of the property. We're safe here."

Nora nods at my assurance over the safety of the house, but doesn't look quite convinced, and I don't blame her. Safety is never an absolute, and considering everything she must be thinking and feeling, her wariness is more than justified.

Standing in the kitchen, the lights over the island are too bright and the hum of the refrigerator sounds like a jet engine. The silence grates against my ears in quiet, damning confirmation of a single fact.

I don't know how to help her.

Other than being here, other than pulling the strings I can to get this investigated and have Sorenson dealt with, I don't know how to help. Though my soul has known her since the moment I first saw her, that doesn't mean I know everything about her yet, and right now I have no idea if she needs more space, or less, if she wants me to say something or do something or just leave her alone to process.

With nothing else to do but trust the instinct that's still tugging gently at the center of my chest, I walk around the island until I'm just a few inches away from her. Slowly, so she has time to stop me or move away if she doesn't want me near, I reach out and pull her to me.

Nora, to my surprise, melts into my embrace, letting out a

long, shaky breath.

"What do you need, little siren? What would make you feel better?"

It's probably an idiotic question to ask. What she needs is Sorenson locked up in a jail cell somewhere.

"A shower, I think, would be a good start," she says.

I nod and take her by the hand, grabbing her bag in the other and leading her from the kitchen toward the bedroom. When we reach her door, I'm ready to kiss her on the forehead and leave her to it, give her some space to process, but I never get the chance.

Just as I'm reaching for the handle to open it for her, Nora's hands land on my shoulders and she pushes me up against the opposite wall. Her mouth follows a second later — hot, hungry, and eager. I respond without thinking, without caution or restraint, completely taken over by the need that floods through me as soon as I have her in my arms.

Nora's moan tastes like surrender and temptation and a thousand things I've waited lifetimes for. Body warm and pliant and willing under my hands, I'm struck with the desperate need to keep her, hold her close, take her somewhere and shift so I can show her just what it means to be a kraken's treasure.

I drop my mouth to her neck, taste the sweet salt of her skin. When her hands tighten in my hair, though, tugging to an edge of delicious pain, it snaps a bit of rationality back into me.

"Nora." I'm torn between caution and mindless want, even as I still have my teeth pressed against her throat. "Nora. We can't."

"We can."

Gods above. I know better than to entertain this.

If one of us is going to keep a level head right now, it should be me. I need to remember all the reasons this is a bad idea. I'd be the lowest of bottom-feeders if I pressed her for intimacy while she's still processing her own emotions.

When I pull back and look down into her eyes, though, it's not grief or fear or uncertainty shining back at me.

No, it's a determination and a steely resolve that nearly knocks me to my knees.

18

Nora

"We can."

Elias's tortured hesitance is clear on his face.

He wants this. I *know* he wants this. He's done a terrible job of hiding it today, and with every glance of those stormy eyes and every time he's touched me, I can feel it there.

What I don't know is whether he wants to try to protect me more than he wants to give into it.

"Nora," he says again, and I can almost hear his defenses crumbling. "We…"

"Can," I finish for him.

And why the hell shouldn't we? Daniel stole my sense of security today. He stole my trust and my confidence for years. Does he get to take this, too?

All the way here, all the way through my confession to Elias, fear and panic have been giving way to anger and certainty. What right? What fucking right does Daniel have to still have so much influence over my life?

Elias pulls back a few inches and regards me warily. "Little siren…"

As much as I appreciate all the care and consideration he's shown me, it's not what I want right now. I want him. I want to choose and to be chosen in return.

Elias told me he's been waiting for me for centuries. Without saying so many words, he's already let me know he's all-in on this, on me.

Now it's my turn.

"Do you know what I was going to do?" I ask him. "Back at my apartment, do you know what I was going to do?"

He shakes his head slowly.

"I was going to invite you inside." A kiss, placed just under his jaw. "I was going to press you up against my door and kiss the hell out of you." Teeth, rasping lightly over his Adam's apple. "Then, I was going to ask if you wanted to take a shower, you know, because we're so sweaty from hiking." A hand, cupped against the growing erection just begging to be released from his jeans. "And then? I was going to ask if you wanted to show me what you didn't this morning."

I drag my fingers over the spot on his hip where he started to shift, making my meaning more than clear.

A shudder runs through the entire length of his body, though he still doesn't relent.

"Nora…"

"Let me have this?" I ask him, taking his face between my hands and making him look me in the eye. "Please? I want this. I want you."

It's not fair to pull on his hesitation like this, to demand more than I should. I know it's not fair. And maybe Elias does, too, but the last thread of his resolve snaps and he buries a fist in my hair, tipping my head back and claiming my mouth with a tortured groan.

He throws open the door to my room and we bump our way inside.

"Do you still want that shower?" he asks, breathing fast and heavy.

"Only if you join me for it."

With another rumble in his chest, he takes me by the hand and leads me through the bedroom into the huge en suite. It's got a jetted tub sunken into the floor, double vanities, and its own small sauna, along with the biggest damn shower I've ever seen.

Tiled with a mosaic of blue and green and gray, it has a wall of fancy shower heads that look like something out of a spaceship and a bench seat that brings a lot of very interesting possibilities to mind, especially with how much space the whole thing provides.

Plenty of room for one human and her kraken.

Elias turns to face me, eyes raking up and down my body, the barest hint of reserve still lingering in his expression. He grabs me by the hips and brings me crashing back against his body.

"You'll tell me," he says, voice low and rough in a way that makes my lower belly coil in anticipation. "If you feel any kind of hesitation, or want to stop for a single moment, you'll tell me."

It's not a question, but I nod anyway.

"Words, Nora."

Another pulse of delicious heat at the command in his voice. "I'll tell you."

We're a mess after that. Tearing hands that leave our clothes in piles on the floor; sloppy, inelegant kisses; stumbling steps; and graceless bodies as we finally make it under the spray of water. We're too eager, and it's ice cold at first, making me yelp and spring closer to him.

Elias's body is incredible.

He saw more of me than I saw of him this morning, and I take my time returning the favor. I don't just look, either. How could I, with this amazing specimen of a man in front of me?

Running my hands over the broad set of his shoulders and the planes of his chest, I find more little scars on him, nicks and cuts and a few larger gashes that tell the story of his long, long life. The muscles beneath those scars jump and bunch as I continue to explore, delighting in the heat and the strength of him, the way my touch seems to make him come undone.

When I reach for the thick, stiff length of his cock, though, he catches my wrist in his hand and pulls my fingers gently away.

"Little siren," he rasps, leaning in to lick a drop of water off my collarbone. "All I ask is mercy."

With that, he drops to his knees, and it only takes a gentle nudge to have me sinking down onto the bench seat. Elias moves immediately into the space between my legs, kissing a trail up one thigh and down the other, then nipping at the inside of a knee before pulling both of them up to rest on his shoulders and leaving me completely exposed to his own mercy.

"Comfortable?" he asks, starting a new, tortuously slow path of kisses down one thigh, inching closer and closer to the place that's already hot and aching for him.

I arch into him, silently demand he stop teasing me, give me some kind of...

"Nora," he murmurs into my skin when I don't respond.

"Yes," I manage to gasp when one of his hands snakes between my legs, thumb pressing up against my clit. "Are you... are you going to shift?"

"You're going to come against my mouth first," he says, lowering his face between my thighs. "And then I'll give you my tentacles. Maybe. If you behave for me."

The sound I make is entirely unintelligible as he catches my clit between his lips and sucks, hard. I buck up off the bench seat, but his hands on my legs keep me still as he feasts on me, alternating between long draws against my clit, and slow, languorous strokes of his tongue. He's teasing me, torturing me, drawing wave after wave of pleasure from me until I'm writhing and mindless, demanding the release he's holding just out of arm's reach.

It doesn't take me long to catch it, not when his damned mouth moves on me more insistently, and two long fingers sink into me. The friction and the fullness have me arching and straining against him, close... so close... until I'm lost completely to a fast, consuming orgasm. My body goes limp on the seat, and my head rolls back. It's only Elias's firm grip on me that keeps me from sliding all the way to the floor.

He holds me through every wave of my climax, stroking my legs and my belly, whispering endearments and praise until my head and heart are swimming with warmth.

When I finally peel my eyes open and look down again, though, my breath catches in my throat.

Where Elias was kneeling on the shower floor, his legs have disappeared. In their place, a mass of curling, expanding tentacles in a deep blue-gray.

Twisting in and over and around themselves, there are more than I can count, and as I watch they expand and contract, moving closer, until one brushes against my ankle.

It's softer and warmer than I thought it would be. Smooth and gentle instead of cool and slimy. I watch, transfixed, as it winds around my leg in a light embrace.

When I meet Elias's gaze again, he's watching me, too.

"Is this alright?"

Some of the sexual edge is gone from his voice. In its place, a note of uncertainty, something vulnerable that reaches out and tugs at the center of my chest.

"Yes," I tell him, leaning forward to drag a hand through his dark hair and bring his handsome, scarred face up to mine. "Yes. You're beautiful."

The sound that breaks from his throat is rough and broken, and when he presses his mouth to mine, I want to take all of that doubt away. Parting my lips for him, devouring him with the same hunger he's always had for me, I put every bit of acceptance I can into that kiss.

Below, there's another tentacle caressing and teasing its way lightly up my other leg, working in tandem with the first to soothe me and get me accustomed to the feel of him. Despite myself, I feel a rash of goosebumps break out over my skin. Elias's tentacles must be sensitive enough to feel them too, because he breaks the kiss to check in with me again.

"Still okay?"

I nod, and when one of those reaching limbs skates a little higher up my leg, brushing against the already-sensitive skin of my inner thigh, I instinctively open wider. The pointed, slippery tip passes lightly over my pussy, dipping just inside, and I gasp.

Elias chuckles. "You're doing so well. My brave little siren."

"Is this... your full shift?" I ask him, breathless, trying to latch onto the details I learned while reading about shifters over the past couple of weeks, but not entirely capable of making my mind focus on anything other than the hypnotic, beautiful, strange sight of him undulating against my skin.

Elias laughs again. "No. I won't shift fully while we're intimate. Even I can understand why having a full sea monster in your bed may not be all that sexy."

I shiver a little at the idea. A sea monster. A fearsome, ancient creature from the depths stalking the mortal world above.

"I'll show you sometime, if you'd like to see," he whispers against my skin, leaning down to brush his mouth over my shoulder before kissing a trail up my neck. "It works best if I'm in the ocean. Maybe I'll put you in a little rowboat and send you out into the deep. Maybe I'll be there, waiting in those depths to strike and carry you off to a sea cave where I can ravish you completely."

Oh, god. The image that puts in my mind shouldn't be so fucking hot.

Neither should the feel of two of those tentacles moving higher still, winding around my waist, pulling me up off my perch and closer into his body. By all rights, I should want to run screaming from this room, from the monster who's got me in his grasp, but this is... Elias.

This is the man who's been so tender and careful with me, the pirate with the wicked gleam in his eye, the kraken who wants to treasure me.

Mine.

I let him move me how he wants, melting into the warm, slippery sensation of being enveloped completely. He's everywhere, all at once. With our torsos pressed together and the rest of me being slowly, deliciously teased and caressed, the last of my reservations slide away with the water cascading over us.

Low against my belly, his front tentacles part, and my hand brushes over another that's different from the rest, stiffer and shorter, with a blunted head and ridges up and down its length.

I stroke it once, twice, and Elias groans out loud. He drops his head to rest against my collarbone, breathing a little shakily.

I run my hand up and down him again. "What is this?"

He takes a few long seconds to answer. His hips thrust into my touch, and the tentacle I'm holding fucks against my hand like he can't help himself.

"My mating tentacle," he says, voice harsh and hoarse. "It functions like... like..."

He's missing beats, not quite able to form a sentence as I continue to touch and explore him.

"Like your cock?"

A shaky nod is all I get in return.

"Is this... is this alright? Touching it like this?"

Again, he can't speak, can't do anything but thrust against my hand and make a low, almost-pained sound in the back of his throat. I take that to mean 'yes', but after how he played with me earlier, I'm not letting him get off that easily.

"Words, Elias," I purr, stilling my hand and smirking at him.

He still doesn't answer right away. Instead, he wraps a tentacle around my wrist, squeezing gently. I glance down at the restraint before meeting his eyes again, blue-black with desire.

"Yes. And I'll show you just how I like it."

Firmly, he guides my hand up and down the length of him, thrusting to meet each stroke. The growl in his chest gets louder, and when he leans in to whisper against the skin just below my ear, it sends a shot of liquid fire through my veins.

"Harder, little siren. Like you mean it."

I'm not gentle with him, not hesitant or reserved in the slightest as I tighten my grip. Groaning, he takes my mouth again, plundering, knotting his hands into my hair and pinning me to him while he continues to fuck into my grasp.

Elias is wild, undone entirely, and the surge of power it gives me to see him like this makes me work him even harder.

In my hands, his mating tentacle is slippery not just from the water, or the smoothness of his skin, but seems to be leaking its own lubrication directly from the tip. Thick and viscous and weeping over my hand, my curiosity gets the better of me. Pulling my mouth from his, I raise my fingers to get a taste, only to have my wrist bound again just a few inches from my eager lips.

"Little siren." Elias's voice is strangled.

"What? Is it toxic or something?" It's all over me by this point, smeared across my hands and arms and stomach, so I really hope it's not.

He gives his head a sharp shake.

"Then what's the problem?"

"There's no... you just don't have to—"

"I want to."

Though he still looks a little pained, Elias nods, and his tentacle drops away from my wrist. I hold his deep blue gaze as I bring my hand up and slip two fingers into my mouth, watching his predator's focus track every movement.

When the taste of him bursts across my tongue, though, I have to close my eyes. I moan at the sharp, impossible flavor of seawater and sunshine and crisp ocean breezes.

I want more.

Pulling back and meeting his startled, feral gaze, I slide my way down his body. He makes a move to reach for me, stop me, pull me back up, but I push his hands away and sink to the floor. All of those writhing, caressing tentacles stay with me, keeping me bound and supported so I don't have to put too much weight where my knees rest on the unforgiving tile.

"Tell me," I murmur, leaning in to brush my lips against the broad, dark tip of his mating tentacle. "If there's anything I do wrong, you have to tell me."

"Sweet Nora," he breathes, leaning back against the tiled wall like it's too much effort to hold himself up. "Nothing you do can be wrong."

"Good." I smirk up at him. "Then I think it's your turn to just relax and enjoy."

19

Elias

I'm not sure if Nora is meant to be my salvation, or my damnation.

Here, now, with her mouth exploring my shifted cock and her greedy, eager hands running up and down its length, she might be either.

As hard as I try, I can't conjure up any of my prior reservations, or pretend for one single second I'm capable of resisting anything she's willing to give me.

Instead, I tangle my hand into her wet hair and lean my head back against the tiles. My whole body is straining to thrust into her, fuck that pretty little mouth of hers, but I'm going to let her set the pace even if it kills me.

She's done so beautifully tonight, accepted me so completely. I don't want to ruin it now.

"Is this alright?" Nora asks, bringing my mating tentacle

—my cock for all intents and purposes when I'm in this form—to her lips and pressing a delicate kiss to the head.

Gods above, like there's a single chance in hell she could do anything I wouldn't enjoy. Still... I can't help but tease her a little.

I love teasing my treasure, love seeing her eyes light up with excitement and feeling the bite of her sharp humor and radiant temper.

"Is that all you'd like to do with me, little siren?"

Just like I thought, her eyes flash and her lips part. Her tongue rolls slowly over the underside of the head and I have to restrain myself again from thrusting into the wet heat of her mouth.

"Mmm." The pleasured, blissful sound she makes in the back of her throat only makes restraint twice as difficult. "You taste different than I expected. You taste good."

Fuck. *Fuck*. Of all the things she shouldn't say to me. Unable to help myself, I clasp a hand around the back of her head and nudge her forward slightly, pushing myself in just a little deeper.

I support the rest of her with my tentacles, keeping her knees off the hard floor of the shower and keeping as much of me in contact with her as I can.

I want all of her. Every inch. For as long as I can have her.

Stroking her softly with the hand I still have tangled in her hair, I use a couple of tentacles to hug her tighter against me. The shift in our positions brings her closer, and with a roll of my hips, she takes more of me, eagerly welcoming me inside.

She works me slowly at first, learning the taste and the shape of me, eyes flicking up to watch my reactions.

When she drags her teeth lightly along my shaft, I can't stop the strangled groan that rasps from my throat. Nora, the wicked creature that she is, pulls off of me with a wet, satisfying pop and smirks up at me before kissing all the way down my shaft to the base and then back up again.

This time, when she takes me into her mouth, her hands come up as well. One settles on my hip in a firm grip, massaging into the gray-blue skin there. The other reaches back and rests over the hand I have in her hair, pressing it more firmly against her.

Pulling back for a moment, she grins up at me. "Show me how you like it."

With those six simple words, my restraint hovers perilously close to its breaking point, straining at the seams of my control.

"Nora..."

She lowers her head, whispers directly into my skin. "I trust you, Elias. Show me."

My restraint snaps.

With one hand clutched at the back of her head, and one gripped firmly around my cock, I feed her more of my length, controlling her movements so it's not too much, too fast. When she hums low and appreciatively in the back of her throat, I chase the sound, pushing in until I feel the muscles there contracting and drawing me deeper.

Nora's beautiful hazel eyes snap up to hold mine and there's undeniable excitement there, satisfaction, eagerness that makes the wild, feral thing in me demand more.

The rest of my tentacles pulse and squeeze her flesh, working over her back and hips and ass, reaching forward to cup her breasts and play with her pink, perfect nipples. Nora responds to each touch, begging so prettily without saying a word, and when I press a tentacle between her legs, her hips rock instinctively over it, searching for friction.

"Do you need to come again, little siren?"

With her mouth too full of my cock to speak, she just sucks harder, and gives me a look that's easy enough to interpret as *'but, it's your turn.'*

Generous, but so am I.

"You can do both, my treasure. Get yourself off on my tentacles while you suck my cock."

I press that tentacle closer to her cunt, watching her eyes go round as saucers as she rocks again, and this time when she moans the sound echoes all the way down to the internal sacs where I'll one day produce eggs for my mate.

And fuck if that doesn't make me burn even hotter. In my three hundred years I've seldom allowed myself to indulge in the fantasy of fatherhood, and I probably shouldn't be doing it now, but being inside my mate has woken something long-dormant in me, and hell if I know how to switch it off now.

Tamping it down the best I can, I concentrate on Nora's pleasure, and on withholding my own. I'm about three seconds of self-indulgence away from coming, but I won't—I can't—reach that satisfaction until I've pleasured her again.

Delving just the tip of my tentacle inside of her, I watch Nora's eyes flutter close and feel another strangled sound of pleasure break in her throat. I do it again, and again, pushing deeper into her hot, tight cunt as I continue to fuck her mouth.

It's too much. Too much sensation. More than my Nora-starved body can withstand.

Concentrating as much as I can around the mindless, relentless pleasure gripping the bottom of my spine like a fist, I unfurl my tentacle slightly inside of her, just enough to get one of my suckers against that spot on the front wall of her cunt, and…

Nora's orgasm rips through her with a groan that vibrates down my cock, and I'm lost. Still gripping her hair tightly, I come into her mouth. My spend drips down her chin and onto her breasts as she pulls back slightly to catch her breath. She's covered in me, marked by me, and entirely boneless with pleasure as I gather her back up in my tentacles and hold her to me.

With effort, I shift back, concentrating on reigning myself in until I'm standing on two feet with my mate cradled in my arms. Nora reaches down and strokes the side of my thigh.

"I like the tentacles."

Sunshine and starlight and every bright thing in the universe pour through me, but I only chuckle. "I could tell. And don't worry, they'll be back."

Later, after we've finished cleaning up and made our way lazy and naked into Nora's bed, I nestle her body against mine. She's still relaxed and pliant, groaning softly as she melts into me.

"God, Elias," she murmurs. "I think you've ruined me for anyone who doesn't have tentacles."

"Good," I tell her, more gruffly than I intended.

She won't be with anyone else from here on out, with tentacles or without, not if I have anything to do with it. Just the idea of someone else seeing her like that, touching her like that, being entrusted with the impossible sweetness of her body and her pleasure... it pulls on a deep, protective instinct, one that has the monster in me ready to do battle if it meant keeping her here by my side.

Still, the beast doesn't have me entirely, and as Nora's breathing slows and her body grows heavier and heavier against mine, a few hard questions bring themselves back to the fore.

Did we go too far tonight?

It feels like we've lived a lifetime in a day. How was it only this morning I tasted her for the first time, and only this afternoon we walked in the sunshine by the water?

Now, as darkness settles outside and the rest of it comes crashing back in—the threat from Daniel, her panic and fear, the tattered threads of restraint I couldn't keep from snapping—guilt settles in along with it.

Should I have put a stop to things? Nora had been so sure, so eager, so willing for every touch. Open to see me for who I am, to share herself, to offer me a level of pleasure I haven't even come close to in all my centuries.

Was it wrong to take that offer?

All those thoughts sit uneasily in my stomach as Nora sighs and adjusts herself against me. Thinking she'd been asleep, I reach down and smooth back some of the damp hair that's fallen over her forehead.

"Is anything wrong?"

She doesn't answer right away, but when she tilts her face up to mine and presses a soft kiss against my lips, her unease shines clearly in her eyes.

"I just... now that we're not..." Her face flushes a little. "I can't stop thinking about what happened earlier. At my apartment."

Guilt surges up hot and accusing in my chest. This. This is why I should have had the sense to prevent things from going as far as they did tonight.

"I'm sorry, Nora. I should have been more considerate of that before we—"

To my surprise, she laughs. "Seriously, Elias. Don't apologize for that. I enjoyed myself, if you couldn't tell."

I open my mouth to speak, but she stops me with a finger pressed against my lips. Deterred, I bite it gently.

"Unless it wasn't something you wanted?" Her brow furrows. "Shit, Elias, I didn't mean to make you feel—"

It's my turn to interrupt her. "Let's just agree that we both wanted it?"

"Alright," she says, letting out a relieved breath. "I'm still sorry, though, that tonight was such a mess."

"You already know how I feel about you apologizing for

that."

"I know. But that doesn't mean I'm going to stop doing it."

As much as I want to keep arguing the point, I know it can rest for now. In time, she'll understand she never needs to feel guilt about asking for or accepting my help, but not tonight.

"About what happened," I say, choosing my words carefully. "I think it would be a good idea to report this to the authorities."

We probably should have already, but between the primal need to get her somewhere safe, and the even more primal need that overtook us both once we got here, the thought left my head entirely.

Nora, however, doesn't seem to share the same idea.

"I don't know if I want to go to the police. Not yet, at least."

"Why not?"

Nora shudders slightly and burrows closer to my side. I push another strand of hair out of her face and hold her tight, waiting for as long as she needs to answer.

"What would I even say to them? My ex left a note for me? How can I even prove it was him? I mean, I know his handwriting, but it's not like my word is going to be enough to arrest him. And if one of my neighbors let him in, it's not exactly trespassing, is it? What would reporting him do, other than piss him off?"

My jaw clenches. "It would get him on their radar, at least. Leave a paper trail in case…"

I can't finish the thought over the wave of breath-stealing anger that moves through me. Nothing's going to happen to her.

"In case he escalates?"

"I won't let that happen."

It's a bold claim, and one I'm still not sure how I'm going to back up—something Nora's probably more than aware of as she props herself up on an elbow and raises a brow as she looks at me.

"Is that right?"

"Yes," I tell her, tugging her back down against my chest.

She lets me, but she's not willing to let the topic rest. "This isn't your battle—"

"Little siren." It's a warning, and maybe I'm overstepping yet again, assuming things I shouldn't, asking her for too much, but I don't particularly care. Not when it's this important. "As long as you're here with me, it's my battle. Since the moment you called and asked for my help, it's been my battle. Let me fight it with you."

The hand she has resting on my chest contracts, nails sinking just a little into my skin, and I welcome the slight sting of pain, even as she realizes what she's done a moment later and relaxes her grip.

"I don't want you to get hurt. And I don't mean just physically. Daniel is a bastard. I don't know what kind of shit he'd pull if he found out you were a part of it."

"I can handle Sorenson."

"Elias," she says, firming up her grip once again. "I mean it."

Feeling her grow tense against me, I stroke a soothing hand down her back. "Would you let me speak with Blair, at least? Sorenson found you somehow, and right now the Bureau seems to be the most likely source. He should know if Sorenson got his hands on any information."

Nora is quiet for a few moments before answering. And even though those moments are fraught, and the idea of Sorenson still out there somewhere, walking free of the consequences he deserves, makes it feel like there's a pallet of bricks sitting squarely in the center of my chest, there's nowhere I'd rather be than right here, supporting her.

"I think that's alright," Nora says finally, laying her cheek against my chest and letting out a long breath.

It's followed by a yawn, and I press a kiss against her temple.

"Sleep," I tell her. "We're safe for tonight. You're here, with me, and that's all that matters."

"Goodnight, Elias," she says, eyes closing as she stays firmly by my side.

"Goodnight, little siren."

20

Nora

I could get used to waking up pressed against my kraken.

Like yesterday, I wake up before Elias, and it gives me a few minutes to savor the enticing, sexy sight of him sleeping.

Neither of us bothered with clothes after our shower last night, and that fact is working to my benefit this morning as I look him up and down.

He truly is a fine specimen of a man, kraken or otherwise.

Long, toned limbs, a sculpted abdomen and chest, deeply tanned skin peppered with coarse black hair. Such a contrast to my own body.

My physique is a lot less toned, and padded with a soft layer of fat I've grown to appreciate these past two years. It's the body I'm comfortable in. A body that loves frozen pizzas and rich chai lattes, that likes long walks but detests running or lifting weights. I've always felt most at home in myself when I look like this, easy and natural, not striving and stressing to be something I'm not.

Something Daniel wanted me to be.

I shudder now to think of the young woman in the photos Elias must have seen. Thin, blond, and attractive, yes, but also so concerned with every bite she put in her mouth and every hour she spent in the gym of the high rise we lived in.

I'd hated the cameras and the attention, the way Daniel would pick and criticize and make unsolicited suggestions about how I could do better, be better, stop disappointing him. It had gotten so bad that I'd avoided those magazines and newspapers altogether, and felt a wave of anxiety any time a camera was present at an event.

Now, though, with a sexy-as-hell kraken pressed up against me, his big hand resting possessively on the soft curve of my hip, I don't feel self-conscious at all.

Like he can sense me thinking about him, Elias stirs beneath me.

"We talked about this yesterday, Nora," he grumbles. "It's too damned early."

"It's hard to believe Morgan-Blair Enterprises is so successful," I retort, allowing myself to be pulled back down against his chest. "With its CEO so lazy and prone to sleeping in, how does any business ever get done?"

Instead of answering, Elias kisses me. Unhurried and decadent, he probes and teases, strokes and inflames, until my body is melting into his.

"We're going to have to do something about all of this sass," he murmurs. "It's really becoming a problem."

There's no true irritation in his voice, nothing but warm, wanting provocation that makes me smile and nip at his lips. "You like it. I think you needed a little excitement in that boring old life of yours."

"Is that so, little siren? And do you intend to provide that excitement?"

My response is lost in the slow heat of his kiss and the unparalleled feeling of tangling my body with his. There's freedom in it, playfulness, permission to be who I am and say what I want without worrying about being judged and found lacking, to indulge in the hunger I know my kraken feels, too.

It's not until a few long, hot minutes later that we both come up for air. Elias's cock—his human cock—is pressed against my lower belly, and he's breathing just as heavily as I am.

Still, when he hesitates for a moment, there's some uncertainty lingering in his eyes. I can't decipher it, but when he leans in to press a quick kiss against my forehead before climbing out of bed, it puts a knot in the bottom of my stomach.

"I'll be back in a couple of minutes."

That knot stays there as he pads toward the door and disappears into the hallway. It stays there while I locate a pair of underwear, some sweatpants and a t-shirt from the bag I packed in my apartment last night, pull them on, sit down cross-legged on the bed, and wait for him to return.

When he finally comes back into the room, he's wearing a pair of worn jeans and a plain black t-shirt. He crosses to look out the wall of windows facing the Sound, and stays there for a few long moments before speaking.

"About what happened between us last night…"

My stomach drops. I know we talked about it a little before falling asleep, but now, in the bright light of day, maybe he feels differently about how everything went down. Maybe he regrets it, or wishes I hadn't pushed him so far.

"I'm still sorry," I blurt. "If you felt pressured, or if I shouldn't have—"

He's across the room in a few long strides, reaching the side of the bed and pulling me into him. "I was a willing and active participant, if you recall."

My cheeks heat up. I do recall. All too well.

"I just don't want intimacy between us to be..." he trails off again, searching for the right words.

"Tainted by everything that's happening?"

His eyes darken. "No, Nora. That's not it at all. But I don't want to rush things. Emotions are high, and all of this is happening much faster and more intensely than I planned."

That last comment has an improbable smile turning up the corners of my lips. "Oh, you had it all planned out, did you?"

He catches my thread of teasing and tugs on it, hands sliding down to squeeze my ass. "Yes, siren, I did. I wanted to court you, woo you, make you believe I was worthy of you."

His words are teasing, but the idea behind them still makes my chest clench painfully.

"You didn't have to, you know," I tell him.

He laughs gruffly. "Be that as it may... I don't know if things should have gone as far as they did between us last night."

"So... what?" I ask, feeling the first stirrings of self-consciousness and doubt creep in. "You want to dial it back on the physical stuff?"

Like he can sense exactly how I'm feeling, Elias pulls me tighter to his chest.

"I'd like us to have the time to get to know each other, to let things develop at what other people might consider a 'normal' pace."

"What part of anything between us has been *normal* so far?"

Elias threads a hand into my hair, gently tipping my head back so he can look into my eyes. "The best parts. Spending an evening with you at the aquarium. Eating breakfast with you in my kitchen. Walking along the seashore and sharing little bits and pieces of our lives with each other."

Unexpected tears prick at the back of my eyes. Elias cups my jaw in his hand, pressing his thumb to my chin and bringing my lips up for a brief, soft kiss.

"You don't know how much I crave normal with you, Nora."

Normal. A normal life. With Elias. What would that even look like?

The answer comes easier than I would have expected. It takes shape like the long exhale of the breath I've been holding for years, like the life I once thought I might have had.

In that life, maybe I'd finally go back to school and finish my degree. Maybe I'd work at a nonprofit like I'd always intended to, instead of sitting on some hands-off board of one because I was with someone important. Maybe I'd come home to a kraken with his tie loosened, jacket discarded, and shirtsleeves rolled up, ready to pull me into a hug and dance with me in the kitchen just because we could.

"Normal, huh?" I ask him. "What's that look like to you?"

Elias's smile is wide and bright and devastating. "Normal looks like days and years and decades with you. It looks like all the freedom to simply *be* without worrying about any shadows waiting around the corner. Normal looks like bliss, little siren."

Elias's arms are steady, his voice is even and measured, his presence here with me enough to have the rest of my doubts sliding away.

"So," I say, kissing a trail up his neck. "What do we do now?"

"Now we enjoy a couple more days together. How does that sound? You don't have to go back to work until Monday, right?"

"Right," I confirm, finally reaching his lips. "And that sounds wonderful."

21

Elias

Monday morning comes all too soon.

Standing in the doorway of Nora's room, watching her put the finishing touches on her makeup for the day, I'm torn between going to her and giving her a kiss that will stay imprinted on her lips until she's home tonight, and simply standing here and admiring her.

I opt for the latter, and wonder for the thousandth time what in the hell possessed me to put the brakes on things. The rational part of me knows it was the right decision, but as she slicks some gloss on her lips and gives her hair a toss, that part has gone strangely silent. It's the kraken at the fore now —wanting, greedy, hungry for her.

Catching my eye in the mirror, my treasure grins at me, and I have to brace my hands on the doorframe to keep myself in check.

"Ready?" she asks cheerfully.

When Nora stands, I want to groan out loud when I see what she's wearing. A pair of tight jeans that hug the swells of her thighs, and a sweater with a neckline that dips low enough to show some tantalizing cleavage.

She walks over to me, and I don't think I'm imagining the way she takes her time, the sway she puts in her hips, or the knowing, taunting look in her eye.

Teasing little siren.

When she reaches me, she raises her hands to grasp lightly at my lapels, and her Cheshire-cat smile lets me know she's well aware of what she's doing.

"I like you in a suit."

I let out a long breath, laced with the faintest edge of a growl. "Remind me again who decided we should take things slow?"

"I believe that would be you, kraken," she says, leaning up to press a brief kiss against my lips.

When she makes a move to pull back, I grasp the back of her neck and drag her closer, giving her a kiss she'll be feeling for the rest of the day.

Nora's eyes are glazed when we part, and her body's slumped into mine, trusting me to hold her up.

If only the rest of her could trust me that much.

Because it's there, right there, in her eyes. Glazed though they may be, there's hesitation there, too, some lingering resistance to give in completely. This weekend has been wonderful, lazy, normal, but throughout, there's still been a piece of her that doesn't believe she should be here.

Whether it's her belief that she's imposing on my hospitality, her reservations about the bond between us, or just her lingering stress and fear over everything happening with Sorenson, I don't know. Whatever the reason, though, it's enough to quiet the monster for now.

"Little siren," I murmur as I brush one last kiss against her lips. "I won't have you late to work on my account."

Nora huffs out a laugh, and even though it seems impossible to leave the safe, quiet peace we've made for ourselves these past two days, I take her hand and head for the door.

After dropping Nora off at the bookstore—with Travis right on time to start her security detail—I don't head to Morgan-Blair Tower.

I don't do anything for a couple of minutes, in fact, as I sit unable to pull away from the parking spot where I dropped her off.

My entire body is thrumming with the wrongness of it, of leaving my mate alone when I know there's danger for her somewhere out there. It's worse now than it's ever been, and it overwhelms me for a few long minutes as I sit in the car and try to get a grip on myself.

Nora is safe. I know she's safe. She's working an 8-5 shift today with two of her coworkers, in a well-trafficked area of downtown, with security on her the entire time.

Nothing is going to happen to her, but I'll be damned if I can get the kraken side of myself to understand that.

Shaking my head to clear my thoughts, I put the vehicle in drive and pull out onto the street. Instead of heading toward the office, though, I have another destination in mind this morning.

The mood inside the Paranormal Citizens Relations Bureau is noticeably subdued from the moment I walk through the door. The whole place is usually a hive of activity and conversation, a hub for paranormal creatures from all walks of life who either work at or visit the Bureau for the various creature services offered as a part of the ongoing effort to integrate our ilk into the human world.

This morning, however, conversations are muted, faces drawn, and as I approach the desk and catch Ruthie's attention, even her usual sunshine is dimmed.

"I'm here to speak with Mr. Blair," I tell her. "He should be expecting me."

She glances at the computer for a moment, and then back at me with a troubled look on her face. "I'll show you up to his office. He may be running late."

When I'm seated in the office a few minutes later, I thank Ruthie for her assistance. She slips from the room quietly, still with that concern in her expression, and I don't know what to make of it.

It's not the same office I was in the last time I visited the Bureau. Blair's apparently back in the Director's office today, one much larger and on the building's top floor, with dark walls and carpet, and heavy wooden furniture. It's an imposing place, one that communicates strength and authority.

The reminder he chose the other, smaller office on the day he met with Nora—likely just to make her feel more comfortable—ratchets my tension down some. A little. Not much.

No matter his own feelings on Sorenson and the politics of the relationship between the Bureau and the larger government, Blair's still firmly on the side of advocating for paranormals and their mates—human or otherwise—and that counts for a whole hell of a lot.

When he finally shows up ten minutes later, Blair's looking more tired and haggard than I've seen him in years. He takes his seat heavily and sets a pile of files and papers off to the side of his desk. With no greeting or preamble, he lets out a long breath and gets right into it.

"I had the distinct displeasure of meeting Sorenson a few days ago," he says. "When he came to Seattle for a nice little visit with his committee cronies."

Unable to sit still, I rise from the chair and walk over to the window at the side of the room. The Bureau is located on the fringes of downtown, still walkable to the city, but a day of mist and drizzle makes it impossible to see much further than the parking garage at the side of the building.

"What were they here for?"

"The same political hardball they've been at since before the Bureau's inception." His voice has an edge to it I can read immediately.

Blair's spent the better part of the past three decades advocating for the advancement of paranormal creatures. Most of the work he's done has been quiet organizing and political lobbying, flexing all the muscle and influence he's built up over the centuries for the benefit of bringing us all out of the shadows.

Knowing what I do about the hurtles and the backlash he's faced, the age-old anger and exhaustion in him is more than understandable.

"Where is the bastard?" I ask him. "I'd like to pay him a visit."

It's not an idle threat, but, as it turns out, Sorenson isn't in the city anymore.

"Vancouver?" I ask, settling back into my chair as Blair gives me a rundown of the last few days.

"They're meeting with a Canadian delegation to discuss the visa process for paranormals. Sorenson was a smug asshole about it when I met with him."

"Prick," I mutter, and Blair snorts his agreement.

"Indeed. And he's swinging that prick of his all over the damn government. Backed by his daddy's money and some other high-profile lobbies."

"What do they want to achieve up there?"

A troubled look passes over Blair's face. "There's

rumblings about a reevaluation of the Acts. Or at least parts of them. The visas are one of the first topics."

"And Canada?"

Blair shrugs. "I don't think he'll make much headway there. The Canadians have much looser regulations in place, and there are rumors about them expanding their amnesty program."

"Montreal's looking pretty good these days. Maybe Morgan-Blair needs to look at an international office."

"Really? I thought you had a few good reasons to stick around Seattle."

Leaning back in my chair, I cross my arms over my chest. "I might have one in particular that will keep me here for the foreseeable future."

Despite the tension of the conversation, Blair cracks a smile. "How's Nora handling everything?"

"She's alright. Shaken over everything that's happening with Sorenson, and she's staying with me until we figure out what to do about that asshole, but she's been very... accepting about everything else."

The wry light in his eyes is familiar, but instead of the ribbing or bawdy joke he might have once offered, he just shakes his head.

"Moved in already? I admit, I wouldn't have given you that much credit for getting her to come around so quickly."

"It's temporary. Now that Sorenson knows where she lives, it's obviously not the best idea for her to be staying there. In the meantime, I've got Travis and a couple of subcontractors on her security detail."

We fall into a few moments of weighted silence. There's another question I want to ask, but I'm not sure I'm ready for either Blair's reaction or his answer. Deciding I need to ask it anyway, I lean forward and rest my elbows on the desk.

"Did he get Nora's information through the Bureau?"

Part of me expects an immediate rebuke, more of that dragon's temper telling me of course not, the Bureau runs a tight enough ship to make sure their case information is protected and secure.

When it doesn't come, it makes his next words all that much worse.

"I don't know," he admits, looking incredibly unsettled over that fact. "We hold all employees to strict standards of confidentiality, but I can't rule it out completely."

"So what are you doing to protect her?"

Again, that he doesn't bite my head off in reply lets me know just how serious this is. "We've sequestered all her digital records under our highest security clearance, and disposed of anything printed. I'm also doing a review of anyone who might have had access to her files."

"Good," I tell him in a clipped tone, even though we're both well aware the damage is already done.

Unless Nora moves, she's at risk as long as she stays in that apartment. Maybe as long as she stays in Seattle. Sorenson's already proven what kind of man he is, and I'm not about to underestimate him or what he might be capable of. Not when it's Nora's safety on the line.

Even Sorenson just being a couple of hours away in Vancouver makes me uneasy. Enough so that I hope Nora will agree to stay with me until he's back in DC.

"And if you can prove he bribed someone or did something illegal to get her information?"

"Then we'll nail the bastard," Blair says, a spark of vengeance in his voice. "I'm not playing this game anymore. We've dealt with the political bullshit for decades, and the Acts and the Bureau were supposed to be the culmination of all of it, the start of a new era for paranormals. I'm not about to let this organization become some kind of pawn on the political game board."

I've always respected the depth of Blair's commitment to this cause, even if I suspect it's deeply rooted in his own need to make amends for his past and live for something other than his own happiness. It's concerned me at times, made me worry about all of that fire burning him out one day.

Not that he'd ever admit to it, or listen to those concerns if I tried to voice them.

"I appreciate your help with all of this," I tell him instead. "And so does Nora. We're both grateful."

Blair nods. "For you, Elias, and for Nora, I'll do anything I can to help. For the sake of you both starting the life you deserve."

It's a testament to the centuries of friendship between us that nothing much more needs to be said. It's there, in the adamance of his assurance and the unspoken recognition of just how far he'd go to keep one of his friends from losing a mate as he did.

At risk of getting sentimental in front of my oldest, most cantankerous friend, I just offer my own nod and stand, straightening my jacket.

"I should be off," I tell him. "A company to run, meetings to have, all of that."

He snorts a laugh at my utter transparency. "I'll be in touch as soon as I hear anything."

With matters as settled as they can be for now, I leave the Bureau and head back downtown, counting the hours until I have my mate safe and back in my arms.

22

Nora

"Fuck that guy."

If I can count on anything in this world, I can count on Kenna to be blunt as hell in a serious situation. I appreciate it, I really do, especially now in this absolute mess I've landed in.

It's Thursday night, and instead of our usual rendezvous at Holly's apartment, we all decided a night out was needed. Tucked into a window booth at one of our favorite sushi places, Kenna stabs a chopstick into a piece of avocado roll and continues her tirade.

"Like, what the actual fuck is his problem?"

"Your guess is as good as mine," I say, picking up a piece of tempura tofu.

I'm glad I told them what's going on with Daniel. Keeping it a secret felt too much like protecting him, and even though it's hard to get over my shame and talk about it, there's no one else I'd trust to listen without judgment.

Well, no one other than Elias, but it's just as nice to have two best friends in my corner backing me up.

"So he, what?" Kenna asks. "Just thought he'd breeze into town, come to your apartment and, what? Kidnap you? This is some scary shit, Nora."

I shake my head slowly. "I don't think he would go that far."

Kenna opens her mouth to argue, but I press on. "I mean, he's a congressman. He comes from one of the most high-profile families in the country. And enough people know about our history and the fact that he was in Seattle to connect the dots if something happened to me. He's an asshole, yeah, but it's hard to believe he'd be that stupid."

It's what I've been telling myself all week, the silent reassurance that keeps me from slipping too far into a panic spiral.

"So, what do you think he wants?" Holly asks gently.

The million dollar question. If I knew, maybe I'd feel comfortable going back to my apartment, stop startling every time I see a brunette man out of the corner of my eye.

I shrug. "I don't really like trying to put myself in his head and guess. And, I mean, it's been three years since I left, so I have no idea why he'd want anything to do with me."

That's not entirely true. I do have some idea why he wouldn't let it go, why he would hate losing the one person he could control completely. Doesn't take a big leap of logic to assume a man like Daniel would take it as a huge blow to his ego to lose that kind of control.

"Anyway," I continue, "Elias is getting some help from a friend of his at the Bureau."

"That's good," Holly says, still in her gentle, soothing tone. "I hope they get all of this settled soon. And in the meantime, let me know if you need some meditation tips or guided affirmations. It's always better to focus on inward reflection and healing rather than directing anger and negativity outwards."

Over the past few months, Holly's been entering her granola era. She's always been a spiritual person, but since her breakup she's been really leaning into it.

Hiking trips all over the state, meditation, eating vegan, all of it meant to cleanse and cut out what she calls the 'spiritual baggage' that she's been hauling around since Cody left.

I'm not sure if it's working, but I don't blame her for trying. I also can't help but smile a little at the contrast her zen attitude poses to Kenna's bombastic one.

"Alright, alright, I know you're getting all 'eat, pray, love' over here, but c'mon, Hol, some people just really need a beat-down." Kenna stabs another piece of sushi and pops it into her mouth, shamelessly talking around the bite. "I mean, a prick like Daniel does, anyway."

Holly frowns and pokes at her seaweed salad. "I just think we should be focused on Nora."

That takes some of the wind out of Kenna's sails. "Well damn, when you put it that way..."

"It's fine," I cut in, then think better of dismissing how I'm actually feeling. "Well, I mean, not fine. But fine. You know? I feel good about having Elias helping me out with everything."

That gets both their attention fixed squarely back on me, and as my face heats up, I mentally kick myself for saying anything at all. I love my friends, I truly do, but their combined powers of interrogation truly are a sight to behold.

Kenna smirks. "Oh? And how are things going with that kraken of yours?"

I chomp down on my piece of maki roll to buy myself a few more seconds, but they're undeterred. Even Holly's eyes light up with interest and she rests both her elbows on the table with her chin in her hands, patiently waiting for me to spill.

"Not *my* kraken," I croak when I finally swallow. "Just *a* kraken."

"The kraken you're dating," Holly chimes in. "I think that makes him yours."

I give her a glare that has no true weight behind it, but Kenna cuts back in before I can speak.

"I've been doing a little research about krakens," she says, grin growing even wider. "Well. Maybe not research in the scientific sense, but it has been... enlightening. Does Elias have any friends he could set me up with? Cousins? A hot brother?"

"Oh, my god." I cross my arms on the table and drop my head down on top of them. "No. He doesn't have any kraken friends I know of."

"A shame," Kenna sighs. "Because, from my research, kraken tentacles really open up a whole world of—"

"Stop!" I say, choking on a laugh. "Seriously. Not going to talk about my sex life with my... well, with Elias."

"So there is a sex life, then?" Holly asks with a wink. "Good for you, girl."

My face is tomato red as I fling a piece of edamame at them both, but we're all laughing as the conversation steers back to topics that are far, far less likely to get us kicked out of this place.

Holly talks about a hiking trip she's planning this January, something that sounds terrifying as hell to me—being out in the woods in those freezing temps—but winter backpacking is next up on her self-reliance bucket list and she sounds really excited.

Kenna, too, is hoping to hear some good news about the artwork she's been working on the last couple of years. She's gotten deep into illustration, and is close to landing a contract with a prolific monster romance writer for a multi-book series she's planning to release over the next couple years.

"If I get this job, I'm pretty much guaranteed more work from the exposure alone. So then I can spend my days just daydreaming and sketching sexy monsters." Kenna sighs and leans back against the booth. "But seriously, though, getting this contract would be so fucking awesome."

"I'm sure you'll get it," I tell her, meaning it. Kenna is talented as hell, and it would be a huge mistake on the author's part not to hire her.

"What about you, Nora?" Holly asks. "You still happy at the bookstore?"

A few weeks ago, I might have said yes. And part of me would have meant it, truly. I'm happy enough with my work, but it's… just a job. Not something I ever dreamed about doing, and not something I see for myself when I think about my life five or ten years down the road.

Still, it's hard to admit that, and even harder when my two best friends are doing such cool things with their lives. But whether it's the confidence I'm rediscovering as I'm forced to confront my fears, or the permission I'm finally feeling to be myself again, I decide to be honest with them.

"It's alright," I admit, "but I've been thinking about going back to school."

It's been there, in the back of my mind, since the moment I got off the bus in Seattle to start my post-Daniel life. Finishing my degree, finally starting the career I'd given up when I dropped out to move to DC.

Both Holly and Kenna smile brightly.

"You should do it," Kenna says, with absolute confidence. "It's never too late to go back."

"She's right," Holly agrees. "I think it would be great for you, Nora."

"Thanks, guys," I tell them both, heart filling up with the relief of saying those words out loud and being met with the support and approval part of me always knew would be there.

We stay at the restaurant for another hour talking and laughing, and when I finally leave and find Travis waiting in an SUV to give me a ride back to Elias's house, I feel lighter than I have in weeks.

There's one more stop I need to make before heading back to Elias's house.

Travis and I pull up to my apartment, and even though one of the additional security personnel on his team has done a sweep of the building, I'm still nervous.

"Thanks for making the stop here," I tell him.

"Of course, Ms. Perry," Travis says, all professionalism. "Would you like me to come in and wait while you pack?"

I shake my head and smile a little, wishing he'd feel comfortable enough around me to use my first name, but sensing that's not really his style.

"It's alright," I tell him, opening the passenger side door. "I'll just be a few minutes."

He looks like he wants to argue, but eventually nods and lets me know to take all the time I need.

Even with the knowledge I'm reasonably safe here, my heart rate still ticks up as I walk to the front door. I can't help but scan the yard around the building, look up and down the street, and try to shake off the feeling of being watched.

The last we heard from Blair, Daniel is still in Vancouver. I trust Blair's info is good, but I'm still jumpy and afraid of my own shadow when it comes to being out in the world.

Especially here, where Daniel invaded my personal space and sense of safety in the worst way. It puts a heavy weight in my gut as I let myself into the building and quickly climb the stairs to my floor.

I don't regret asking Elias not to go to the police. My years with Daniel taught me there's a different set of standards and expectations for wealthy, powerful people dealing with law enforcement. Pair that with the thin evidence we have and the fact that Daniel hasn't actually done anything to get himself arrested yet, and it makes me more than a little skittish to involve any cops at this point.

Opening the front door of my apartment and inhaling the familiar scent of home, the pit in my stomach grows even bigger.

I'm proud of this place. It's small, but cozy and tidy and mine. It's the first place I've lived by myself, the first place I've made my own, and the realization I might never feel totally comfortable here again makes my heart heavy.

Doing a quick lap of the apartment, I fill up my watering can and water my plants before heading into the bedroom to pack the things I want to bring to Elias's place. More clothes, a couple pairs of shoes, and some of the makeup I didn't already have with me is nearly enough to fill up the small duffel I grab from under the bed, but as I pull it out, something else comes with it.

It's a manila envelope stuffed full of all the personal papers and photos I was able to take with me when I left DC. On a whim, I tuck that into the bag as well. It's been a while since I went through it, and the idea of sharing those memories with Elias chases away some of the lingering gloom.

Satisfied I've packed what I need, I pause once more at the front door before flipping off the lights, taking a long look at my little haven. With a sigh, and with no idea when I'll be back here for good, I shut the door and lock it before heading back down to the waiting car.

Pulling up outside the front door of Elias's house, I thank

Travis again for the ride and for taking the time to swing by my apartment. And, like I expected, he brushes aside the thanks with a gruff answer that equates to 'no problem, just doing what I'm paid for.'

I don't really get the vibe that it's me he has a problem with, he just seems like a quiet person. A demi-fae who looks essentially human—minus the slightly pointed ears—with an incredibly broad frame, neatly trimmed wheat-blond hair, and a brooding, tough guy demeanor that just screams the fact that there's probably some hidden softness lurking beneath.

Or, maybe not. Maybe he just thinks babysitting his boss's new girlfriend is beneath him.

Whatever the case, I'm determined to endear myself to him. Elias puts a lot of trust in him and respects him immensely, and I'm realizing I'd like to get along with everyone in Elias's life, just like I can't wait to introduce him to Kenna and Holly someday soon.

"Well," I say, hopping out of the car. "I still appreciate it, Travis. Really. All of this is way outside what you guys are probably paid for, and I can't tell you how much peace of mind it's given me to have your protection."

His eyes widen a little, like he wasn't expecting to deal with that much emotion today. Before he can brush it off again, though, I pipe back up.

"Do you like cookies? Or brownies? Or... I don't know, maybe something healthier, like granola bars?"

"What?"

If I weren't trying so hard to win him over, I would laugh out loud at the look of absolute confusion on his face.

"To eat," I clarify. "I'm going to bake you something, and I can either guess, or you can let me know what you like."

His only reply is confused silence, but I'm not going to be deterred. I just shrug and toss him a winning smile before shutting the door.

"Think about it," I tell him. "And let me know."

I'm halfway to the house when I hear the passenger window rolling down, and almost pump my fist into the air in triumph when he calls after me.

"Banana bread," he says simply. "I like banana bread. With walnuts."

"Banana bread with walnuts," I confirm. "Done."

And then I get a smile, an honest to god smile, before he rolls the window back up and drives off, and I am one hundred percent taking that as a victory as I practically skip up to the front door.

The house is mostly quiet as I step inside, but with the faint sound of music and a light shining from the kitchen, I head in that direction.

I don't find Elias there, but am greeted by Marta's cheerful face as I walk into the room.

Marta looks like she's somewhere around fifty or sixty, though with her being part nymph and part orc, I'm not exactly sure how that translates to her actual age.

What I do know is that she exudes a calming, warm energy that makes me feel at ease anytime I'm around her. With her sage-green skin, soft silvery hair, and serene smile, it's hard not to feel comforted by her presence.

Tonight, she's finishing up in the kitchen before heading home to her longtime partner, Maud, and smiles brightly when I come into the room.

"Nora," she says. "I was hoping I'd get to see you before I left. After today I'm off until Tuesday."

"For your and Maud's anniversary, right?" I ask, sliding into one of the seats at the island. "Elias mentioned the two of you were getting out of town for a few days."

"Yes. Thirty years together, can you believe it? I know she'd rather not make such a fuss, but I'm too sentimental not to."

I grin at that. I haven't gotten to meet Maud yet, but from how much Marta talks about her, I can imagine the reserved, salt-of-the-earth wolf shifter is probably all too happy to make Marta happy.

"Well, I hope you two have a wonderful time."

We chat some more as she gets ready to leave, and just as she's packing her things up to go, a kettle I hadn't noticed on the stove starts to whistle.

"Oh!" she says. "I almost forgot. There's a new tea from Ruthie I wanted you to try."

It turns out Blair isn't the only one who reaps the benefits of Ruthie's tea-making experiments. Elias comes home with a new blend every time he visits the Bureau.

Marta sets the mug down in front of me, and like every other blend I've tried, it smells incredible.

"Did Elias bring this one home today?"

Marta nods. "He did. He got home just about an hour before you did."

I take a deep sip, and an incredible floral taste blooms on my tongue. The tea has an almost effervescent quality to it, like if I closed my eyes and opened them again, I might find myself in a forest clearing filled with wildflowers and sunlight.

"It tastes like summer," I say, smiling even wider.

Marta just nods, like she knows exactly what I mean.

"Has Elias tried it? And is he around here somewhere?"

"Not yet. And that restless creature went into a workout straight after work. But I think he finished some time ago."

If he's following his usual routine, he probably hopped right in the shower after his workout. The idea of a wet, naked Elias just waiting to be ambushed is incredibly appealing, but I keep my thoughts in check.

Marta and I chat for a few minutes more before she pulls

her coat on and gets ready to leave.

"Thanks, Marta," I say with a smile, raising my mug of tea. "And not just for this, either, but for all the help you've given me since I came here. I really appreciate it."

She tries to brush aside the thanks, but looks pleased all the same, and with a last goodbye and good wishes for her upcoming trip with Maud, she leaves.

I grab my tea and head for my room, not so sneakily taking a small detour to press my ear up against Elias's door. I don't hear anything from inside, and even though I'm aching and to go in and find him, I hesitate.

It's not that I think he'd be unhappy to see me, or that he'd ask me to leave. Actually, it would probably be exactly the opposite.

We've been keeping each other at arm's length this week, and the tension has been nearly unbearable. It's there, in the lingering kisses and the way we find any excuse to touch each other. In the absolutely wonderful misery of him sliding into bed with me at night—even though he always, *always* grumbles about how he should give me some space—and having to keep myself from saying the hell with it and jumping him.

It's getting really, really hard to remember why slowing down was such a good idea. Even if we have been spending the time getting to know each other, getting comfortable just being together, it doesn't erase the fact that I still want my kraken so much it makes me ache.

With all those frustrations hounding me, I carry my duffel and my mug into my room and toss the bag down on the bed before taking another long sip of delicious tea. Shooting off a quick text to Elias, I let him know I'm here and that he can come find me when he's done with his shower.

Bored, restless, impatient, I reach for the duffel with the vague thought of getting all my stuff put away, but I'm stopped by the item laying right on top.

The manila envelope is heavy in my hands, its edges worn smooth with time.

It's filled with photos and documents and little scraps of the life I used to lead. There are more pieces I can hold on to now—art prints and framed photographs in my apartment, little trinkets I've picked up during the past couple years—but once upon a time this single envelope held all the things I could claim as uniquely mine.

The first photo I pull out of the envelope is a snapshot from my freshman year of college, taken in the dorms. I'd been so eager to get away from a mother who I loved dearly, but who never quite bounced back after dad left, so ready to start something for myself in a new place with new people.

I run my fingers over the glossy photo paper, smiling at the younger version of myself with my arms wrapped around my two roommates, friends who I haven't spoken to now in over five years.

I look happy. And I had been. For the first two and a half years of university, I'd felt more like myself than I ever have.

Other photos follow that one, snapshots from my childhood, one of which makes me pause and study the two figures in it.

It's my seventh birthday, and I honestly can't remember who would have taken the photo—maybe my aunt Patty, maybe one of the neighbors in the small rental bungalow my mom and I lived in for most of my childhood—all those memories are a little hazy now. There's a cake lit with candles in front of me, and my mom is crouching down next to me. She has a hand on my shoulder and a smile on her face, but also a tired, blank look behind her eyes.

That's one of the things I remember most about growing up, mom always being tired. Well, that and the fact she was always working, always doing what she had to do so she could provide for us. Even if sometimes I'd catch her looking at me like I was the problem, like maybe she wouldn't have to work so hard or be so tired if I didn't exist.

She never said the words out loud, and never really talked about my dad. By the time I got to my teenage years, started being more independent and relying on her less, things got better. We cohabited more or less like roommates until I left for college.

It took me a long, long time to realize it's not my responsibility to fix my mom. I wanted to, for so long I wanted to. When I was young, I thought if I was good enough and cheerful enough, I could make her smile. I'd thought if I followed all the rules, never got in trouble, and brought home good grades, it would make things easier for her, and she might stop looking at me like I was a problem she couldn't solve.

Shaking my head, I set the photo aside and flip through a few more. Middle school volleyball, a stiffly posed photo with my date for Junior prom, little bits and pieces of the girl I'd been and the young woman who'd had so much in front of her.

When I've had enough of my stroll down memory lane, I tuck everything back inside the envelope and stand up from the bed. All the reminiscing has made me unsettled in a way I can't quite put my finger on. I check my phone to see if Elias has texted me back and find no new messages.

Feeling even more restless, I cross over to the wall of windows at the opposite side of the room and look out into the dark, not really seeing anything beyond the glass.

I'm still seeing all of those photos, lost in the memories they've dredged up, and struck again with the realization that since the time those pictures were taken, I've never felt this free to decide who and what I want to be.

The realization hits me with breath-stealing clarity.

Despite all the other shit going on—or maybe *because* of all the other shit going on—I've been waking up these past few weeks, realizing what I want to dictate my life and what I don't.

Making a split-second decision and not giving myself any time at all to second-guess, I cross the room and step out into the hallway. As I approach Elias's door, I knock softly and put my ear to the dark wood, but I can't hear anything and don't get any reply, so I try the handle. It opens, and I step inside.

Elias's room is enormous. I've only been in here a couple of times, but walking in now still takes my breath away.

A wall of windows lines the far side of the space, looking out over the backyard all the way to the water's edge. Also at the side of the room, a large saltwater pool that goes from in-to outdoors through a glass partition.

Padding softly inside, the tile floor is cool beneath my feet, made of dark gray slate that sets the tone for the rest of the colors in the room. Everything is decorated in dark grays and blues, and with the lights in the pool shining through the softly rippling water, it gives the whole place the feeling of being at the bottom of the sea.

This place feels like Elias.

The darkness of him, the cool kiss of the ocean, the steadiness and comfort of being cradled by the gentle push and pull of waves.

"Hello?" I call out, venturing a little further inside. "Elias?"

I don't get an answer, and it doesn't take me long to figure out why. The surface of the pool ripples slightly, and I can just make out the distorted shape of something huge and dark beneath the water.

My breath catches in my throat.

There's no reply, no sound but my soft footsteps on the tile floor and the water lapping at the side of the pool. When I get closer, I see a couple of tentacles resting on the edge of the pool, but with the shifting water, I can't fully make out the kraken beneath the surface.

If the size of him is any indication, though, he's in a full shift, and I'm not sure I'm breathing at all as I lean in to get a better look. His words about being fully in his other form echo in my mind.

I'll show you sometime, if you'd like to see... Maybe I'll be there, waiting in those depths to strike and carry you off to a sea cave where I can ravish you completely.

Heart thumping in deep, aching beats, I crouch down low.

Like he can sense I'm near, the tentacle on the side of the pool unfurls and stretches toward me. I reach out, stroking his cool, soft skin with my breath still caught in my throat.

"Elias?"

Faster than I can react, that same tentacle snaps up and bands around my wrist, tugging me toward the water.

23

Elias

When Nora's hand strokes my tentacle, I'm in a full shift.

I don't often indulge in the shift, at least not here, but after the last few days I desperately needed to get out of my own head for a while. Being so close to Nora, keeping a leash on myself—though make no mistake, I'd be as careful as she needs me to be for as long as she needs me to be—after a while it starts to grate.

Letting the kraken take over usually eases some of that tension.

The monster isn't exactly separate from me, but he's got his own mind and his own concerns. He's protective of our mate, too, but also tuned in to other things. In the open ocean he hunts, stalking his prey through the deep, and the feeling of that freedom is incomparable.

However, when he feels Nora's gentle fingers stroking,

seeking, he's just as greedy for her as I am.

I'm able to pull back into a half-shift before I send her careening into the pool, but I still sputter a little as I come up for air and release her wrist.

"Nora," I say, coughing around a mouthful of water. "I'm sorry, I didn't mean to—"

"It's okay," she says quickly. "I shouldn't have snuck up on you like that."

Unbelievably, she doesn't look horrified at what I've just done, or by the fact that standing above the water, she must have gotten at least a glimpse of me in my full shift. Instead of disgust, she has a smile on her face as she reaches out again to close her hand around my tentacle, stroking it lightly.

"I didn't mean to stay in so long," I tell her, trying to ignore the feel of her skin on mine.

She laughs softly. "Don't be sorry. Having this around my wrist gave me... ideas."

Fuck, just the thought of that... of keeping Nora bound, completely at my mercy... I shouldn't entertain it for a single second, not when we're meant to be taking a step back and taking things slowly.

She seems to clock that conflict on my face, because she stays quiet, still touching me and waiting for me to reason things out on my own time.

Like that's even possible right now.

With Nora here, in this space, it's all I can do to keep a grip on my sanity.

This is the closest thing to a lair I can claim. Muted grays and dark blues to mimic the hues of sea caves on remote islands. Cool, smooth tiles on the floor. An enormous saltwater pool to disappear in for a while.

On my more stressful days, I sleep submerged, fully shifted and cradled by the water. In eras past, my ancestors wouldn't have kept more than a sea cave above the water for a dwelling. Even that would have mainly served as a repository for treasures, with the bulk of their lives lived beneath the sea.

And now that my own treasure is in my lair, still touching one of my tentacles, still with that wicked little smile fixed on her lips...

A thrill of primal, undeniable instinct pulses through me, and I grit my teeth to keep from reaching for her.

It's the reason I've mostly kept her out of this space. Not because I don't want her here—quite the opposite, actually. I want her here too much. The monstrous part of me would wrap her up and keep her safe, tuck her away somewhere she can't be harmed. It would have me be greedy with her here, worship her here.

But if my little siren wants to be worshiped, if my treasure wants me to be selfish and greedy with her...

I give my head a sharp shake, and Nora frowns.

"What is it?"

"I... I don't want to go back on my word to provide you the time and space you need, or pressure you for anything you're not ready to give."

Her frown vanishes in an instant, replaced once more by her teasing grin.

"Is that all?" she asks, leaning closer.

Every single one of my muscles tense at the invitation in her voice, in her eyes, in the sway of her body toward mine. Without my willing it to, the tentacle she's touching wraps around her wrist once more. The hold is loose, but an unmistakable warning.

She glances down at where I have her bound. "Do you want me to go?"

I should say yes. I need to say yes. For both our sakes.

"No, Nora. I never want you to leave."

This room. My home. My life. I'm not sure exactly which

I'm referring to, probably all of them, but she's got a place in each as long as she wants.

"Alright," she whispers. "I've had a long day. A swim sounds pretty good right now."

If there was any doubt left in my mind that Nora was mine—my mate, my siren, my biggest temptation—it evaporates instantly. In its place, a warm, inexorable heat and a primal command spreading through my veins.

"You're welcome to join me," I tell her, bringing another couple of tentacles up to play with the hem of the blouse she's wearing. "But you're wearing a few too many clothes."

Nora nods and reaches down to lift it up.

"How much do you like this shirt?" I ask, voice lower and more gruff than I intended.

"Not much."

It shreds with a quick jerk of my tentacles, and the pieces land somewhere near the corner of the room as I toss them aside with a careless flick.

"The bra?"

Nora laughs. "That one I think I'll keep."

"Off. Now."

She's no doubt got more control over her fine motor function right now than I do, and I'm not enough of a brute to destroy her things just because the need to have her bare is pounding through me with every beat of my two hearts.

"Pants, too," I tell her, in case she'd like to keep those as well. "All of it."

My little siren is in no hurry. Smirking at me, she takes a step back and tugs her wrist from my grasp. When she reaches for her waistband and unfastens her pants, her movements are too slow and deliberate for there to be any misunderstanding her intent.

Nora is teasing me. Taunting me. Paying me back in kind for the frustration I've put us both through this week. And I'm more than willing to let her have her fun. For a while.

With a tug and a shimmy, she slides her jeans off and kicks them aside. Her socks follow, leaving her in just her bra and panties. With more of that deliberate slowness, her bra goes next, baring her full, perfect breasts and rosy pink nipples already hardened with excitement. When she pauses with her hands tucked into the waistband of her panties, though, I find my patience wearing thin.

Raising two tentacles in warning, I give her a long, hard look. "I am more than capable of dealing with those, if you aren't."

A pulse of delight from my treasure, smiling brightly as she continues to toy with them. "I think I can manage."

"That may be," I tell her, grasping onto the fabric at her hips with those two tentacles. "But I don't know if I can wait that long, little siren."

The lacy thing tears from her body like tissue paper, making Nora gasp and leaving her entirely bare before me. I want to grab her, pull her into the water, but leaning back and giving her a long, admiring look seems like almost as good an option. With the added benefit of letting her choose to come to me, and giving her any last time she might need to reconsider.

But it would seem my siren's mind is made up.

She wades slowly into the pool, getting used to the temperature of the water, and when her eyes meet mine again she laughs. Standing on the third step down, the water laps at her waist, leaving her torso bare and dappling her body in shifting, rippling light.

"What?" I ask, staring spell-bound and the impossibly erotic sight she presents.

Nora shakes her head and laughs softly again, then gestures to herself. "I feel like some kind of sacrifice coming to you like this."

My blood races, and I reach a tentacle out under the water to tease against one of her thighs. Nora gasps, but leans into the touch and takes another step into the water.

"A worthy offering," I tell her, wrapping that tentacle around her waist. "Any ocean god would be pleased with such a gift."

She comes to me willingly, eagerly, running her hands over the tentacle that has her bound and relaxing into my hold as I reel her in. Pressed against my body, the warmth of her radiating through every part of me, she leans up and nips at my ear.

"What about a terrible, fearsome sea monster? Would I make a worthy sacrifice for him, too?"

"That depends on whether you were a willing tribute."

"And if I was?"

"If you were, little siren..." I say, winding two more tentacles around her and lifting her out of the water. I keep her there, hovering just over the surface at the perfect height to feast on. "Then I would have no choice but to worship you."

The words are low and rumbling, spoken into the soft skin of her inner thigh as I inch closer and closer to her cunt. Nora gasps again and shifts for me, opens for me, trembling with anticipation. And with the first swipe of my tongue over her damp, warm, swollen flesh, she cries out and arches against my hold.

The sight of her bound in my tentacles is more erotic than anything I ever could have imagined. Wrapped around her soft, plush body, squeezing her tight, keeping her still when she bucks and writhes with pleasure, it draws on that same dark instinct howling up from the bottom of my soul.

Claim her. Keep her. Fuck her.

I settle for devouring her instead, savoring the offering she brings to me so sweetly.

The taste of her only stokes those instincts higher,

stronger, closer to the brink of blissful oblivion. Her thighs bracket the sides of my head and I grunt in approval, tightening my grip on her and sinking my fingertips into the curve of her ass.

It doesn't take long until her body is taut and straining, cries growing louder and more insistent. When I bring a tentacle up to work in tandem with my mouth, to tease around her wet, pulsing entrance, breaching her just enough for her to feel the stretch, Nora implodes.

I stroke and ease her through every spasm of her climax, keeping her firmly held as she comes apart against my lips.

When she's finally settled down, I lower her into the water and shift her against me, turning her in my tentacles so she's got her back pressed to my chest. She leans into me, arches her neck to claim my lips in a long, scorching kiss. Wrapping her hair around my fist, I tug her head back and plunder her mouth as my tentacles continue to caress and explore.

She's only taken the smallest parts of me—the tip of a tentacle, the slow draw of one of my suckers—and I monitor her every reaction as I give her a bit more. A tentacle, delving deeper into her; a sucker, wrapped around her clit. Any sign of displeasure, any hint of hesitation, and I'll pull back, but Nora gives me nothing but sweet moans and wordless pleas for more.

All of it makes my mating tentacle throb where it's pressed snugly against her ass. It's no secret she can feel it, too, as she grinds herself against me. Over and over, she rubs against the length of it, tempting and taunting and making me want things I'm not altogether certain she's ready for.

Taking a deep breath and getting a handle on myself, I pull my tentacles away from her cunt and lean down to murmur into her ear.

"How much of me do you want, little siren?"

I have to ask her. I have to know where my boundaries need to be. If it were up to me, I'd give her everything I have. I'd fill her so completely there would never be room for anyone else. I'd keep her here for hours—fucking her, making her see stars, giving her orgasm after orgasm until she was begging for mercy.

Nora doesn't answer right away, still moving her hips against my shifted cock, chasing the pleasure I'm more than willing to give her. When I press my teeth into her skin in a small reminder, though, she leans her head back to look up at me.

And fuck, is she beautiful. Eyes glazed with pleasure, lips swollen and parted on a gasp, cheeks flushed, she looks every inch the siren that she is.

"All of you," she whispers. "I want all of you, Elias."

24

Nora

I'm still coming down from the earth-shattering orgasm Elias just gave me, but with his cock pressed against my ass and those damned tentacles of his already stoking me back up, I mean every word.

"All of you. I want all of you, Elias."

His answering groan echoes all the way down to my aching pussy.

"Are you sure?"

Craning my neck back, I catch his lips in a deep, slow kiss. I hope he can taste my certainty. I hope I'm telling him what I need when the words don't seem like enough.

Maybe it's what I've always needed. Someone to be patient with me. Someone to be careful with me. Someone who's shown me time and time again that what I want matters more than anything.

Elias moves us into the shallow end of the pool with my back still pressed to his chest. He has a tentacle wrapped around each of my thighs, holding me open, and another banded around my waist to keep me still and pinned against him. When a fourth winds its way up my neck, gently tipping my head back so he can nip at my lips, I taste the ocean.

"Do you trust me?"

"Yes," I breathe. "Yes, I trust you."

The tentacle around my neck shifts slightly, tipping my head forward. "Look down, Nora. See what you do to me."

Between my legs, his mating tentacle is thick and hard and pulsing against my damp pussy, and it's not the only thing that wants in.

I've entirely lost track of the number of appendages my kraken has, but when yet another tentacle probes against me, all I can do is buck and rear back into him, crying out at the unfamiliar sensation. He hasn't gone this deep before. He's only given me light, teasing touches and shallow dips inside, nothing like the deep, insistent way he's stroking into me now.

"That's it," Elias grates out when I bear down and shift open to take him deeper. "Just like that, Nora."

Warmth floods through me with his graveled praise. Warmth and trust and painfully sweet tenderness that only ratchets up every other sensation.

The feeling of Elias's tentacle breaching me, filling me, diving deep and branding me from the inside out, is like absolutely nothing I've ever felt before. Pulsing and alive, twisting and shifting and fitting itself to the shape of me.

I look down, and the sight of that blue-gray tentacle disappearing inside of me sends an impossibly erotic thrill to the bottom of my belly and the tips of my toes.

Elias follows my gaze. "So pretty, my treasure. Do you think you can take some more?"

I nod, but he brings a hand up to cup my chin, tilting my

head back toward him.

"Let me hear your words."

"Yes! I want more."

"Ask, and it's yours," he rasps, and pushes in another few inches.

My thighs shake from the impossible, building waves of pleasure and Elias tightens his hold on me, spreading me even wider as his tentacle dives deep and retreats.

His shifted cock bumps up against my inner thigh, and a small pulse of uncertainty moves through me. I have no idea how I'm going to take all that. Long, thick, and already weeping from the tip, my core tightens just looking at it.

Elias seems to read my hesitation, because he leans in to whisper low and dark into my ear.

"I'll make sure you're ready for me, little siren."

Inside of me, the tentacle he's impaled me on shifts and twists, growing thicker somehow, like it's curling in and doubling over on itself. The stretch of it boarders on too much, makes me squirm and moan and press back against him, but I'm not about to ask him to stop. When I tangle my hands into his hair and pull his head forward to claim his mouth, he growls and presses even deeper, fitting himself against the spot he drove me wild with last time.

His tentacle shifts again, and I feel the pressure of one of his suckers latching onto me. There, right *there*, hitting that sensitive spot inside and ripping another scream from me as my climax crests and breaks. He works me through every spasm, drawing the pleasure out until I'm half-certain I'm going to pass out from it.

I don't, but it's pretty damn close as he eases out of me, hugs me tightly to him, and kisses every bit of bare skin he can reach.

"Have you had enough for tonight?" he murmurs against my shoulder.

"No. Not nearly enough."

"Little siren," he whispers. "You don't have to—"

"I *want* to." To emphasize my point, I rub my ass against him where he's still hard and ready for me. "Unless you don't want—"

My words cut off at his sharp growl and his lips crashing into mine. He's ravenous as he strokes his tongue deep, hand on my throat, keeping me pinned in place. And when he notches his cock against my entrance, the clawing need to have him inside steals my breath.

Elias breaks the kiss and looks down over my shoulder. Expression rapt, he watches himself nudge against me once, twice, before sliding the blunted tip inside.

Just that—just the smallest part of him—is already enough to make me feel stretched and full. Elias's shuddering breath breaks against my shoulder as he drives his hips forward another inch, then another, until I'm meeting him thrust for gentle thrust, groaning at the impossible feel of him sliding deeper.

"Easy, my treasure," he says. "Let me take my time with you."

I hear him, and I want to agree, but with each inch gained I'm getting more impatient. Letting out a small moan of protest, I shift my hips, straining to take more of him, and his answering growl rumbles all the way through me.

"Greedy. So greedy, my Nora. Shall I be merciful and give you what you want?"

"Please," I gasp. "Please, Elias, I—"

I don't get to finish begging.

With a powerful upward thrust, he fills me up entirely and wrenches a ragged scream from the back of my throat. He's there, bottomed out, sunk to the hilt in me. I'm stretched so full that for a few long moments all I can do is drop my head back against his shoulder and close my eyes, trying to adjust to the feel of him.

"Beautiful siren," he murmurs, rolling his hips in a way that makes another moan rasp from my throat. "Look at you taking me so well, my mate."

I know Elias is mindless at this point, too far gone into the magick being woven between us to think about what he's saying. And I know I should be more off-put by him using that word, but I can't seem to make myself care.

No, when I look down and see myself stretched around him, feel the insistent pulse of him inside of me and the light press of his teeth against my neck, there's no part of me that shies away from that word.

My mate.

Elias drops a hand to rub slow circles around my clit as he eases gently in and out of me. It's not enough, not nearly enough. Reaching up and back to wrap an arm around his neck for leverage, I grind into his thrusts and move restlessly against him, begging for more. More pleasure. More touch. More of the wild, incredible feel of him.

I must moan at least some of it out loud, because Elias growls low in his throat. "You need more from me, little siren?"

"Yes! *Please.*"

When he pulls out of me, I cry out sharply in protest. It's only a couple of seconds, though, before he's got me turned around and pushed up against the smooth, tiled edge of the pool, one of his thick tentacles banded around my body to keep me supported as he slams back into me. The rest of those tentacles embrace me, too, sliding over my skin, caressing me, toying with my nipples and my clit.

Elias is... everywhere. In me, around me, enveloping me completely until the outside world might have disappeared. The entire universe has narrowed down to the feel of his cock filling me up, his tentacles teasing and massaging and keeping me bound to him, the beating of both our hearts, the rasp of our breath, and the splash of the water around us.

Through it all, my kraken keeps me anchored, even when another orgasm builds from the very center of me outwards. It's more intense than before, heavier, deeper, burning me up from the inside out until it breaks with a ferocity that blanks my vision out for a few long, ecstatic moments.

Elias comes just after I do, driving deep and exploding in me with a wash of heat that makes my belly flutter and my body go lax against his.

25

Elias

Floating aimlessly with Nora in my arms, I'm filled with a sense of soul-deep peace.

I'm still lodged deeply inside of her, and every so often I feel her spasm and grip around me in waves of pleasure that draw little moans and sighs from my siren. She's tucked against my chest, still held firmly in my tentacles, and as the haze of lust recedes, I'm struck by how very right this feels.

She was magnificent. *We* were magnificent, together. I knew we would be, never doubted for a single moment that joining my body with hers could be anything less than a gods-blessed miracle, but nothing could have prepared me for the emotions that would follow.

Nora fills me up from the soul outwards. Her body, her mind, her sweet spirit.

She was always meant to be mine.

If I believed it before, it's branded on me now. In my blood and bones, weaving itself into the fabric of everything I've ever been or will be.

When I finally ease out of her, she gasps a little at the feeling of release, and then her face goes crimson.

"What is it?" I ask, stroking a hand over her wet hair. "Are you sore?"

"No," she says quickly. "I just... we didn't talk about, uh, birth control or anything. Before we started. I mean, I'm already on the pill, so it should be fine, but... I just..."

She's adorable when she's tongue-tied, but I take mercy on her by squeezing her tight and taking her chin in my hand to tilt her face up toward mine.

"I can't get you pregnant, Nora."

Her face falls a little, and I'm not sure what to make of that, but I quickly elaborate.

"At least not right now. My kind, krakens, go into a heat of sorts when we're ready to mate with our partners."

"Oh." Her brow furrows, clearly confused. "And what happens during this... heat?"

I chuckle. "What you might expect. A frenzy, of sorts, driven by the biological need to reproduce."

At the word *frenzy*, she shivers a little against me. "And then you'd... get me pregnant?"

Yes, the kraken's voice inside me croons. *Yes, I would, my mate. I'd fill you so completely there would never be any doubt who you belong to.*

"Not necessarily," I say instead, beating back the unreasonable beast. "There are precautions we could take to make sure that doesn't happen if it wasn't something you wanted. There's no pressure for you to ever take an egg from me."

Her head snaps up. "Hold up. That's going to need some more explanation. An *egg*?"

Tightening my grip on her waist, I brush a tentacle over the swollen heat of her cunt and delight in the way she bucks her hips instinctively to meet my touch.

"When I'm in heat. I'll create eggs I can pass to you. Sex during a heat, sex meant for breeding, is a bit... different. More intense. I'd secrete a chemical that would make it possible for you to accept an egg and carry it to term."

Nora shivers again, though I don't think it's out of fear as her bright eyes meet mine. "So would it just be like... a replica of you? If it's your egg?"

That she doesn't immediately reject the idea, that she's not disgusted and pushing herself away from me and getting the hell out of the pool, is all the encouragement I need to lean in and capture her lips for an adoring kiss. When I pull back, she keeps her arms around me, smiles up at me, and for a moment that beautiful, impossible future we might have stretches out in front of me.

"It would be a part of you, too, little siren. Don't ask me to explain how the biology or magick of it works, but our child would get just as much from you as they would from me."

I imagine a little kraken girl with my black hair and Nora's incredible eyes, who might inherit my own youthful proclivity for mischief and make us both old and gray before our time. Or perhaps a little boy with soft brown hair and sea-blue eyes who'd be every bit as sensitive and thoughtful as my mate.

Nora remains silent for a minute, contemplating what I've told her, then reaches up to cup my cheek in her palm. "Is that something you'd want one day? Kids? A family?"

"I would."

She nods. "It's always seemed a little abstract to me, becoming a mom, but I think... I think I'd want that too."

Something small and fragile and wonderful blooms in the center of my chest.

"It's not something we have to decide anytime soon," I tell her gently, tucking that feeling away for now. Keeping it somewhere it will be safe.

I shift back into my human form before carrying Nora from the pool to my bed. We're both still dripping wet, but it hardly matters in the haze of exhausted, blissful satisfaction.

She's relaxed in my arms, completely sated, and I can't help but internally purr in pleasure to see her so undone.

My mate. Satisfied. Happy. Utterly fucked-out and *mine*.

"Alright," she murmurs, curling into my side and settling her head in the crook between my neck and shoulder. "No kids right now. I'm, uh, also clean. Do krakens get STDs?"

"I'm immune from most normal human illness. Including STDs."

"Oh," she says. "Well. I got tested after I moved here, and there hasn't been anyone since then."

I look down, brow furrowed. I suppose it makes sense, given what she went through in her last relationship, but the idea she hasn't had that type of companionship in so long is... well, hard to believe, for one.

On the other hand, the feral, kraken part of me hisses in pleasure that there are no other males walking around Seattle who have intimate knowledge of my treasure.

Nora, perhaps mistaking my expression for something else, blushes a little. "Which is just my clumsy way of saying I'm not seeing anyone else. Romantically. I mean, you probably already guessed that, but... I thought it might be worth mentioning."

Her cheeks turn a darker shade of pink as she speaks, and the primal satisfaction in my chest grows even more pointed.

Good. It's good there's no one else. There won't be from now on if I have anything to do about it.

"There's no one else for me either, Nora," I tell her. "And there won't be, as long as we're together."

And even if we're not, there may never be anyone for me again. I don't say the words aloud, but they ring just as true in the back of my mind.

Nora laughs softly. "Does that make you my boyfriend, then?"

I have to laugh as well. *Boyfriend*. Gods. What a thing to be called by my mate, the piece of my own heart living and breathing and walking around outside my body.

"I'm whatever you want me to be."

Mate, husband, boyfriend, friend. It hardly matters to me. As long as she'll have me, I'll be here.

"Whatever I want you to be..." she murmurs. "That seems like a pretty broad promise."

If she only knew how broad the promises I'd make to her could be.

"What would you like me to be, little siren?"

Nora leans back and studies me. "On the first morning we spent together, you said we had all the time in the world for our relationship."

"I did."

"I was wondering if you meant that literally? Blair said something the day we met about krakens living to be a thousand years old. And I've read a few things about mating bonds. Kraken mating bonds, in particular, and how they affect humans who form them."

Nora looks a bit abashed, like she's confessed to doing something she shouldn't. I just chuckle, leaning forward to press a kiss against her temple.

"I'm glad you've been curious enough to do some research. And yes, you're right. A human who bonds with a kraken will have an extended life span. For lack of a better way to explain it, we would meet in the middle and live to be roughly the same age."

I hadn't wanted to drop that bit of information in her lap

for fear it might scare her, and perhaps that fear was not unfounded. When I glance back down at her, Nora looks unexpectedly distraught.

"You'd live a shorter life because of me? That's awful, Elias. Why would you want that?"

I shake my head in immediate denial, trying to assuage her worries. "If you're asking me whether I'd live a thousand years without you, or take a couple hundred less and get to spend them with you by my side? That's not even remotely a choice for me, little siren."

Her concern doesn't leave her eyes. "I still don't see how that would be worth it."

I still don't see how I would be worth it.

The implication in her words is clear enough, and it makes me ache on her behalf as I take her hand in mine and raise it to my lips.

"I would be more concerned with how it might affect you." When she gives me a questioning look, I explain. "I've lived centuries, Nora. And with that comes more and different types of heartbreak than you might expect. It's not a small thing for me to ask of you, taking on a life like that."

Nora is quiet, but she puts her hand over my hearts and presses lightly. Her cheek follows, resting on my chest as she listens to the beat there. The beat that's now only for her.

"It's not something you have to think about tonight," I tell her gently. "Like I said, we have time."

"All the time in the world," she murmurs.

She's quiet for a little while after that, and when the sound of her breathing grows slow and even, I can't stop the pulse of painful tenderness in my chest. So much, I've asked of her, and so much she still has to decide.

Still, there's nowhere else I'd rather be tonight than here, right here with Nora. And as sleep pulls me under a little while later, I drift off feeling more peaceful and content than I have in any of my three hundred years.

26

Elias

On Nora's next day off from the bookstore the following Wednesday, I indulge in some time off as well. It's a rare occurrence for me to take time away from the office that doesn't involve business travel of some sort, but the idea of spending an entire day uninterrupted with Nora is too great a temptation to pass up.

In the back of my mind, I'm aware this time is temporary. It would be insane to assume she'd want to continue living here after the threat from Sorenson is dealt with, and even more insane to ask her if she wants to.

Not that I'm thinking about it. Not at all.

I'm absolutely not imagining what it would be like to have Nora here permanently when we curl up together in the living room in front of a fire to spend an evening reading and cuddling. I'm not imagining it when I wake each morning and have her nestled against my side. It's not right at the forefront of my mind when I pull her into the pool or the shower and have her moaning and writhing against my tentacles, making it all too easy to picture keeping my treasure here forever.

No, I'm not imagining it at all.

We haven't talked about being mated or taking any next steps since that first night together in the pool. It's not unreasonable for her to need some time to process the information, and at the very least it hasn't sent her running in the opposite direction, so I suppose that's something.

And, all of that aside, we have today. A normal, glorious day to spend with my mate.

We sleep late, and I wake my treasure up with a trail of warm, wet, biting kisses down her neck. She moans herself awake, and it's not long before she's got her hands tangled in my hair, pushing me down even further so I can bring her to bliss.

That particularly pleasant interlude is followed by a shower that involves very little actual washing up, breakfast back in bed, and a slow, simple morning of kissing and touching, laughing and talking and lounging in bed together.

After lunch, we walk down to explore the shorefront at the edge of my property. It's a gray and chilly day, but we're bundled up and Nora's cheeks are glowing pink with the cold. Her whole face lights up when she sees the beach and the views, and it's just one more thing I hope might convince her to move here one day.

She grabs for my hand as we walk, smiling up at me with trust and affection and a relaxed joy that seems to glow from the inside out.

Late in the afternoon, we walk back to the house. There's an unfamiliar vehicle parked in the driveway, and I instinctively step in front of Nora. That instinct only lasts a second, though, before I pick up on the scent trail leading from the car to the house and groan out loud.

"What is it?" Nora asks.

"An unexpected guest."

Her entire body tenses, and I kick myself for not explaining better and frightening her.

"A friend," I assure her. "I didn't know he was planning to drop by."

She still looks a little wary, but takes my hand as we walk up the front steps and into the house. As soon as we're inside, a male voice carries from the direction of the kitchen.

I know that deep, smooth laugh and the elegant cadence of that voice, just as surely as I know the vampire it belongs to will be charming the tail off Marta like he always does when he comes to my home. At almost sixty, already partnered, and with a no-nonsense attitude I've always admired, Marta's perfectly capable of putting the centuries-old denizen of darkness in his place when she needs to, but that doesn't stop him from trying.

When we get closer to the kitchen, the words get easier to make out. And, as I take a step in front of Nora and peer around the corner, my suspicions are confirmed.

"Dearest," Casimir says, leaning over the counter with a wicked smile on his face. "You get more and more beautiful every time I see you."

Marta titters and clucks her tongue, but doesn't do anything to discourage him as she moves around the kitchen, putting some groceries away.

Nora leans forward and tries to get a look, but I put a hand on her shoulder. "It's just Casimir. I can tell him to leave if you'd rather not have company today."

Her eyes brighten. "The vampire? I'd love to meet him."

She strides into the kitchen without waiting for me to answer, and I send up a quick prayer to any gods who might be listening that he'll behave himself with her.

That, as it turns out, ends up being a completely useless endeavor.

"Ah," Casimir croons as she walks into the room. "The little human who's hooked our kraken. Let me get a better look at you, goddess."

Nora shoots me a glance over her shoulder that clearly says, *Is this guy for real?*, before continuing on into the room, stopping to stand opposite Casimir at the island.

"It's nice to meet you, Casimir," she says brightly.

"'Cas' is just fine," he says with a wink, and then inhales deeply.

Scenting her. I let out a short warning growl and his deep red eyes snap to me, sparkling with amusement.

"My congratulations to you both," he says. "And may I say, I'm not surprised. With as delectable as this little one smells, it's no wonder you—"

"Enough," I say, crossing to stand beside Nora. "Go find your own mate to sniff."

It's a small slip, calling Nora my mate when we're still dancing around the use of that word, but either she doesn't notice or doesn't mind as she smiles, rolls her eyes, and gives me a soft elbow to the side.

Good. I hope she gets used to me calling her that. Especially around other monsters, it's going to be difficult not to.

Part of it is the urge to claim, the primal thing inside of me that won't be satisfied until the whole world knows she's mine. The other part of it, though, is pure pride. Pride in Nora, pride that this lovely, strong, beautiful creature belongs to me. It's a pride that, if and when she ever decides to truly become mine, will probably inflate my already swollen ego to a truly concerning size.

"Is this how you treat guests in your home?" Cas asks, putting a hand over his heart in mock-injury. "With growls and derision? Here I was, expecting a warm welcome and some refreshments after traveling all the way from Boston, only to be so sorely treated."

"Oh, you great lout," Marta says from inside the pantry. "You know I already offered."

Nora studies him for a moment, tilting her head to one side. "Do you eat? Or do you just, ya know…"

She makes a slicing motion across her throat, and Cas is silent for one wide-eyed moment before breaking out in deep, booming laughter. Nora joins him, flashing me a wink in reassurance that makes something warm and pleased take up residence near the center of my chest.

"I do occasionally indulge in a rare steak or a deep red wine," Cas says through his chuckles. "However, if you're offering…"

My snarl is only half-hearted as I snake an arm around Nora's waist and draw her close.

"Help yourself to the wine cellar, bloodsucker, and leave my mate out of it."

"Beast," she hisses under her breath at my possessive touch.

"Yes," I murmur into her ear. "Your beast."

We're interrupted from further conversation by the doorbell ringing. I'm not expecting anyone else, but when I hear Travis's heavy-booted footsteps from the foyer followed by the opening of a door and the murmur of another familiar voice, I want to groan again.

Travis and Blair walk into the kitchen a few moments later, the former shrugging apologetically and the latter grinning to find us all there. When Blair throws a pointed look at Cas, I narrow my eyes at them both.

"You two planned this, didn't you?"

The dragon and the vampire share another knowing, not at all guilty look, and I've got the answer I need.

"You really should be careful to whom you extend an open invitation into your home," Cas says.

"I called your office," Blair adds, unapologetically. "They said you were out for the day, and since it's been a decade since you took a personal day, I had an idea where I could find you."

"And you took that as your cue to stop by uninvited?"

Another couple of shameless glances, and I sigh, knowing it's a lost cause.

"Well," Nora says. "I'm glad to see you, Blair. And you too, Travis."

Travis smiles at Nora. "The banana bread was wonderful, by the way."

Her grin lights up her entire face. And just like that, the rest of my irritation slides away. If she's glad everyone's stopped by for a visit, then I can stop being so surly that my peaceful day with my mate has been interrupted.

Blair clears his throat. "This isn't just a social call. I wanted to speak to you both about some developments on Sorenson's movements."

All my instincts hone in at those words, and my hold on Nora tightens. Her smile fades, and Blair has the good grace to lose all his teasing humor as he takes a seat at the island and folds his hands in front of him.

At the other side of the room, Marta says something quietly to Travis, and he nods. She catches my eye and gives me a small, reassuring smile as the two of them slip out the side door of the kitchen.

Cas, the only one still in the dark, frowns. "Who is this Sorenson?"

I tense up at the question, and I'm about to ask him for some privacy, too, when Nora speaks up.

"It's alright," she says, giving my hand a squeeze. "You can tell him. All of this is on Daniel, and I'm not going to feel ashamed about it anymore."

Squeezing her hand in return and leaning down to press a kiss against her temple, I gesture toward the island and the rest of us sit.

I give a rundown of the past few weeks, and Nora offers a brief explanation of her history with Sorenson. Not everything, of course, but enough to get the gist of what happened between them. Blair supplements what he's learned about Sorenson's involvement with the Paranormal Oversight Committee, and some updates about what he's been doing in Vancouver.

According to Blair, the summits up in Canada have been unproductive, with the Canadian government having little to no interest in engaging with the group of American lawmakers on this set of issues.

When we've finished filling Cas in, he's silent for a few long moments, staring at his entwined fingers with his red eyes narrowed in contemplation.

"Is this man coming back to Seattle?" he finally asks, voice low and serious.

"And if he is?" Blair asks.

Cas's lip curls back, showing his fangs. "There are ways to put the fear of death into men like this."

Blair just snorts. "Don't know if the bastard's heading back to the city, but he is still in the vicinity for now until he's done with whatever he hopes to accomplish in Vancouver. A whole crock of shit, that is, what with—"

"Let's save it for another time," I cut in smoothly when I feel Nora go a little stiff on her stool beside me.

Between talk of Sorenson, and ominous threats from a vampire who I know is more than capable of carrying those threats out, it's more than enough darkness for today.

Blair and Cas both agree to set the subject aside for now, given that as long as Sorenson stays up in Canada, there's no immediate threat. Still, I'm worried for my mate, uncertain how she's taken this latest update and the fact that he's still walking around out there somewhere completely free of any consequences for his actions.

Nora, however, surprises me when she perks up and smiles broadly at our guests.

"Would you guys like to stay for dinner?"

"That depends," Cas croons, still with his fangs exposed. "What would be on the menu?"

"For you?" I say. "I'm sure we could find you a squirrel to suck dry."

Nora elbows me in the side, though is obviously smothering a giggle when I look back down at her.

"I could eat," Blair says, shooting a conspiratorial look at the vampire.

Nora, entirely unfazed, just smiles brightly as she heads toward the fridge. "Great! Let's see what we can scrounge up."

And that's how we somehow end up with Casimir and Blair staying for dinner, sitting around my dining room table with Marta and Travis joining in for the meal.

We're a motley crew of monsters, and Nora fits in like she was always meant to be here.

Watching her laugh and sip her wine, admiring the way the candlelight dances over her rosy cheeks and sparkles in her hazel eyes, she seems so peaceful, so content, like she knows she's safe here. Like she knows she belongs.

I want to give her that.

I want to give Nora a place where she knows she'll always be welcome. I want to give her a family, however patched together and frayed at the edges that we may be. I want her to know there's nothing she needs to do or fix or change to deserve it. All she needs to do is be here.

"Elias," she murmurs, and I realize I've been staring off

into space for the last few minutes, checked out of the conversation completely. "Is everything alright?"

I don't need to catch Casimir's or Blair's eyes to know they're both probably smirking, smug as hell but genuinely happy for me, as I reach over and squeeze her hand.

"Everything's wonderful."

27

Nora

The next few days pass in a happy, comfortable blur.

Things feel different after dinner with Elias's friends. Maybe because seeing how he was with them, being invited into his world and feeling right at home, made me finally start to picture how a future between us could look. And maybe Elias can see it, too. Maybe having me here with the people he cares about most in the world does the same thing to him.

Well, that, or the insane amount of fantastic sex we're having.

Tentacles really aren't hard to get used to at all. Not when I'm stuck in some kind of temporary, sexy limbo of being a guest in his house and suddenly having a live-in boyfriend I can't keep my hands off of. And who could blame me, really? Now that we've opened that particular pandora's box, there's really no way to button it back up again.

The question of what Elias and I are to each other is still hanging in the back of my mind, but I don't feel the need to answer it. Not right now. Not when all I want to do is savor this time with him.

I like Elias. I *really* like Elias. I like being here with him, and not just because of how incredible his house is. It's the peace and security of this place, the comfort of having someone who seems able to read my mood with a glance, giving me space when I need it and easy, endless affection when I don't.

Even his friends are growing on me. Marta and Travis, obviously, but I'm starting to be more comfortable around Blair as well after the less than stellar start we had.

The vampire is a slightly different story, but as he ends up being a house guest after the dinner party, it gives me a little time to acclimate to him. Cas hangs around for a couple of days before heading out on a trip to Alaska to connect with a coven of his kin who live there.

He really is... something else. Even more than Elias and Blair, he speaks like he's from a different time entirely, with another hard to place accent that makes me think vaguely of Dracula.

He's taller than either Elias or Blair, and thinner, with careful, graceful elegance to his movements. His platinum blond hair is always perfectly styled, and his face is made up of sharp, angular features and sinfully full lips that are quick to smile or scowl, always pulling back to show off two truly shocking fangs.

I don't really know what to make of him, but he seems loyal to his friends, and though some things he says are clearly meant to shock and provoke, it seems to be more out of good humor and honest teasing than any kind of malice.

He leaves with the dark promise that any time I need his help with problem ex boyfriends, I'm more than welcome to give him a call. What that means, I don't even want to guess, but after the whole 'putting the fear of death' into someone comment, I don't doubt for a second he's got the bite to back up his words.

"Finally alone," Elias murmurs, wrapping his arms around my waist from behind just after the door shuts with Cas's departure.

"'Finally'?" I ask, leaning into him and shivering with pleasure as his lips brush over the back of my neck. "Like having him around has stopped you from pouncing on me every chance you got the last few days."

Those lips on my neck turn into a soft bite, and I moan and squirm against him.

"Yes, but I much prefer doing so when there isn't a four hundred-year-old vampire in my house scenting and hearing it."

Scenting... and... hearing?

Elias must sense the horror in my stiffening posture, because he spins me around and chuckles at my expression.

"He did not!" I sputter, glancing back over my shoulder at the door. "Seriously. Tell me Casimir did not spend the last three days listening to and... smelling us have sex."

Elias just laughs again. "Alright. If it makes you feel better, he had absolutely no idea."

He's lying, I know he's lying, but I can't stop the flush on my cheeks or the disbelieving giggle that creeps up my throat. "That's terrible, you know. You could have said something. What must he have been thinking about having to deal with that?"

"I'm sure he was thinking how nice it would be to have a tasty little morsel of his own." He leans in, bringing his lips to my throat.

"So that's what I am?" I ask, breathless. "A snack?"

"You're a whole damn meal, little siren." Without warning, he reaches down and grabs me, lifting me up and tossing me over his shoulder. "And I'm famished."

And that's how I find myself carried off to my kraken's lair, stripped bare and pulled into the water. He's got me bent over the side of the pool in the shallow end, legs held open with two of his tentacles while he buries his face in me from behind.

Elias takes his time with me, savors me, teases and nips and builds my pleasure up and up again, only to pull back when it's about to crest. He's tormenting me in the sweetest, most delicious way possible, and I'm so mindless with it I almost don't notice the new sensation.

One of his tentacles strokes over my ass, dipping in between my cheeks, and I can't help but tense up a little. Elias, missing nothing, pauses.

"Too much, little siren?"

I swallow hard. "I've just never, uh, had anyone. There."

"Should I stop?"

He withdraws his tentacle without waiting for me to answer, and I unconsciously buck my hips back, chasing the sensation.

"Not necessarily," I squeak out.

Elias shifts up and over me, pressing his broad chest against my back, rubbing his cock against my ass, and letting out a gruff, rumbling chuckle.

"You don't have to take this, my treasure," he says, running the length of his shaft against me. "Or anything, if you don't want. But I think you might enjoy it, if you'd like to try."

"Yeah," I say, breathlessly. "Okay. Yeah. We can try that."

With another deep laugh, he teases that tentacle up my inner thigh and stops to dip briefly into my pussy before working it up to my ass. The slippery, soft feel of it against me, prodding and gently massaging, is unfamiliar, but not unpleasant. And when it dips just inside—stretching me, filling me, joined by another that plunges deep into my pussy —I cry out and slump down against the cool tile at the pool's edge.

Elias keeps me supported as he works in and out of me, making it so my breasts don't get crushed against the hard surface. He whispers to me the whole time about how lovely I look stretched around him, how beautifully I'm taking him, little bits of filth and praise and affection that make my toes curl and a slow, insistent heat spread from the center of my chest outwards.

When he pulls his tentacle from my pussy and replaces it with his cock, I swear I can see stars. Elias works me in tandem, plunging in and out, deeper and harder, and when one of his suckers draws sharply on my clit, I'm lost.

"Let me feel you, little siren," he whispers. "Let me feel you come apart for me."

All the sensation crests and breaks in an orgasm that rips a sob from my throat. Elias follows, thrusting deep and spilling into me with a hoarse shout of his own. He stays pressed into me for a few long minutes as both our breathing returns to normal, chest draped over my back, dragging hot kisses and whispering more praise over my shoulders and neck.

The beat of his hearts against me, the warmth and the weight of him, the feel of his cock still pulsing and filling me, the words he's saying, all of it overwhelms me and washes over me in waves of bliss.

And after, when he eases out of me and tends to me, cleaning me up and lifting me from the water, wrapping me in a plush robe and carrying me to bed, there's nowhere else in the world I'd rather be.

28

Elias

Sitting in my office during a few blissfully unoccupied minutes before lunch, I stare at the stack of papers in front of me without really seeing them. My mind's tied up in other concerns, playing and replaying conversations from the last few days, and bogged down with the unexpected complications that have cropped up with the news about the Paranormal Oversight Committee's dealings up in Canada.

A few more human partners Morgan-Blair works with are concerned about our ability to keep doing business as normal. It's not entirely unexpected, but disheartening all the same. There will always be fear when something upsets the status quo, and there will always be those who would rather see their own interests protected at the expense of others.

As always, my primary concern is for all the beings who make up Morgan-Blair Enterprises. Keeping our contracts, protecting our business, it's all for the same reason Blair and I set up shop after we left the seas behind, and the principle that's guided me even after he left the company.

Standing and crossing to stand in front of the windows, I peer out at a city that's changed so much in the time I've been here, and can't help but wonder what's coming next. Not just for this company or this city, but for all of us paranormals as we strive for something better than we've had for so many millennia.

I also can't help but wonder where in this rain-soaked city my mate is at the moment.

I rub a hand idly over the center of my chest, appreciating the warmth that seems to have taken up residence there. An instinctual thread of awareness, soft and ever-present. A thread I might tug and follow all the way to her.

I won't, of course, even if that gentle pull stays with me whenever we're apart, and even if I never truly stop worrying about her and looking forward to the next time I'll get to see her.

Fortunately, I don't have long to wait as my cell buzzes with an incoming call. It's reception with a notification that Nora's stopped by for lunch, and some of the tension I've been carrying in my neck and shoulders slides away.

Smiling to myself like the lovesick fool I am, I turn and head toward the door so I can meet her at the elevator.

Nora steps out carrying a pizza box and with a wide smile when she sees me waiting there for her.

"Bertrosa's," she says, lifting the box. "I hope you're hungry."

"Starving."

We settle in to the seats in front of the windows, grab our slices, and Nora launches into a story about a book club of little old ladies who just put in a big order for a series of erotic romance novels, followed by one about a new fantasy author who's hosting his first book signing at the store next week.

This Nora is so different from the woman I met that first day at the Bureau. So different from our first date. When I see her like this—comfortable and relaxed and shining with happiness—it's like peeking through a window to see the woman she must have been before Sorenson.

The woman I hope she'll have the freedom to be for the rest of her life.

When she catches me admiring, she pauses and raises a brow.

"I'm being boring with all the work talk, aren't I?"

Shaking my head, I reach over and give her knee a reassuring squeeze. "Not at all. I know how much you enjoy your work, and I love listening to you talk about it."

She shrugs. "It's alright, I suppose. It's a job."

There's something lurking beneath the lightness of her tone. "Is it not where you want to be?"

Nora frowns a little, takes a sip of water, and seems to contemplate what she wants to say for a few seconds before finding the words she needs to.

"If I'm being honest? I really love Tandbroz, but I've been thinking about going back to school."

She seems almost shy about it, like she's not quite certain how I'll respond. Other than mentioning that she dropped out of college when she moved to DC with Sorenson, she hasn't talked all that much about any desire to go back. But from the tentative, hopeful look on her face, it's easy to guess it's still something important to her.

"Are you?" I ask, setting down my food and turning to give her my full attention. "What would you like to study?"

"I was a business major. Nonprofit management and communications, specifically. I don't know if any of those credits would transfer anywhere, though, or how it would feel to be back on some campus now that I'm older."

Little lines of thought and worry spring up between her brows.

"We could figure all of that out."

Those lines disappear, replaced by a wry smile. "We?"

"Yes, *we*. Like it or not, little siren, I'm your boyfriend now. So that means I get to help you out with whatever it is you need to do to achieve the things you want to."

"My boyfriend," she murmurs. "Seems like kind of a weird word for what we are, doesn't it?"

"Maybe," I say with a shrug. "But I admit it's growing on me."

She laughs at that, and we steer back toward the topic at hand. We talk about a few of the schools in Seattle she's considering, along with some good online programs. She doesn't mention going back to her college in Dallas, or looking at other schools outside the area, but I try not to read too much into that or assume it means more than it does about why she'd be interested in staying here in this city.

We finish eating, and I get up to throw away our plates. When I turn around, Nora has stood up as well. She's paused in front of my desk, staring down at the wood-carved ship.

"This is you?" she asks, running a finger along the wooden tentacles coming up from the carved water.

"Indeed," I murmur, running my lips over her neck and trying not to let myself be run away with any fantasies.

"And the boat?"

"The *ship* was the one Blair and I sailed during our... ah... days on the wrong side of the Royal Navy."

"Your pirating days," she says with a laugh, tilting her head to give me better access to her neck. When my teeth press lightly into her skin, she shivers.

"Yes, little siren. My pirating days. When I was accustomed to taking exactly what I wanted."

I reach up to bracket her throat lightly, and Nora's heart

is pounding hard and fast. Her breathing speeds up, and she presses into my hold.

"What if you'd found me on one of those ships you plundered?"

The idea of that shouldn't be so erotic. It shouldn't make me tempted to toss my treasure over my shoulder and carry her away, to act exactly like the pirate I once was and claim the prize I've won.

Instead of answering her, I tighten my grip on her throat and bring my other hand around to splay against the bottom of her stomach, just over the fastening of her jeans.

When her breath hitches, I chuckle and lean in to whisper in her ear, to ask her just how willing she'd have been to be the spoils of my victory.

However, before I can, a soft knock at the door makes both of us freeze.

Regretfully stepping away, I clear my throat. "Come in."

Veronica pokes her head around the corner of the door and smiles apologetically. "Another visitor for you. I can tell him to leave, if you'd like."

Knowing just how few people would warrant such an interruption, I shake my head. "You can show him in. Thank you, Veronica."

She ducks back out, and a few moments later Blair appears, eyes immediately locking onto the two of us as a knowing smirk spreads across his face.

"Apologies," he drawls. "I didn't mean to interrupt."

Beside me, Nora's cheeks go a lovely shade of pink. I watch as it spreads down her neck, into the collar of her shirt, and I wonder just how far that delicious blush goes...

Blair clears his throat. "If you don't mind, I've got some news that might interest you both."

The smile on Nora's face dies. "About Daniel?"

Blair nods, and the mood in the room abruptly changes. I

take Nora's hand and squeeze it gently before the three of us take seats around my desk.

"He's back in DC," Blair says. "A contact I have on the Hill let me know he arrived back in town yesterday for the start of the new session."

The news he's no longer in this part of the country is welcome, but I don't really take the time to hear or process it for myself. My eyes are on Nora, watching her posture relax a little, and feeling my own do the same as she lets out a long, relieved breath.

"That's... good to hear," she says finally. "Did you find out how he got my information in the first place?"

A dark look crosses Blair's face, smothered quickly for Nora's sake. "We're still investigating, but the Bureau is the likeliest source at this point."

Nora nods, looking down at where her hands are folded in her lap, and I meet Blair's eyes.

A flash of that anger, centuries-old and molten, and I know he's telling the truth. I also know it probably kills him to have someone within the organization he helped build from the ground up betray everything the Bureau stands for. The protection of paranormal creatures, and their mates. An organization dedicated to helping us all find our footing in a world that's not always welcoming. It puts a heavy weight in my chest.

At the core of it, too, is my gnawing guilt that if it weren't for me, Nora would never have been put into this position. There would have been no record to be leaked, no threat to her safety, no upending of the peaceful life she fought to build for herself.

I hold Blair's gaze, and some of that guilt is echoed back in the hard set of his jaw and the glint in his amber eyes. After all, who would know better than him the feeling of absolute helplessness and self-loathing that comes with being culpable in the harm of someone you only ever wanted to protect?

"So," Nora says cautiously. "What next?"

"Next we keep an eye on him," Blair says, reverting to the soothing manner it's always so jarring to hear him use with others.

I'd call it manipulative, but I've never seen him use it for any purpose but a good one, and anything that might keep Nora calm and reassured is alright in my book.

Blair continues. "Sorenson's proven he's going to be a thorn in the Bureau's side, so it won't be a stretch or cause any suspicion if I keep in touch with my contacts about his meetings and activities on the Hill. We should have plenty of word if he leaves DC again on official business or takes any time away from his office."

Nora nods, still thinking, and when she looks at me, there's a question in her eyes.

What does that mean for us?

It's not a discussion I want to have in front of Blair, so I stand from my desk and clear my throat, looking meaningfully toward the door.

The dragon's not the only one who can exercise his right to kick monsters out of his office when he feels the conversation is over.

Thankfully, he takes the hint, stands, and gives a few more reassurances that we'll be notified if and when anything changes, but that it seems like Sorenson will be out of our hair for a while. Following him to the door, I shut and lock it behind him before returning to Nora.

Taking the seat beside her, I reach over and grasp her hand. "Talk to me, little siren. What do you need right now?"

29

Nora

"What do you need right now?"

What a question.

What I need right now is to never have met Daniel Sorenson. What I need is a damn time machine that could take me all the way back to picking out a college somewhere far from home. Maybe I would have gone to one in Seattle. Maybe I would have made different friends and had a different life and at just the right time, I would have run into my kraken in a coffee shop on a rainy day.

But, since none of that is an option, I stand up from my chair, gently disentangle my hand from Elias's, and cross to stand in front of the wall of windows so I can gather my thoughts.

I start with the things I know for sure.

Daniel's not in Seattle anymore. He's a couple thousand

miles away from here, but he *does* still know where I live. Even with all the distance between us, there's still a small but persistent thread of dread about that fact tugging at the back of my mind.

But I also know I'm not alone. Not anymore. I've got someone in my corner who's shown me time and time again he's willing to go to bat for me, protect me, give me a place where I can feel safe.

Next, I move on to the decisions I have to make.

Where I'm going to be staying. How I'm going to get back to something that feels even slightly like my normal life. Though, with how much Elias has already shaken that small, normal life to its core, maybe there's never any going back to it.

These past couple of weeks have felt like borrowed time. Normal people don't do this. They don't have to face these issues before they've barely gotten to know each other. They don't have mates and all the expectations that entails.

I rub a hand absently across the center of my chest as I think, over the dull ache just behind my breastbone.

My mind is spinning with all of it, and I try to focus on what I have to deal with right now. Which, first and foremost, is where I'm going to be staying tonight.

As much as it pains me to admit it, I'm still not entirely comfortable with the idea of moving right into Elias's house.

Or, maybe the better way to phrase it is that I'm a little uncomfortable with just *how* comfortable I am with the idea. I shouldn't want all of this so soon, and all the emotions and the heightened stakes are probably making it hard for me to see things clearly.

It's not that I don't trust Elias, or that I have any reservations about my safety with him. It's my own judgment I don't trust, my ability to sort through everything that's happened in my past and everything that's happening now and make the right choice for myself.

Still, that doesn't make it any easier to say what I need to say next.

Turning from the windows, I find Elias standing back near the desk, waiting patiently for an answer. Walking over and stopping just an arm's length away from him, I reach out and run a hand idly over one of his lapels.

"I think I'd like to stay at my apartment tonight, if that's alright with you. And, I also think I'd like the whole security thing dialed back a bit."

Part of me expects him to push back against that, insist on keeping my security or continue staying at his house. Elias, however, surprises me.

"If that's what you need, then that's exactly what's going to happen," he says. "I have a couple of requests, though."

"And what would those be?"

He wraps an arm around the small of my back, tugging me to him. "I'd like to have Travis install some extra security measures in your building and apartment."

I frown. "You'd probably have to ask my landlord about that."

When Elias doesn't answer right away, I glance up and find a guilty expression on his face.

"You already did, didn't you?"

"Technically Travis did. And nothing's been installed yet."

Laying my head back against his chest, I decide not to fight him on that one. "Fine. I'm okay with that. Any other requests?"

"I'd like our relationship to continue as it has been."

Frowning even more deeply, I'm about to open my mouth to ask him what he means by that, why he thinks it wouldn't, when he swoops down and kisses me.

"What I mean," he says when he pulls his lips from mine. "Is that I'd like our relationship to continue in a way that feels right for us both. Selfishly, I'd prefer if we still spent as much time together as possible, and hope you'll see my home as being open to you whenever you'd like and for however long you'd like to stay."

The words ease some of the lingering ache in my chest, settling it to a mellow warmth. I kiss him again, slow and unhurried at first, but with a spark that comes back to life immediately, reminding me all too well just where we'd been headed before Blair knocked on the door.

Elias, whose thoughts are apparently following the same path as my own, breaks the kiss and cradles my face in his hands.

I think he'll pounce on me, kiss me again, fan those sparks into an open flame, but he takes a step back and looks me up and down slowly.

It's always so unnerving to have his full attention on me like this, but in the very best way. The darkening blue of his eyes, the quirk of those full lips into a roguish smile, the sensual promise in every look and touch.

Knowing full well he's already got me on his hook, Elias takes his jacket off and tosses it onto a chair, then slowly, deliberately, unbuttons his cuffs and rolls both sleeves up to the elbow. When he reaches up to unfasten his top button and loosen his tie, a warm anticipatory heat courses through me.

"Where were we?" he murmurs. "Before we were so rudely interrupted?"

"You might have to remind me."

He hooks his fingers into the belt loops at the front of my jeans and tugs. "I think I was about to do something about these. And then I think I was going to toss you onto that desk and put it to an entirely inappropriate purpose."

I glance around the office, confused. "You're going to shift? In here? I thought you needed water to do that."

Elias laughs. "I don't. Well, not strictly speaking, it is a little uncomfortable to shift on dry land. Chafes against the tentacles."

"I don't want you to be uncomfortable. We don't have to —"

"Have I spoiled you on my kraken cock, little siren?" His voice is lower now, and taunting. "Do you not have any interest in the man separate from the monster?"

"Not a monster," I whisper, excitement coiling low in my belly. "Or, if you are, then you're my monster."

To prove my point, I reach down to stroke the rapidly growing bulge under his pants. He thrusts into the touch and buries a hand in my hair, tugging my head back so I have to look up at him.

Elias takes one step forward, then two, keeping his hold on me as he backs me into the desk and only letting go so he can reach down and grab my ass to lift me up. Setting me down on the desktop, he plants his hands on either side of me, caging me in with his body.

I spread my legs to make room for him and tangle both my hands into his hair to take the kiss I've been aching for.

He responds with a low, rumbling groan, thrusting his tongue deep and grabbing my legs under the knees to wrap around his waist. He's just as ravenous as I am. Plundering, demanding, nipping at my lips until I'm breathless for him.

When he breaks the kiss, we're both breathing hard.

"Up," he commands, unfastening my pants and giving my hips a squeeze.

I obey, and he deals with my jeans and underwear, tossing them aside before dropping to his knees in front of me. I barely have time to catch a breath before he hooks both hands around my hips and tugs me forward so I'm sitting right on the edge of the desk, and I don't have any time at all before he's there, diving between my legs, taking a slow lick up the very center of me.

My arms give out, and I slump back against the desk. I'm sure I'm making a mess of whatever papers and folders and other super-important CEO stuff he's got laid out, but I'm way beyond caring right now.

Elias, it would seem, doesn't particularly care either as he growls his approval and continues making a meal of me. His hands join his mouth, and when he sinks two long fingers into me, I bow up off the desk and clap a hand over my mouth to stifle my moan.

"None of that," Elias says, nipping at my thigh. "Let me hear you."

"Everyone... outside... won't they hear?" I pant, still grinding and bucking against his hand and face.

"Sound-proofed doors and walls for privacy. No one can hear you here but me, little siren. All those sounds you make are just for me."

Lowering my hand, I do nothing this time to stifle my moan when he drops his mouth to my clit and catches it between his tormenting lips. He works me relentlessly, making his own noises of satisfied pleasure as he brings me higher and higher toward my peak.

Just as I'm about to come, though, he stops. He ignores my garbled, desperate protest as he pulls away and stands in front of me, looking down at where I'm still sprawled across his desk.

"Please," I moan. "I need—"

"I know what you need, little siren. And you're going to get it, but it's going to be on my cock."

There's an edge to his voice, something that has me propping myself up on a shaky arm and reaching for his belt buckle. He's still so fucking hot with his shirt and tie all rumpled up and his sleeves pushed back to show the thick, corded muscles in his forearms, but there's something dangerous about him right now, too. Something sharp and dark and a little unsteady as I dip my hand inside his pants and draw his cock out.

Elias groans when I wrap my hand around his length and stroke him, hard. Just the way he likes it. Or, at least the way he likes it when he's shifted, but from the open-mouthed expression of pleasure on his face when I do it again, it would seem those preferences carry over into this form as well.

Apparently teased enough, he reaches down, draws my hand away, and gives his pants a rough shove down to his knees. He grazes the tip of his cock against my clit, and everything in me lights up. I cry out and press closer to him, silently begging.

Elias chuckles and repeats the motion, still with that edge to him. "Is this what you wanted?"

"Yes," I say between gritted teeth.

"Tell me, little siren. Tell me what you want me to do."

Oh, it's going to be like that, is it?

Before he can stop me or pull back, I lunge for him, grabbing at his hair, wrapping my legs tighter around his waist, and kissing him hard. When I sink my teeth into the pad of his bottom lip, he snarls into my mouth.

"I want you to fuck me," I rasp out in a voice I hardly recognize. "I want—"

I lose the words on a scream, but Elias throttles it with his lips as he sinks into me fully with one powerful thrust.

Fuck, he's good like this. I'll always appreciate the tentacles, but having him like this is incredible, too.

Elias gives me no mercy, slamming into me, letting me feel all of him. I cling to the soft fabric of his shirt, pant and cry out with each thrust. He dips his head down to my neck, running lips and teeth along my sensitive, over-heated skin.

"You're going to come for me, Nora. And when you go back to work this afternoon, you're going to feel me here all day. All night, too, when you go back to your apartment."

The words, spoken in a harsh whisper against the hollow of my throat, have something cracked and broken in them that cuts through the sensual haze I'm lost in.

Elias keeps moving in me, dragging his teeth over my skin, and breathing hard as he grinds his hips against mine at just the right angle to make me breathless. When I finally pry my eyes open, though, his expression is tight, almost pained, as he meets my gaze and pins me in place with that deep, fathomless blue.

"You take just as much space as you need, little siren, but know that I'm right here whenever you want me."

To emphasize his point, he picks up his pace, driving me out of my damn mind until it's all I can do to cling to him and chase after the release he's holding just out of reach.

"Yes," I tell him, barely able to speak but wanting to say something, anything, to soothe the note of pain in his voice. "Yes. And I'm here, too."

He groans into my neck and shifts our angle slightly so my hips tilt up. When he brings his thumb to my clit and starts stroking me in firm, commanding circles, all that pleasure builds to a breaking point. I shatter for him, and revel in the hard pulse of his body as he comes apart inside of me.

We stay like that for a minute, and then two—panting, shaking a little, clinging to each other—until we finally recover the capability for speech.

Elias presses his lips against my damp forehead. "Nothing's changed, Nora. The way I feel for you. The things I want for us. None of it's changed."

"I know," I whisper, leaning into his touch. "Nothing's changed for me, either."

Only… that's not entirely true. Because now, besides the cloying worry and constant anxiety over Daniel, there's another little pinch of pain in my chest. It's one that would have me stay with him, say the hell with it all and just move in with him like I'm almost certain he'd prefer.

I know it's crazy, and I know I can't give in to it. Not now. Not so soon. But that doesn't stop it from hurting as we clean ourselves up and straighten our clothes as best we can.

It doesn't stop hurting as he walks me out of the office and to the elevator. And just before I go, as the doors slide shut between us, there's a moment where I can see all of that pain and uncertainty echoed back on his face, too.

Elias and I fall into a new pattern over the next week.

I work, he works, we see each other in the evenings most days. We flirt over text. We meet for lunch and have a very ill-advised makeout session in the alley behind the bookshop that nearly gets us caught by my boss. He comes to stay at my apartment and we find out the hard way that my tiny shower-tub combo is barely big enough for two, and absolutely not big enough for two plus tentacles. Despite finding that out, we somehow make it work in an awkward tangle of limbs and laughter as we collapse naked and panting into the tub, vowing to never take the pool in Elias's bedroom for granted again.

And the next morning, when he cooks me breakfast in my little kitchen and we drink coffee on the couch together, snuggled up and just enjoying each other's company, it fills my heart up with a quiet, aching sort of peace.

It's... normal. This is what normal people do.

I should be happy with it. I really should. And most of me is happy with it. Almost all of me, really, except the small deranged voice in the back of my head and the persistent twinge in the center of my chest that keeps drifting away from me, daydreaming, wondering what my kraken is up to and unconsciously counting down the hours and minutes until I see him again.

I'd call myself smitten, say that I've got a wild crush on

Elias Morgan, but I know better than that. This isn't a crush. I'm not just smitten.

Still, as the week goes on, some of that same edge of discontent worms its way in. It's there when we say goodbye, when we face a night apart. And even though Elias has kept a tighter leash on himself since our little tryst in his office and not let it show like it did when he was fucking me, I know he feels it, too.

Despite that inner turmoil, the week passes. I'm just finishing up a shift, ready for three whole days away from work.

Getting ready to leave the bookstore, a fine misty rain is falling over the city, and a chill immediately settles into my bones as I glance out the front window of the shop. The thought of the walk to the bus stop, the wait in the cold, the long ride home, all of it makes me long for the luxury of a warm car and a ride to Elias's place.

This is what you asked for, Nora, I remind myself as I put on my jacket. *This is what you wanted. Distance. Normalcy.*

Not that it stops me from dreaming about Elias's enormous bed and his saltwater pool as I say goodbye to my coworkers who are closing and leave the shop. It doesn't stop me from missing him as I huddle underneath the bus shelter and shiver a little in the cold.

I'm so wrapped up in those thoughts that I take a few seconds to hear the approaching footsteps, and a couple more to realize that a tall figure in a dark coat has come to stand right in front of me.

Every single hair on my body stands on end, and even before I look up, I already know what I'm going to find.

The face of my nightmares, staring back at me.

Daniel smiles. "Hello, Nora."

30

Elias

It's been a hell of a week.

All the rumblings being stirred up by the Paranormal Oversight Committee are coming back on our community in spades, and Morgan-Blair hasn't been unaffected. The meeting I had with Thoreson and Rutelege seems to be some sort of canary in the coal mine, and I've spent this past week navigating several similar conversations with other important partners.

All of it sits uneasily on my shoulders, but that's not my only ache right now.

Seattle is cold and rainy tonight, and as I stand and look out my office windows, I can't help but let my thoughts drift to Nora. The city lights dance and distort behind the rain-speckled glass, but I keep staring and staring like maybe if I look hard enough I'll be able to see her.

It's only a few minutes after the end of her shift, and we don't have plans to meet tonight, but I can't stop thinking of her out walking in the rain and the darkness. The image of her hood pulled high and her shoulders stooped against the cold makes my hand twitch toward the phone in my pocket.

Just calling to offer her a ride home wouldn't be crossing a line, would it?

Gods above, I don't even know anymore.

It's been damned near impossible to keep myself on a leash these past few days.

I want to give Nora what she needs. If that's time and space, so be it, but I also can't do anything about the fact that holding back has been agony. I want Nora's nights and her mornings. I want every quiet moment in between.

It's been there, right there, since the first moment I saw her—the recognition of the other piece of my soul walking around somewhere in the world. Every moment I've spent with her since has made it abundantly clear.

I want Nora's forever.

Not that I can tell her that. Nora isn't ready to give everything I want from her. It's not fair of me to assume she would be, or even to put that option on the table before I'm reasonably sure I know what the answer will be.

Still, it doesn't stop me from wanting it as I turn away from the windows and cross back to my desk. It doesn't stop me from pulling out my phone and hovering my thumb over her name in my contacts list for a moment before thinking better of it.

I put the phone face-down on my desk and turn back to my computer to sort through some high-priority emails, losing myself in the work for a few minutes before a persistent tug in the center of my chest has me reaching back for my phone.

Deciding that caution can wait tonight, I dial her number,

listening to it ring for a few seconds before going to voicemail.

It shouldn't make me uneasy. She could be on the phone with one of her friends, or making one of her infrequent calls home to her mom. Or maybe she's still at work, busy and staying past the end of her shift, and screened my call.

There's a reasonable explanation for it, I'm sure, and I put my phone back down and turn my attention to the work in front of me. It's what I've been doing on the nights we don't spend together. Staying late, getting as much off my plate as I can, so when I'm with her we can spend as much uninterrupted time together as possible.

It's what I should be doing now, but I still can't concentrate. My eyes keep darting to the phone, half-certain Nora's about to call me back.

She doesn't, and when I try her again a few minutes later, it goes straight to voicemail.

All my unease coalesces into a restlessness that has me grabbing for my jacket and heading to the elevator.

It's just a short walk to Tandbroz, and though I have no idea if she'll see it as an invasion of her space or and overstep of the boundaries we've been forging this week, no part of me can stop myself from hitting the button to take me down to the lobby.

No, the further I descend, the more my chest aches, and the more certain I become that something isn't right. And it won't be right until I find her, see her, reassure myself she's okay.

All those thoughts hound me as the elevator glides to a stop and I cross quickly through the lobby and head out into the cold Seattle night.

31

Nora

"What are you doing here, Daniel?"

I surprise myself a little with how calm and steady my voice is. As if my heart wasn't pounding so hard in my chest it's threatening to crack my ribs. As if my lungs didn't feel like they've lost about ninety percent of their capacity to hold air.

His smile widens, and it's like the last three years haven't even happened. I know that smile. Soft and deceptive, it usually showed up right before he delivered a scathing comment or casually devastating criticism.

"I'm here to see you, Nora. I want us to talk."

"You need to leave," I tell him, moving out from under the bus stop shelter and trying to walk away. I don't know where I'm going, other than back toward Tandbroz, somewhere safe.

I don't even make it three steps before his hand closes around my upper arm.

"Not until we talk."

Even through the layers of my jacket and the sweater beneath, my skin crawls at his touch. It crawls even more when I glance up from beneath my hood and meet his gaze.

His light green eyes never had much of a soul in them, but tonight they're especially empty. He stares down at me with nothing, absolutely nothing in his expression that would suggest how deranged it is for him to be here right now. His face is blank, totally calm.

It's a calm that chills me to my bones.

"A lot has changed since you left," he says casually. "I've been assigned to two new committees in the House. One in particular that might be of interest to you."

I bite down hard, stubbornly setting my jaw and refusing to engage with this bullshit.

"The Paranormal Oversight Committee has some interesting issues on the table right now," he continues. "Ones that concern some of your new friends, I think."

The rolling in my stomach turns into cartwheels. Elias told me all about what's been going on—changes to the laws, how it's starting to affect his company. Still, I try to keep my face as blank and neutral as possible.

Enough. Enough of this.

"What concerns me absolutely doesn't concern you," I tell him, but when I try to wrench my arm away, he holds on tight.

"Doesn't it?"

Again, I don't answer, and the hold he has on my arm doesn't let up.

"I'd like some time with you," he says. "Just for a conversation."

I'm about to try to break his grip again when he reaches over and sweeps his jacket aside. It's only a slight movement, but enough to flash the gun he's got at his waist.

"Let's go get a drink, Nora."

I stop fighting. I stop doing anything, completely frozen where I stand. We're still on a public street, and although it's quiet tonight, there are a few other people out and about. If I called for help, what would he do? Would he shoot me? Would anyone else get hurt?

"How does that sound?"

Not knowing what to do, not knowing what I can do without risking my own life or someone else's, I numbly nod my head.

"Good," he says, leaning down to speak softly near my ear. "I've been waiting for this day for three years. I suppose I should thank the clerk at the Bureau who tipped me off and let me know just where I could find you."

My heart drops, but I still can't speak as he uses his hand on my arm to steer me down the street. I don't know where we're going, but we're headed in the opposite direction of the well-trafficked downtown.

"You looked so pretty that night at the bookstore," Daniel goes on, and bile raises up in the back of my throat at the confirmation I was right. I wasn't just seeing things that night. "Not that you should be working in a place like that when you have other options."

Other options. Being with him. Being accessible and accountable to him every single second of every damn day. Only having as much money and freedom as he gives me. Depending on him entirely.

We turn down another street, one that's even darker and emptier than the last, and a bolt of fear courses through me.

Fuck. I made the wrong decision, didn't I? This is exactly what to do if you want to get murdered. Don't scream. Don't fight. Let him get you alone.

Fuck. Fuck. Fuck.

I'm about to take my chances and just start screaming

when Daniel stops outside a small, unassuming looking bar.

"We should have some privacy here," he says, reaching for the door.

Before he can open it, my phone buzzes from inside my coat pocket with an incoming call. Daniel's eyes zero in on the spot, and he holds his hand out wordlessly. Not sure what he'll do if I refuse, I fish it out and hand it over.

A brief glimpse as I give it to him shows Elias's name, plus the two little heart emojis I added next to it in my contacts list just a week ago. When Daniel looks down at the screen, a flash of rage breaks over his features before he's able to hide it.

Without a word, Daniel drops the phone to the sidewalk and steps on it, shattering the screen. The buzzing stops, Elias's name goes dark, and Daniel smiles back down at me, firmly behind that chilling mask of his once more.

"Let's go," he says, taking me by the elbow and leading me inside.

32

Elias

Nora isn't at the bookstore.

Her scent is, and her coworkers let me know she left here almost a half-hour ago, apparently on her way home.

Stepping outside, the rain has picked up now, and any traces of her scent that might have followed her to her bus stop have long since been washed away. And that's probably precisely where she went. Home. She's probably home and safe, and all of this is an overreaction.

Still, I'm rooted to the sidewalk just like I was the day we bumped into each other. Why I can't accept the likely truth, I don't know, but everything in me is screaming that there's something I'm not seeing.

Something is wrong.

I feel it with every breath I take. The ache in my chest is too pointed to ignore, and I step back under the bookstore's awning and pull my phone from my pocket to try calling her again.

Nothing.

Dialing Blair next, he answers on the third ring.

"I need you to do a check on Sorenson."

Whether it's the tone of my voice or his own lingering suspicions about the bastard, he says he'll try to get in touch with his contact in Washington and call me back in a few minutes. We disconnect, and I shift from one foot to the other, restless energy coursing through me.

I could drive to her apartment, see if she's there, but the idea of it feels wrong. Leaving downtown feels wrong, like I'd be taking myself further away from her rather than closer.

Closing my eyes, I try to tap into the instinct I haven't fully let myself connect with. I've held back, pushed it down and kept it quiet for fear of it leading me to make a mistake with Nora. Better I denied that part of myself and dealt with the consequences alone than do something that might frighten her or drive her away from me.

But now? Now it's the only thing I can think to do.

All the feelings come rushing back immediately. The wave of possession and protectiveness I felt when I first saw her. The instinct to find her, keep her, shelter her, I felt the morning we ran into each other at the Bureau.

It's an awareness of her that seems etched into my blood and bones. It tugs at something deep in the center of my chest, something that tells me she's not too far from here.

Before I can make a move to head back out into the rain and start searching, start following that pull to her, my phone rings again.

When I answer and hear Blair's clipped, angry tone on the other end of the line, all of my restlessness and my need to protect my mate crystallize into one single instinct.

Find her.

33

Nora

The fact that Daniel didn't just kidnap me, or shoot me, or do whatever the hell it is he intends to do with me, is so, so much more chilling than any of the alternatives.

Sitting at a table in the back of the bar, two untouched drinks on the tabletop between us, Daniel crosses his arms over his chest and leans back in his chair. He looks so casual, like this is any normal date we might have gone on while we were together.

God, this is so fucked.

This game, whatever he thinks he's going to accomplish, the disgusting power trip he must be on right now. He still thinks I'm the same Nora he knew. He still thinks I'm pliable and easy to manipulate, that he can spin pretty lies around me and I'll nod my head and agree.

Or maybe it's just about control. The freak probably gets

off on it.

"I was thinking about pressing charges," he says, reaching forward and picking up his old fashioned off the table. "For the jewelry you stole when you ran off."

The jewelry was mine. Gifts, all of it. He knows that, but I'm not about to argue with him. I stay silent and wait for him to finish the sip of his drink.

"How did you get out here, anyway? I've always wondered. You never really worked, so I can't imagine you had much cash lying around."

I didn't work because you said it was more important for me to support you. The words simmer in the back of my throat. I swallow them.

"A bus."

"Ah," he says, taking another sip. "That explains it. I can't imagine that was very comfortable for you."

No. It wasn't. Neither was struggling to start over in a city where I knew no one, or trying to pick up all the pieces of myself you shattered.

"Do you remember when we first met?" he asks, abruptly changing the topic.

My stomach rolls at the question. Of course I do. We met when I was in the middle of my third year of college. I was volunteering with a voter registration organization doing outreach to get young people registered to vote. Daniel had come to one of the events and singled me out almost immediately.

He'd been so handsome to me back then. Older, charming, so much more sophisticated than anyone I'd ever met. He'd asked for my number that day, and when I went back to my dorm that night I remember laying down in my bunk bed, staring up at the ceiling with butterflies flitting through my stomach, wondering what it was he saw in me.

I'd assumed it was because he could somehow see *me*. I thought maybe he'd admired my passion for advocacy and community service, that he'd been able to see past my shy, awkward exterior and recognize something that made him like me.

Now, though, with time and hindsight, I know exactly what he saw.

He saw a young woman who was eager to please, who wasn't confident in herself, who didn't really even know herself, and who was desperate for approval, *anyone's* approval.

He saw someone he could manipulate and control completely, and I'm sure it was a slap in the face to his ego when I finally showed him I wasn't.

"It was at that rally, right?" I ask, still trying to drag this conversation out, give myself time to find some way out of this. "The voter registration rally?"

His eyes narrow a bit at getting an answer that's more than a couple of syllables long, and he takes another sip of his drink before setting it down and resting his hands on the table.

Still, he smiles at whatever the memory holds for him. "You fell in love with me so quickly."

Another wave of stomach-lurching regret. He's not wrong about that.

"You had it good with me, Nora. I gave you everything."

I'm sure he wants to believe he did.

"And to find out you've been living in that shoebox of an apartment. Taking the bus. Working in some store. Pretending to be someone else and getting by with so little. Make it make sense to me, Nora."

A sick, sinking feeling settles into the bottom of my gut.

I'll never be ashamed of the life I made for myself here. I'll never regret the decision I made to leave and the hard work it's taken to get this far. But something about what he just said clings on and won't let go.

Pretending to be someone else.

While I don't want to listen to anything this monster has to say, that insult hits a little too close to the truth for me to ignore it completely. Is that what I've been doing? I'm not the same woman I used to be, but I've been making decisions like I am. I've been playing my cards small, afraid, cautious.

It's what I've been feeling these last few weeks, isn't it? As I've come back to life, come back to myself, it's put all the rest of it into shocking clarity.

I don't know exactly who I am. I don't know who I'm going to be. But I do know that I'm going to survive whatever's happening here.

Meeting Daniel's eyes fully for the first time since we sat down, I really study him.

He's looking right back at me, and as I stare him down, I see the first crack. A pulse of uncertainty in his eyes, maybe surprise at whatever he finds in my own. He covers it quickly with another blank look and a polite smile, but not quickly enough for me to miss it.

"I've been living the life I want," I tell him quietly. "On my own."

"That's not entirely true, though, is it?"

His placid smile is gone. In its place is cold, inhuman flatness, a sharp, brittle-edged rage threatening in the tightening of his features and the hard set of his mouth.

"You've found someone else, haven't you?"

Ice pours through my veins, and I'm desperate to keep Elias out of this. "I haven't."

Daniel takes a piece of paper from his pocket, unfolds it, and lays it on the table between us. It's a copy of a report with bold lettering printed across the top indicating where it came from.

The Paranormal Citizens Relations Bureau.

He only leaves it on the table for a few seconds before

picking it up and pretending to read it, like he hasn't probably already done so a dozen times, but a few words jump out immediately.

My name. Elias's. Kraken. Mate.

Keeping my face as neutral as I can, even while my heart is racing, my eyes dart unconsciously to the hip where the gun is still hidden under his jacket. Luckily, Daniel doesn't notice as he folds the paper up and tucks it back into his pocket.

"Is he coming for you, mouse?" Daniel asks, using the nickname he gave me years ago.

Mouse. Small, quiet, easy to trap or step on.

"No. He's not."

I'm not sure if that's a lie. We weren't supposed to meet tonight. My phone is shattered somewhere on the ground outside the bar, so I have no idea if he's tried calling me again or if he's figured out something is wrong.

Without thinking, I tug on that stubborn, tangled thing in my chest. It's been hovering there for days, maybe weeks, maybe since that very first day at the Bureau.

A warmth, a knowing, some small thread of gentle awareness.

I haven't been able to look at it too closely, haven't really been able to acknowledge it exists at all, but right now the instinct comes to me as naturally as breathing.

Wherever he is, I only hope Elias can feel it, too.

Daniel seems to run out of patience as he gives his head a sharp shake and drains the rest of his drink. He drops a fifty on the table before standing, taking me by the elbow, and pulling me to my feet. Reaching around me, he grabs my coat from where I draped it over the chair's back.

"Coat on, mouse," he snaps, shoving it into my hands. "My father's plane is waiting at the private airstrip, and we're going back to DC. Tonight."

He's insane, actually insane, if he thinks kidnapping me like this is going to lead anywhere but to him in a jail cell. Still, I'm unarmed, and the only thing I want to do right now is survive this, so I do what he says. I put my coat on and let him march me out of the bar. Somewhere between here and wherever he's taking me, there will be an opportunity for me to get away.

Won't there?

There has to be. I have to survive this. I absolutely refuse to let this be it.

It's still raining outside, and the night air has dropped by several degrees in the last hour. In the dark and the gloom, Daniel starts walking to a sedan parked halfway down the block.

I can't let him get me into that car.

It's how-not-to-get-murdered 101, isn't it? Don't let them take you to another location. I don't believe for a moment he'd feel any need to be honest with me about where we're going, and the possibility that there's no jet waiting, that he's going to drive me out of Seattle, kill me, and dump my body somewhere no one will find me is very real.

I don't *think* Daniel's stupid enough to do it. Not when it would be easy enough to trace my disappearance back to him. Not when a bunch of people just saw us in that bar.

But I also don't know that for sure. I don't know what the last couple of years have done to him, how deep his hatred of me runs.

With no guarantee of my safety and nothing else I can think to do but risk it, I twist my body with all my strength and rip my arm from his. I barely have half a plan in mind—get back inside the bar, start screaming, pray that it will be enough to scare him off—but I don't even make it two steps before Daniel catches me. Roughly taking me by the arm, he curses and starts pulling me toward the car.

I drag my heels on the concrete, and have just opened my mouth to scream when another voice calls out from the darkness.

"Let her go, Sorenson."

34

Elias

I've never known what rage feels like.

Not truly.

I've seen it in Blair, in the depths of his ancient, focused capacity for dominance and vengeance, in the aftermath of losing his mate, but I've never felt it myself.

But watching Nora struggle against the man who's had her terrified for years, watching his fingers squeeze hard enough on her arm to leave bruises, seeing the flash of the gun he's got holstered at his waist, I know rage.

I know it down to the depths of my soul.

"Let her go, Sorenson."

It's Nora's eyes I meet first, big and round and shining with tears, and all that rage in me doubles.

Still with one hand on her, Sorenson reaches for the gun, and every muscle in my body tenses. I'm unarmed. I'm not one to carry a weapon on any normal day, and even if it would have occurred to me to procure one from Travis or elsewhere before setting off to find Nora, I probably wouldn't have spared the time to do so. Not when I could sense she was in danger and needed me.

"Think about what you're doing," I say, voice low and calm. "Really think about it, Sorenson."

There's a moment of indecision in his face, a brief crack that shows the coward he is. Driven by pride and ego and the belief he can have whatever he wants, and the weakness beneath rotting it all from the inside out.

Still, he pushes that doubt aside and pulls the gun, pressing it to Nora's side. Her whole body goes rigid, and the pulses of her terror echo in me through the ties that bind us.

"This has nothing to do with you, monster," Sorenson sneers, taking a step backward toward the car he no doubt has waiting nearby.

He's not taking her anywhere.

Letting my rage coalesce into a focused, icy calm, I take a step as well. He pulls the gun from her side and points it toward me, and a pained cry breaks from Nora's throat.

Because of me. Because she's scared for me.

He glances at her in sharp understanding, then laughs. The sound of it is cruel and unhinged, like he's just put together the last piece of whatever deranged puzzle he's been building in his mind.

"Are you scared for him, mouse?" he asks, putting the gun back to her.

Mouse. The way he spits it at her puts a violent crack down the center of my chest. It's there, in his mocking, in the cruel glee at the idea he might be frightening her.

This is what she lived with for years.

This is what she's being forced to live through again, because he found her through me.

When Nora meets my eyes again, I hope she can see the strength and reassurance I want to give her.

Just a little longer, my treasure, I want to tell her. *Just hang on.*

I'm watching Sorenson, waiting for another tell, some slight slip up I can take advantage of.

I want to believe if he truly intended to hurt her, he would have by now. But with the way his expression grows more wary and desperate, I don't want to give him any more time to decide.

"Let her go," I say again. "You know how all of this ends if you don't."

He tightens his hand on her, enough that Nora flinches, and a deadly certainty settles over me. No matter how this ends, Sorenson will never know a day of peace for as long as he lives. Even if he walks away from this, he'll never know another day of happiness or safety.

He'll live the rest of his life exactly how he made Nora live hers.

Sorenson's eyes are wild, his movements uncoordinated and jerky as he pulls Nora backwards again. His hand shakes where he's holding the gun, and realizing how close he might be to accidentally shooting her, I know time is up.

I don't make it more than a couple of steps toward them before a booming noise from above has us all looking skyward.

A terrible, ground-shaking roar splits the night sky. It startles Sorenson enough that he loosens his hold on Nora. Not entirely, but enough for my brave mate to wrench her arm out of his grasp and take a stumbling step away from him.

He lunges for her, but a moment later a flash of golden scales and enormous wings and long, black talons dives from the darkness above and knocks him aside.

The gun goes flying, Sorenson screams, and though she

nearly topples to the ground as well, Nora keeps her feet and runs to me. A shadowed figure appears from a nearby alleyway, kicking the gun away from where Sorenson's sprawled on the pavement and closing in on him.

"You made a mistake tonight, my friend," Casimir's low, melodic voice taunts as he stalks toward where Sorenson is scrambling to get up. Another roar splits the air as Blair turns and descends back toward the scene.

I hardly see any of it. No, my attention is entirely on Nora.

As my friends deal with Sorenson, she crashes into me, and my soul has never known the depth of shattering relief that courses through me.

As soon as she's in my arms, I don't wait around to see what Cas and Blair do with Sorenson. I don't really care. Not when Nora's still shaking and has tears running down her cheeks, and not even when my instincts are telling me to stay and eviscerate the male who would dare threaten my mate.

Nora comes first. Her safety comes first. Everything else can wait.

And by the quieting commotion behind us, it sounds like my friends have things well in hand. Sirens wail in the distance, and there will be more chaos to confront in the aftermath, but not now. The only thing that matters is getting her away from here.

Sweeping Nora into my arms, I take off running.

35

Nora

I can't stop shaking.

My whole body is still strumming with adrenaline and my teeth are chattering, and though I can hear Elias distantly speaking to me, I can't grasp onto any of the words he's saying.

He gets us into a waiting car, says something to Travis where he's sitting in the driver's seat, and keeps me cradled against him while we take off into the Seattle night. The whole time, he murmurs to me, but the blood pounding in my ears makes it impossible to hear him.

After a while, I think he realizes that because he stops talking and just holds me. He strokes my back and runs his lips over the top of my head. His heart is beating fast and heavy where I've got my cheek pressed against his chest, and the steady strength of his arms around me is the only thing keeping me from falling apart completely.

We pull into an unfamiliar parking garage, and he lifts me out of the car and carries me into an elevator. In the quiet, the shaking only gets worse, accompanied by a tightness in my chest that makes me feel like the walls in the tiny space are closing in around me.

"Nora," Elias whispers, pressing his forehead into mine. "You're safe. Everything's going to be alright."

It calms me down. Not a lot, but enough that I can close my eyes and make it the rest of the elevator trip up to wherever he's taking me.

The doors open with a soft ding and we step out into an unfamiliar apartment. Sleek, modern, with the same dark blue and gray color scheme as Elias's house.

"My city condo," he explains when he sees me looking warily around the space.

The memory of that conversation surfaces dimly, and I lay my head back down against his chest as he carries me through the foyer and into a vast, open living space that's connected to the kitchen and dining areas. Flipping a switch on the wall, the space fills with warm light.

On the opposite side of the room, a full wall of windows looks out on downtown, and the city lights shining in through the droplets of rain scattered on the glass make the rest of the world seem distant and small. It's a welcome feeling, to be so far away from it all, and I concentrate on that view as Elias carries me to one of the plush, cream-colored sofas in the living space and sits down.

He doesn't speak, and I'm not sure if that's because he knows I'm not quite ready, or there just simply isn't anything to say right now, but I savor a few more moments of peace.

The adrenaline is ebbing, my heartbeat is slowing, and everything that happened over the last couple of hours starts to creep back in.

Daniel forced me to go with him at gunpoint.

Daniel was going to kidnap me.

Elias and his friends stopped him.

And now I'm safe, held by my kraken.

The last I saw of Daniel, he was being pummeled by a vampire and a freaking dragon, which... good. He deserves everything he has coming to him. But I don't want to think about that right now. I don't want to think about any of it.

Instead, I focus on the arms still holding me. Silent and stiff, I can feel the tension rolling off Elias in waves.

"How did you find me?" I ask, voice coming out croaky and hoarse.

Elias startles a little when I finally speak and pulls me closer to him. "I followed our bond."

That thing in my chest. The one that doesn't ache now, but sits like a mellow, comfortable warmth somewhere near my heart.

"I felt it too. Or at least I think I did."

He lets out a harsh breath. "I thought you... I didn't know if I'd be able to..."

When his words trail off, I reach up to cup his cheek. "You found me."

"Always, Nora. I'll always find you."

I kiss him, and there's no urgency in it. There's not even much heat. Just a slow, tender caress and all the words I can't say. Reassurance and comfort, calm and reunion. There's nothing more I want in this moment than to remind him, and myself, that I'm here, safe and alive.

"Where did Blair and Cas come from?" I ask, pulling back a little.

He lets out a huff of breath that might have almost been a laugh if he wasn't so tense right now. "Blair took to the skies and started searching for you as soon as we realized Sorenson had left DC. And Cas just got back into Seattle this afternoon.

He also came as soon as I called."

I nod, chest tightening a little to know how quickly his friends sprung into action for me.

Elias pulls back, reaching up to smooth some of my hair away from my face. He shifts me slightly in his hold and accidentally jostles the place on my arm where Daniel grabbed me. I wince a little and his eyes zero in on the reaction.

Face white, he pulls his hand away immediately. "Fuck. You're hurt. I shouldn't have—"

He moves like he's going to slide me off his lap, and I clutch both hands in the front of his jacket.

"Don't. I'm fine. It's—"

"Little siren," he warns, voice low and serious. "If you're about to say 'nothing' I—"

"—not that bad," I finish. "I mean, yeah, it's bad. But I'll live."

Jaw tight, like he's holding back all the arguments he wants to make, Elias tugs gently at the front of my jacket. "Off. I want to see."

Carefully, he helps me take off the jacket and the sweater I'm wearing beneath it. The tank top I've got on as my bottom layer leaves both my arms bare, and we both stare for a few silent seconds at the distinct set of hand-shaped bruises just starting to appear on my upper arms.

Elias's curse is harsh, but muffled as leans his forehead into the spot between my neck and shoulder, taking a few deep breaths. When he comes back up for air, it's impossible to miss the carefully leashed rage in his blue eyes. Not at me, never at me, and when he leans in to press a kiss on my forehead, he's shaking slightly.

"Stay here for a minute?" he asks.

I nod, and he shifts me off his lap and onto the plush couch cushions. He gets up and walks toward the kitchen, followed shortly by the sounds of a few drawers opening and closing, and a sink running before he returns.

In his hands, he has a glass of water, a couple of pain pills, and an ice pack. He kneels on the floor in front of the couch, hands over the pills and the water, and presses the ice pack to one of my arms.

"I don't know if this will help," he says gruffly. "I'm not sure there's much else you can do for bruising."

There probably isn't, but the cool press of the ice pack feels nice, and being tended to feels even better. I'm about to tell him that, try to soothe away some of those deep worry lines still creasing his forehead and bracketing his mouth, when his cell phone rings.

He glances at it, frowns even more deeply, and hands me the ice pack. "I should take this."

I nod, pressing the pack to my arm and watching him cross the room to the windows and answer. He's speaking too quietly for me to hear, but his expression hardens and he shakes his head at whatever's being said on the other end of the line. After another minute of back and forth, he sighs in irritation and hangs up.

"I'm so sorry, Nora," he says as he sits back down beside me. "That was Travis. He let me know the police are on their way up, and they'd like to speak with you."

Just like that, the reality of everything that happened tonight crashes back into me.

"Have they... have they arrested Daniel?"

Elias nods. "Yes. They have him in custody."

"Good," I say, setting the ice pack aside and scooting to the edge of the couch.

I want to say it with courage and conviction, but the slight tremble in my voice is unmistakable, and Elias puts a hand on my knee before I can stand, face still creased in concern.

"You don't have to do this tonight. We can—"

The sound of the elevator opening cuts off whatever he was about to say. Travis steps out first, followed by a man and woman wearing street clothes, with badges displayed on their belts.

Elias stands before I can, putting himself in front of me as he stares the officers down. One of them, a woman in her late forties with an air of authority that makes me feel like she's probably the one in charge, steps forward and clears her throat.

"Ms. Perry," she says, tilting her head a little to see around Elias. "My name is Geraldine Harris, and I'm a senior detective with the Seattle PD. I'd like to ask you a few questions about what happened tonight with Daniel Sorenson."

"Can't this wait until morning?" Elias asks.

I appreciate that he's trying to protect me, I really do, but I take a few deep breaths and concentrate on that small spot of warmth in my chest, feeling some of my reemerging panic die down. As I do, Elias glances back over his shoulder at me, and when I give him a reassuring smile, I actually mean it.

He defended me tonight. He *saved* me tonight. Now, it's my turn to finally say what I need to, start getting the justice I'm more than owed.

"We'd like her to come to the station and make a statement tonight," Detective Harris says, still trying to peer around Elias to where I'm sitting.

Elias tenses like he's going to keep arguing, but I stand and lay a hand on his shoulder.

"It's alright," I say, finally working up the courage to speak. "I'll come to the station."

Elias immediately turns to face me taking, my face in his hands. "You don't have to."

Leaning into his touch, I let out a long breath. "I know. But I need to."

36

Elias

It's just after midnight, and the waiting room at Seattle PD headquarters is a ghost town. I've been sitting here for the last few hours while Nora speaks with the detectives to give her statement and provide photographic proof of her bruising.

They didn't allow me back with her. Whether that's because we're not married, or because they'd rather speak to her own her own, I'm not sure, but after giving my own statement, they directed me to wait here. It's a little slice of hell, sitting and waiting and wondering what she's going through right now.

The only solace I can take is that Sorenson is fucked ten ways from Sunday, and not just over the attempted kidnapping.

It's no coincidence that two detectives, rather than uniformed officers, were the ones to take this case. According to the call I took from Blair just after I finished my interview, Sorenson's been on the radar of federal law enforcement for a few years. Fraud and insider trading and who knows how much more shady shit he was no doubt certain he could get away with as a congressman and the son of a billionaire.

Maybe it's what made him so desperate, feeling that noose of consequences closing in on him. The idea makes my blood run cold. What would he have done with Nora if given the chance? If she'd tried to fight him, tried to run like she had just attempted to when I caught up to them, what would he have done?

The long, solitary hours give me time to think. Too much time to think.

I play those moments outside the bar over and over in my mind. Recalling Nora's terror, how close I'd come to getting there too late, Cas and Blair arriving just in time, how easy it would have been for all of it to go wrong.

I could have lost my mate tonight. Nora could have been killed. And even though she wasn't, she's still going to deal with the mental and emotional ramifications of this night for the rest of her life.

All those thoughts swirl and coalesce until they land on a single, powerful emotion. Guilt.

How much pain has my presence in Nora's life caused her? How much trauma has she endured because of me?

If not for me, Daniel may never have found her. She may never have had to confront the horrors of her past and endure what she did tonight. If not for me, she may have been able to continue healing in her own time and eventually built the life she wanted without having to deal with any of this.

A short time later, the door to the waiting room opens and Nora walks in, accompanied by Detective Harris. Even though she gives Harris a small smile, shakes her hand, and doesn't appear to be in any acute distress as she walks over to me, it's not hard to guess she's exhausted. She looks pale, and there are dark circles forming under her eyes.

"All done," she says as she reaches me, attempting another little smile.

I stand, wrap my arms around her, and simply savor the feel of her against me for a few long moments. Wracked with guilt or not, there's no feeling in the world that can compare.

"Can I give you a ride home?" I ask her.

Nora looks up at me, confused. "Home?"

"To your apartment."

She frowns, and I wonder if I've made a misstep. Maybe she doesn't want to go back there tonight. But would she want to come to my place instead? I could offer her the condo, or to put her up in a hotel if either of those would be a better option.

"You..." I start, hoping I don't fuck things up further. "You were planning to have some time and space for yourself tonight. Before everything happened. I didn't want to presume you would... after everything... I..."

My words trail off, and I swallow hard. Nora, still frowning in confusion, reaches up to brush a hand over my cheek, waiting for me to finish.

"I can understand why you'd want some space from me, Nora. After the part I played in all of this. If you'd prefer to go somewhere other than your apartment, I can take you wherever it is you'd like to be."

Her eyes go soft with understanding. "I think we need to talk. But not here. Can I come back to your place?"

Our place, the kraken's voice inside of me instinctively wants to correct. *Your place, for as long as you want it to be.*

"Of course," I say instead, stepping back from her embrace and taking her hand in mine. "Let's go."

Walking into the house with Nora, I can't shake the feeling that this is... right.

On the days she's not here, the rooms seem empty and quiet. My bed is too big without her, and though I'll always appreciate the blessing of having a place like this to come home to, there's something about it now that doesn't feel complete without her in it.

In hindsight, maybe it's always felt like this. Perhaps all the years I spent waiting to find the other piece of my heart made me numb to it, so blind to what was missing all along.

Beside me, Nora's quiet as we step inside and I lock the door behind us. She was quiet on the drive here, too, resting her head against the seat and letting her eyes drift shut. I don't know if she was truly sleeping or if she just wanted the peace and quiet, but I let her take the lead. Whatever she wants, whatever she needs tonight, it's hers.

We walk down the hallway leading toward the bedrooms, and she passes the door to the guest room, opening mine instead.

Despite it all, the second that door closes behind us, a wave of soul-deep calm washes over me. It's the kraken in me roaring his approval, the monster more than satisfied to have our mate safe in our lair.

"I'd like to rinse off," Nora says, breaking the silence and startling me out of my thoughts. She gestures down at her clothes. "Just feeling a little gross after everything that's happened."

"Of course," I tell her, turning to head into the bathroom. "I can—"

"Not in there."

Without giving me a chance to ask her what she means, she takes a step toward the pool, tugging the sweatshirt she's wearing up and over her head. I'm rooted to the spot, watching her step to the edge and slide her pants and panties down over her hips, kicking them aside.

"Nora," I say hesitantly, even as my body sparks to life at

the sight of her exposed skin.

"Are you coming, kraken?" she says over her shoulder as she wades in. "Or are you just going to stand there and stare?"

Helpless to do anything but follow, I get to work on my own clothes.

37

Nora

The embrace of the water is a welcome balm on my aching body. After our first time together, Elias adjusted the temperature of the pool to be a little warmer and more comfortable for me, and it's just right tonight.

The tension I've been carrying during the last few hours finally starts to recede as I dive in and take a few slow strokes out into the middle of the pool. I'm laying on my back in the water, staring up at the ceiling, when I hear another soft splash as my kraken enters the pool.

Still, when I shift up to tread water and look over at him, his hesitation and guilt are still clear as day on his face, and in the faint pulses of emotion I can feel through the bond between us.

Like some kind of switch I turned on and can't seem to flip back off—not that I *want* to flip it back off—I've been able to feel Elias these last few hours. It's still a little confusing, a little overwhelming, but the longer I sit with it and explore it, the more natural it feels.

It just feels like... Elias. Like the steady beat of his hearts and the strength he's always given me.

My kraken swims closer, already in his half-shift with his mass of blue-gray tentacles undulating gently below the water's surface. He doesn't touch me, though, and stays just out of arm's reach like he's waiting for me to decide what I need from him.

It's a decision that's as easy and natural as the pulse of our bond in my chest. "Just... hold me?"

Elias nods and reaches one of his tentacles out to curl around my waist in a gentle embrace. A few more follow, wrapping around my body and tugging me toward him. I loop my arms around his neck and bury my face in his shoulder, dragging my lips over his skin and inhaling the familiar scent of him. His breath hitches as he cradles my head in one hand and rubs soothing strokes up and down my back with the other.

I'm entirely wrapped up in him, and more than anything else, it's exactly what I need to feel right now.

Safe. Held. Protected.

Giving my statement against Daniel was powerful. Knowing he's locked up for tonight is a colossal weight off my shoulders. But all of it pales in comparison to the knowledge that I'm taking what I want. I'm choosing my kraken, choosing Elias and the comfort and strength he's more than willing to lend me tonight.

Leaning into him, melting into his sturdy embrace, it's all I need.

Still, it's not all rainbows and butterflies. Not yet. Just like last time, I know coming back from something so fucked up is going to take months, maybe years. And that was before, when I arguably wasn't dealing with something *this* fucked up.

Right now, I'm still riding the high of relief. Daniel, everything that happened tonight, the whiplash of being here and safe, all of it still feels like it's being held at arm's length in the back of my mind. Eventually, it's going to come back around in waves that will catch me off guard, devastate me, and leave me a mess.

"The detective, Harris, she gave me some information on trauma counselors in Seattle. I think I'd like to see one."

Elias's arms tighten around me. "That sounds like a good idea. Whatever support you need, I want to help you find it."

The weight of that support is already settling on me like a warm blanket, just as steady and real as the feel of Elias holding me.

"But I'm... alright," I tell him, trying to think how I can explain. "Right now. Fuck, I mean, I'm probably not. But I feel okay. I want to be here with you."

"Nora..." Elias starts, leaning away a little so he can look at me. "I want to apologize for everything. For the part I played in making it so Sorenson could find you. If it wasn't for me going to the Bureau and having them track you down, he wouldn't have."

There it is. Some part of me already knew that's what he was feeling guilty about, but I'm still glad he's able to be open and honest enough to tell me.

I reach up to run my fingers through his hair. "Do you remember what you said to me the first time I told you about Daniel?"

"What part?"

"You told me it wasn't my fault. What he did. The way he treated me and made me feel. You told me it wasn't my fault."

He nods, but the wariness doesn't leave his face.

"I've never blamed you," I continue. "For any of it. I mean, yeah, I was pissed and scared at first, and even more pissed that Daniel violated both our privacy by finding me the way he did, but none of that was on you."

Elias tugs me back against his chest. "You're better to me than I deserve, little siren."

I can't help it, I have to laugh at that. "And you've been absolutely wonderful to me from the day we met."

"I keep thinking about it," he confesses. "Everything. All of it. What I could have done differently. How I could have protected you better. Wondering if you might have been better off if I'd never seen you in the coffee shop that day."

"I wouldn't have been," I say, absolutely certain. "Sure, maybe Daniel wouldn't have found me, but I also might have stayed in the place I was for who knows how much longer. Afraid. Hiding. I'm never going to claim it was good that things happened like they did, but you finding me will never be a bad thing."

Elias nods, thinking that over, too, but still doesn't look convinced.

It's a strange sensation, feeling his indecision like this. It's like two opposing strands wrapped around each other—one that wants to reach out and claim me, keep me with him forever, and one that still pulses with a guilt and regret I somehow know he feels to his core.

Even more strangely, the combination of the two calms me even more than I already was. It's been like this with him since the beginning. Nothing forced, nothing owed to or expected by him. Even now, it's my choice where we go next.

It seems almost silly, honestly, after everything that happened tonight, to still have that be an open question.

It's one I have no hesitation in answering now.

"Elias." I lean up to press a soft kiss on his lips. "I don't want this to touch us, not anymore."

We've been a pair of fools. Too careful, too cautious, and I'll be the first to admit I can take the blame for most of it.

Not that he'd ever blame me.

"Tell me what you want," I say, curling my fingers into his damp hair. "Without being worried you're going to freak me out. Tell me what you really want."

Elias's eyes dart back and forth across my face. Whatever he finds there, it makes him take a long, deep breath before he answers.

"I want you with me, Nora. I want you here when I fall asleep and when I wake up. Always. I want you here always."

The warmth of his words echoes the warmth in my chest as I burrow into him.

"Alright," I whisper, pressing another soft kiss against his neck. "Alright. Thank you for telling me. And I have a counter-offer."

With the first genuine smile he's had on his face tonight and a low, relieved laugh rumbling in his chest, he kisses my forehead before answering. "And what would that be?"

"I don't think I'm ready to move right in, but my lease *is* up in a couple months, and I can go month to month after that. In the meantime, I wouldn't be opposed to spending a whole lot of time here. Or having you stay with me."

"You know I'd never say no to a night with you, little siren."

"And until then," I say, cautious optimism breaking through, "maybe we can try out a little bit more of that normal you wanted for us? I mean, *actual* normal this time. Would that be alright with you?"

By the way his arms tighten around me and the soft laugh rumbling through his chest, I suspect it might be, but the expression on his face when I lean back and look at him for confirmation steals the breath from my lungs.

38

Elias

"Would that be alright with you?"

Would it be alright? She's asking for something as simple as time together, wondering if that's what I want, too. As if she doesn't know I'd hand her the whole damn world if she asked for it.

"Is that a question, Nora?" I ask her. "Do you really not know?"

With a wicked little smile on her lips, she leans up and nips at mine. "Yes. I know. But answer it, please."

My siren. As always, I'm powerless against her.

"I'll give you years of normal," I tell her with a kiss to her cheek. "Decades." Another kiss, this one on the tip of her nose. "All the time in the world and all the years of my life, they belong to you." A kiss on her jaw. "We could have the most normal, boring life in the world, and I'd be the happiest being alive." My teeth scrape along her throat and she shivers. "But I'd also like to give you more than that, my mate. I'd like to travel with you, and show you some of the places I've known. I'd like you to meet some of my kin where they live in their far corners of the seven seas. I'd like to build a life and a family with you, but only when you're ready."

Maybe it's more than she's ready to hear, but it's nothing less than the truth.

I want Nora, all of her, for the rest of our lives.

Still, I'm not sure how she'll react or if she feels anywhere near the same for me, but when her smile spreads even wider and she surges up to claim my mouth in a long, possessive kiss, I have my answer.

"I think all of that sounds wonderful," she says. "And we have all the time in the world, right?"

"All the time in the world," I agree.

Laying back in the water and taking her with me as I push us deeper into the pool, I'm struck once more by the same sharp instinct that hit me the moment I first saw her.

Right. This is right. The two of us together.

We stay like that for a while, letting the water hold us steady, hearts beating in sync, with nothing much more that needs to be said right now.

Well, perhaps there is one more thing that needs to be said.

Looking at my treasure, I pause and consider for a moment. It might be too soon, yes, but she's asked me to be honest with her, to give her the truth about how I feel and what I want. Even if she's not yet ready to say it back, I could no sooner stop the words from breaking free than I could stop myself from loving her.

"I love you, Nora."

She goes absolutely still against me for a few heartbeats before pulling her head up from my chest.

A slow, brilliant smile breaks over her face, and in that moment it's as if the sun and the stars and all the centuries I've waited for her fade away. Here's my new center, the soul I was always meant to find in whatever grand scheme conspired to bring us together.

"I love you too."

She kisses me again, and all I know is peace.

39

Nora - Eight Months Later

I'm adrift at sea, being hunted by a kraken.

When Elias brought the idea up a few weeks ago, it took me a moment to remember the taunt he'd made the first time I'd seen him shifted. I'd half written it off as sensual teasing or empty boasting, but it turns out he was absolutely serious.

The cool fall and winter prevented us from playing out this particular fantasy of his, but now that it's finally summer here again in the Pacific Northwest, my kraken's not going to be denied.

He sent us off from shore and rowed out into a calm little bay before disappearing into the water with a roguish grin and a dark promise in his eyes. Even though I lunged for the side of the boat and peered into the water, he was already gone.

The whole thing is absurd, really. Here I am in a tiny

wooden boat, struggling with the oars and drifting further and further from shore, all while some gigantic sea monster stalks me from the depths.

It's absurd. Absolutely absurd... and undeniably hot.

A faint splash sounds from somewhere behind the boat and my heart starts racing even faster. I whip my head around to look, but there's nothing there. No sign of my kraken.

Struggling with the oars, I manage to get a few good strokes in before the noise echoes out through the stillness of the bright, sunny afternoon once more. My core clenches and a wave of goosebumps breaks out on my skin at the pulse of awareness that skitters through me.

He's close. Really close, if the strong tug in the center of my chest is any indication.

Letting all my emotions pour into that bond, I push onwards. I'm really giving it my all now, dragging the boat through the water and breathing heavy, but only until the first massive, blue-gray tentacle breaks the surface of the water. It wraps around the boat's bow and stops me in an instant.

Elias is so much bigger in this form.

He warned me about it, of course, when he walked me step-by-step through how this whole scenario would play out. But hearing about it and seeing it in the flesh are two very, very different things.

When a second tentacle joins the first, snaking up around the side of the boat and looking for weak spots—or, more likely, looking for me—I scramble to my feet in sheer, delighted fright. The boat rocks beneath me, but when I peer into the water all I can see is the shadow of something dark and massive.

A heartbeat later, one of those enormous tentacles jerks me back down onto the wooden seat in the center of the boat as it wraps around my waist. It's joined by another banded around both my thighs, and two more to cuff my wrists. The rest envelop the sides of the boat as he begins dragging it slowly but surely toward one of the sea caves set into the rocky coast.

I pull a little at my bonds, testing, teasing him, only to be held even tighter. The tip of the tentacle wrapped around my waist unfurls upward, dipping under the hem of my shirt and seeking out my breasts. It latches a sucker onto the very tip of one of my nipples and gives a sharp tug, the slight stinging pleasure of it an unmistakable reminder to behave and remember who's in charge here.

It sends a corresponding pulse of heat straight down between my thighs. Even as we pick up pace and move closer to shore, even as the wood of the boat starts to creak and crack under the pressure of his tentacles, my excitement only grows.

I'm still a little nervous, but I know my monster will take care of me. Just like I know the word itself doesn't have any fear in it unless I decide it does.

Monster. My monster. Not the kind hiding under the bed or lurking in the shadows of my past, but the wild force of nature who's claimed me for his own.

Beneath me, the wood finally gives way just as we reach the mouth of the sea cave. I'm hoisted into the air and out of the way as the wooden planks crack and shatter, and even though I know I'm still safe, I can't help but cry out in surprise.

The tentacles holding me tighten as the darkness of the cave closes over us. It's a long, narrow crevice in the shoreline cliffs with a bottom deep enough for Elias to navigate through, and a flat rock ledge at the very back perfect for storing away plundered treasure.

We reach the back of the cave, and he sets me down on the damp stone, all of those tentacles retreating back beneath the water. I walk carefully to where the edge of the rock meets the water, and peer down at the kraken waiting for me.

From this angle, I can see all of him, and even though the dim of the cave still obscures him a little, it can't hide the sheer massive size of him, the power, the graceful way his limbs move through the water.

Once upon a time, I might have been frightened at the sight of him, but now all I see is beauty. All I see is Elias.

"My kraken," I whisper, voice filled with affection and awe as I look at him. "My mate."

All those tentacles shudder and shift, and a moment later Elias's head and shoulders break the surface of the water as he transforms back into a half-shift. With a wave of seawater that breaks onto the rocks and washes all the way up to my knees, I surrender completely and let my monster pull me into his arms.

Elias

I've captured my treasure at last.

Nora lets herself be caught so beautifully, offers herself to me with an enthusiasm and a sweet surrender that spreads like fire through my veins.

My mind is still half-kraken, still half-feral with the need to claim her, keep her, fuck her, and the urge to have her bare has me surging forward onto the damp floor of the sea cave. It's the perfect spot, one I spent weeks searching for once I had her agreement.

I needed everything about this day to be perfect.

And it has been. From Nora's openness and enthusiasm, to the beautiful day, to the unending waves of excitement and the slightest hints of trembling, nervous anticipation I've been feeling from her since the moment I disappeared beneath the waves.

Nora has done beautifully. She's been perfect. Not that I ever expected anything else from my little siren.

Unable to wait a moment longer, I twine my tentacles beneath the shirt and the skirt she's wearing, searching for seams that tear easily away from her warm, delicious body. Beneath, she's not wearing anything else, a naughty little detail I wasn't even aware of until I had her writhing in my grasp.

Once she's bare, I can't help but wrap her up in a couple of tentacles and hold her out in front of me, taking a few long moments to admire her. Everything about Nora is glowing. Her creamy skin accented by splashes of flushed pink, her magnificent hazel eyes glazed over with lust, her golden brown hair wild and wavy with sea salt.

Drawing her to me, I twine a hand into her hair and tip her head back. She moans a little at the sharp tug, and presses herself closer.

When I wrap two tentacles around her thighs, I'm greeted with the warm, damp feel of her arousal and a pulse of sheer lust through the bond between us. I could thrust into her now and she'd already be wet and ready for me.

Still, I hold back. It's not time. Not yet.

This ritual we've acted out today has another purpose as well. One that's much, much more meaningful than sex.

Not that sex with Nora is ever meaningless, but there's something else I want from my mate today. Something I'm more than certain she's ready to give me.

"Little siren," I croon, wrapping her up more securely, holding her still and open for me, legs spread wide and wanting little cunt positioned just over where my shifted cock is ready to drive into her. "I've captured you, and I would claim you."

I'm ready for my mate to belong to me completely. To bind

herself to me. To spend the rest of our days as one.

In my grasp, a shiver runs through her, no doubt a response to everything pulsing through the bond between us. The tenderness, the love, the trust, the simmering lust and the promise of forever. It fills me up and leaves no more room for doubt, no capacity to wait another day, another hour, another minute for her to be mine.

Where the bond comes from, and the magick it offers those it chooses, is still a mystery. From our gods or the cosmos or fate itself, who's to say?

What I do know is that Nora is breathless and smiling at me, trussed up so prettily in my tentacles, with love shining clearly from every inch of her.

"I accept your claim, Elias," she says. "And I'd claim you as well."

"Yes, little siren" I murmur, sliding her down onto my cock. "For as long as my two hearts beat they're yours."

Nora cries out as I fill her, and my entire being hums with vibrant awareness of her as the last threads of our bond weave themselves together.

"Who do you belong to, Nora?" I ask as I bottom out inside of her. "Who holds your soul?"

"You do!" she moans, back arching with pleasure. "I'm yours."

With that final acquiescence, I lose myself in her completely.

There are times when I'm more than happy to let my little siren take the lead. To ride me and claim me how she wishes. But today? Today she's mine. Still holding her firmly, I move her up and down my cock.

We've decided on a word—*chai*—she says it, and I'll stop, but in our prior discussions she was open to this, eager for this, and by her reactions now she's having no second thoughts. Her body is limp and trusting, lax and pliable as I glide her up and down, reveling in the slick slide of her cunt on me.

It's not until I reach for her clit with another tentacle, covering it with a sucker and drawing sharply on its stiff, sensitive peak, that she tenses back up. When she arches and writhes against me, I start moving as well, meeting the push and pull of her body with hard, deep thrusts into her. Ratcheting up the pressure on her clit, I lean forward and graze my teeth over her throat.

"My mate," I murmur. "My beautiful siren."

Another tentacle reaches around to cup her ass, dipping between the two firm, round swells to tease against the tight ring of muscle between.

"Will you let me claim you completely?"

I almost think Nora's beyond the capability of providing a reply, and am about to draw back when her eyes flutter open and meet mine, the entirety of my soul contained within them.

"Yes," she breathes, claiming my mouth in a searing kiss and murmuring against my lips. "Please."

I drive into her there, too, and it sends her over the edge. Her inner muscles clench down, her body is wracked with spasms of pleasure, and I devour the scream of bliss from her lips.

All of it, combined with the unimaginable sensation of her through our bond and the soul-shattering feeling of joining with her completely, throws me over my own precipice. I spill myself within her, groaning into her mouth and losing myself completely in the joy of claiming my mate.

It's not until a few minutes—or hours, or days, who's really to say?—later, when I'm sprawled out on the floor of the sea cave with my mate stretched out on top of me, that some semblance of sanity returns.

It's sanity laced with joy, with peace, with boneless exhaustion and an ache in my muscles I know I'll gladly be feeling for days. On top of me, Nora props herself up on an elbow and smirks at me.

"Well," she says, voice filled with laughter. "That's one way to round out a weekend. I don't know how in the world I'm supposed to just get back to normal life with a regular Monday after this."

It's Sunday afternoon. A peaceful, ordinary Sunday afternoon, one that seems wonderfully incongruent compared to the magnitude with which both our lives have just changed.

"I suppose you only have yourself to blame for that," I tease her. "Since you were the one who didn't want to take a big, extravagant trip for the occasion."

She smacks my arm lightly. "Oh, sure, put the blame on me. Because you're not the one who has to stick around Seattle for classes."

It's just one more thing I admire about my mate. Once she decided on the college she wanted to attend, one right here in Seattle, she didn't want to wait for fall semester. She jumped right in with a few summer courses in addition to her job at the bookstore.

Watching her pick that dream back up, hearing her speak so enthusiastically about her teachers and classmates and plans for after she graduates, has been a joy. It lights her up from the inside out and gives her something positive to focus on, especially with the ongoing prep for Sorenson's trial.

Thanks to his own stupidity, greed, and hubris, Sorenson hasn't seen the outside world since the night he tried to kidnap Nora, and based on the mounting evidence against him it's unlikely he ever will again.

We don't let it take up more of our thoughts than it has to, and have both decided to move on from it with pointed determination. Sorenson is in our past, and he won't detract from the happiness of our future.

"We could have waited," Nora says, shifting her hips around where she's still impaled on me in a way that makes us both groan. "Maybe gone somewhere over my fall break, or waited until Christmas."

"Absolutely not," I grumble, pulling out of her with a wet slide that draws more groans.

Shifting back into my human form, I walk to the dry area further back in the cave and pick up the duffel bag I stored here earlier this morning. I take out a towel and return to my mate, cleaning her up before pulling out the fresh sets of clothes I packed for us both. We pull them on and get ready to head home, to *our* home, as it has been the last few months.

"Impatient, as always," she teases.

I sling an arm around the small of her back and draw her to me. "Can you blame me? I've waited three centuries for you, my treasure."

Another wide, bright smile lights up her face. "I suppose that's true. And now you get to spend another three hundred ordinary, normal years with me."

"There's nothing on this earth that sounds better to me than that, little siren."

And truly, how could I ever ask for more? The mundane and magickal all mixed up together in the kind of life I never even knew to dream of. A string of endless tomorrows stretching out in front of us.

My mate, my treasure, my Nora.

Truly mine at last.

Printed in Great Britain
by Amazon